The Missioner

"DO YOU MIND EXPLAINING YOURSELF?" SHE ASKED.

[Page 23.] FRONTISPIECE.

The Missioner

By
E. Phillips Oppenheim

Author of " Anna, the Adventuress," " Mysterious Mr. Sabin,"
" A Lost Leader," " The Great Secret,"
Etc.

Illustrated by Fred Pegram

Boston
Little, Brown, and Company
1909

Published January, 1909.

𝔓𝔯𝔦𝔫𝔱𝔢𝔯𝔰
S. J. PARKHILL & CO., BOSTON, U. S. A.

CONTENTS

BOOK I

CONTENTS

BOOK II

LIST OF ILLUSTRATIONS.

THE MISSIONER

BOOK I

CHAPTER I

MISTRESS AND AGENT

THE lady of Thorpe was bored. These details as to leases and repairs were wearisome. The phrases and verbiage confused her. She felt obliged to take them in some measure for granted; to accept without question the calmly offered advice of the man who stood so respectfully at the right hand of her chair.

"This agreement with Philip Crooks," he remarked, "is a somewhat important document. With your permission, madam, I will read it to you."

She signified her assent, and leaned wearily back in her chair. The agent began to read. His mistress watched him through half closed eyes. His voice, notwithstanding its strong country dialect, had a sort of sing-song intonation. He read earnestly and without removing his eyes from the document. His listener made no attempt to arrive at the sense of the string of words which flowed so monotonously from his lips. She was occupied in making a study of the man Sturdy and weather-beaten, neatly dressed in country

clothes, with a somewhat old-fashioned stock, with
trim grey side-whiskers, and a mouth which reminded her somehow of a well-bred foxhound's,
he represented to her, in his clearly cut personality,
the changeless side of life, the side of life which she
associated with the mighty oaks in her park, and
the prehistoric rocks which had become engrafted
with the soil of the hills beyond. As she saw him
now, so had he seemed to her fifteen years ago.
Only what a difference! A volume to her — a
paragraph to him! She had gone out into the
world — rich, intellectually inquisitive, possessing
most of the subtler gifts with which her sex is endowed; and wherever the passionate current of life
had flown the swiftest, she had been there, a leader
always, seeking ever to satisfy the unquenchable
thirst for new experiences and new joys. She
had passed from girlhood to womanhood with every
nerve of her body strained to catch the emotion
of the moment. Always her fingers had been
tearing at the cells of life — and one by one they
had fallen away. This morning, in the bright
sunshine which flooded the great room, she felt
somehow tired — tired and withered. Her maid
was a fool! The two hours spent at her toilette
had been wasted! She felt that her eyes were
hollow, her cheeks pale! Fifteen years, and the
man had not changed a jot. She doubted whether
he had ever passed the confines of her estate. She
doubted whether he had even had the desire. Wind
and sun had tanned his cheeks, his eyes were clear,
his slight stoop was the stoop of the horseman rather
than of age. He had the air of a man satisfied with

life and his place in it — an attitude which puzzled her. No one of her world was like that! Was it some inborn gift, she wondered, which he possessed, some antidote to the world's restlessness which he carried with him, or was it merely lack of intelligence?

He finished reading and folded up the pages, to find her regarding him still with that air of careful attention with which she had listened to his monotonous flow of words. He found her interest surprising. It did not occur to him to invest it with any personal element.

"The agreement upon the whole," he remarked, "is, I believe, a fair one. You are perhaps thinking that those clauses ——"

"If the agreement is satisfactory to you," she interrupted, "I will confirm it."

He bowed slightly and glanced through the pile of papers upon the table.

"I do not think that there is anything else with which I need trouble you, madam," he remarked.

She nodded imperiously.

"Sit down for a moment, Mr. Hurd," she said.

If he felt any surprise, he did not show it. He drew one of the high-backed chairs away from the table, and with that slight air of deliberation which characterized all his movements, seated himself. He was in no way disquieted to find her dark, tired eyes still studying him.

"How old are you, Mr. Hurd?" she asked.

"I am sixty-three, madam," he answered.

Her eyebrows were gently raised. To her it seemed incredible. She thought of the men of sixty-three or thereabouts whom she knew, and her lips parted in one of those faint, rare smiles of genuine amusement, which smoothed out all the lines of her tired face. Visions of the promenade at Marienbad and Carlsbad, the Kursaal at Homburg, floated before her. She saw them all, the men whom she knew, with the story of their lives written so plainly in their faces, babbling of nerves and tonics and cures, the newest physician, the latest fad. Defaulters all of them, unwilling to pay the great debt — seeking always a way out! Here, at least, this man scored!

"You enjoy good health?" she remarked.

"I never have anything the matter with me," he answered simply. "I suppose," he added, as though by an afterthought, "the life is a healthy one."

"You find it — satisfying?" she asked.

He seemed puzzled.

"I have never attempted anything else," he answered. "It seems to be what I am suited for."

She attempted to abandon the *rôle* of questioner — to give a more natural turn to the conversation.

"It is always," she remarked, "such a relief to get down into the country at the end of the season. I wonder I don't spend more time here. I daresay one could amuse oneself?" she added carelessly.

Mr. Hurd considered for a few moments.

"There are croquet and archery and tennis in the neighbourhood," he remarked. "The golf course on the Park hills is supposed to be excellent. A great many people come over to play."

She affected to be considering the question

seriously. An intimate friend would not have been
deceived by her air of attention. Mr. Hurd knew
nothing of this. He, on his part, however, was
capable of a little gentle irony.

"It might amuse you," he remarked, "to make a
tour of your estate. There are some of the outlying
portions which I think that I should have the honour
of showing you for the first time."

"I might find that interesting," she admitted.
" By the bye, Mr. Hurd, what sort of a landlord am
I? Am I easy, or do I exact my last pound of flesh?
One likes to know these things."

" It depends upon the tenant," the agent answered.
" There is not one of your farms upon which, if a
man works, he cannot make a living. On the other
hand, there is not one of them on which a man can
make a living unless he works. It is upon this principle that your rents have been adjusted. The
tenants of the home lands have been most carefully
chosen, and Thorpe itself is spoken of everywhere
as a model village."

" It is very charming to look at," its mistress
admitted. " The flowers and thatched roofs are
so picturesque. 'Quite a pastoral idyll,' my guests
tell me. The people one sees about seem contented
and respectful, too."

" They should be, madam," Mr. Hurd answered
drily. " The villagers have had a good many privileges from your family for generations."

The lady inclined her head thoughtfully.

" You think, then," she remarked, " that if anything should happen in England, like the French
Revolution, I should not find unexpected thoughts

and discontent smouldering amongst them?   You
believe that they are really contented? "

Mr. Hurd knew nothing about revolutions, and
he was utterly unable to follow the trend of her
thoughts.

" If they were not, madam," he declared, "they
would deserve to be in the workhouse — and I should
feel it my duty to assist them in getting there."

The lady of Thorpe laughed softly to herself.

" You, too, then, Mr. Hurd," she said, " you are
content with your life?   You don't mind my being
personal, do you?   It is such a change down here,
such a different existence . . . and I like to understand everything."

Upon Mr. Hurd the almost pathetic significance
of those last words was wholly wasted.   They were
words of a language which he could not comprehend.
He realized only their direct application — and the
woman to him seemed like a child.

" If I were not content, madam," he said, " I
should deserve to lose my place.   I should deserve
to lose it," he added after a moment's pause, " notwithstanding the fact that I have done my duty
faithfully for four and forty years."

She smiled upon him brilliantly.   They were so
far apart that she feared lest she might have offended
him.

" I have always felt myself a very fortunate
woman, Mr. Hurd," she said, " in having possessed
your services."

He rose as though about to go.   It was her whim,
however, to detain him.

" You lost your wife some years ago, did you not,

Mr. Hurd? " she began tentatively. As a matter of fact, she was not sure of her ground.

" Seven years back, madam," he answered, with immovable face. " She was, unfortunately, never a strong woman."

" And your son? " she asked more confidently. " Is he back from South Africa? "

" A year ago, madam," he answered. " He is engaged at present in the estate office. He knows the work well —— "

" The best place for him, of course," she interrupted. " We ought to do all we can for our young men who went out to the war. I should like to see your son, Mr. Hurd. Will you tell him to come up some day? "

" Certainly, madam," he answered.

" Perhaps he would like to shoot with my guests on Thursday? " she suggested graciously.

Mr. Hurd did not seem altogether pleased.

" It has never been the custom, madam," he remarked, "for either my son or myself to be associated with the Thorpe shooting parties."

" Some customs," she remarked pleasantly, " are well changed, even in Thorpe. We shall expect him."

Mr. Hurd's mouth reminded her for a moment of a steel trap. She could see that he disapproved, but she had no intention of giving way. He began to tie up his papers, and she watched him with some continuance of that wave of interest which he had somehow contrived to excite in her. The signature of one of the letters which he was methodically folding, caught her attention.

" What a strange name! " she remarked. " Victor Macheson! Who is he? "

Mr. Hurd unfolded the letter. The ghost of a smile flickered upon his lips.

" A preacher, apparently," he answered. " The letter is one asking permission to give a series of what he terms religious lectures in Harrison's large barn! "

Her eyebrows were gently raised. Her tone was one of genuine surprise.

" What, in Thorpe? " she demanded.

" In Thorpe! " Mr. Hurd acquiesced.

She took the letter and read it. Her perplexity was in no manner diminished.

" The man seems in earnest," she remarked. " He must either be a stranger to this part of the country, or an extremely impertinent person. I presume, Mr. Hurd, that nothing has been going on in the place with which I am unacquainted? "

" Certainly not, madam," he answered.

" There has been no drunkenness? " she remarked. " The young people have, I presume, been conducting their love-making discreetly? "

The lines of Mr. Hurd's mouth were a trifle severe. One could imagine that he found her modern directness of speech indelicate.

" There have been no scandals of any sort connected with the village, madam," he assured her. " To the best of my belief, all of our people are industrious, sober and pious. They attend church regularly. As you know, we have not a public-house or a dissenting place of worship in the village."

" The man must be a fool," she said deliberately. " You did not, of course, give him permission to hold these services? "

" Certainly not," the agent answered. " I refused it absolutely."

The lady rose, and Mr. Hurd understood that he was dismissed.

" You will tell your son about Thursday? " she reminded him.

" I will deliver your message, madam," he answered.

She nodded her farewell as the footman opened the door.

" Everything seems to be most satisfactory, Mr. Hurd," she said. " I shall probably be here for several weeks, so come up again if there is anything you want me to sign."

" I am much obliged, madam," the agent answered.

He left the place by a side entrance, and rode slowly down the private road, fringed by a magnificent row of elm trees, to the village. The latch of the iron gate at the end of the avenue was stiff, and he failed to open it with his hunting crop at the first attempt. Just as he was preparing to try again, a tall, boyish-looking young man, dressed in sombre black, came swiftly across the road and opened the gate. Mr. Hurd thanked him curtly, and the young man raised his hat.

" You are Mr. Hurd, I believe? " he remarked. " I was going to call upon you this afternoon."

The little man upon the pony frowned. He had no doubt as to his questioner.

"My name is Hurd, sir," he answered stiffly.
"What can I do for you?"

"You can let me have that barn for my services,"
the other answered smiling. "I wrote you about
it, you know. My name is Macheson."

Mr. Hurd's answer was briefly spoken, and did
not invite argument.

"I have mentioned the matter to Miss Thorpe-
Hatton, sir. She agrees with me that your proposed
ministrations are altogether unneeded in this neighbourhood."

"You won't let me use the barn, then?" the
young man remarked pleasantly, but with some
air of disappointment.

Mr. Hurd gathered up the reins in his hand.

"Certainly not, sir!"

He would have moved on, but his questioner stood
in the way. Mr. Hurd looked at him from underneath his shaggy eyebrows. The young man was
remarkably young. His smooth, beardless face was
the face of a boy. Only the eyes seemed somehow
to speak of graver things. They were very bright
indeed, and they did not falter.

"Mr. Hurd," he begged, "do let me ask you
one question! Why do you refuse me? What
harm can I possibly do by talking to your villagers?"

Mr. Hurd pointed with his whip up and down the
country lane.

"This is the village of Thorpe, sir," he answered.
"There are no poor, there is no public-house, and
there, within a few hundred yards of the farthest
cottage," he added, pointing to the end of the street,

"is the church. You are not needed here. That is the plain truth."

The young man looked up and down, at the flower-embosomed cottages, with their thatched roofs and trim appearance, at the neatly cut hedges, the well-kept road, the many signs of prosperity. He looked at the little grey church standing in its ancient walled churchyard, where the road divided, a very delightful addition to the picturesque beauty of the place. He looked at all these things and he sighed.

"Mr. Hurd," he said, "you are a man of experience. You know very well that material and spiritual welfare are sometimes things very far apart."

Mr. Hurd frowned and turned his pony's head towards home.

"I know nothing of the sort, sir," he snapped. "What I do know is that we don't want any Salvation Army tricks here. You should stay in the cities. They like that sort of thing there."

"I must come where I am sent, Mr. Hurd," the young man answered. "I cannot do your people any harm. I only want to deliver my message — and go."

Mr. Hurd wheeled his pony round.

"I submitted your letter to Miss Thorpe-Hatton," he said. "She agrees with me that your ministrations are wholly unnecessary here. I wish you good evening!"

The young man caught for a moment at the pony's rein.

"One moment, sir," he begged. "You do not

object to my appealing to Miss Thorpe-Hatton herself? "

A grim, mirthless smile parted the agent's lips.

"By no means! " he answered, as he cantered off.

Victor Macheson stood for a moment watching the retreating figure. Then he looked across the park to where, through the great elm avenues, he could catch a glimpse of the house. A humorous smile suddenly brightened his face.

"It's got to be done! " he said to himself. "Here goes! "

CHAPTER II

THE HUNTER AND HIS QUARRY

THE mistress of Thorpe stooped to pat a black
Pomeranian which had rushed out to meet
her. It was when she indulged in some such movement that one realized more thoroughly the wonderful grace of her slim, supple figure. She who hated
all manner of exercise had the ease of carriage and
flexibility of one whose life had been spent in
athletic pursuits.

"How are you all?" she remarked languidly.
"Shocking hostess, am I not?"

A fair-haired little woman turned away from the
tea-table. She held a chocolate éclair in one hand,
and a cup of Russian tea in the other. Her eyes
were very dark, and her hair very yellow — and
both were perfectly and unexpectedly natural. Her
real name was Lady Margaret Penshore, but she
was known to her intimates, and to the mysterious
individuals who write under a *nom-de-guerre* in the
society papers, as "Lady Peggy."

"A little casual perhaps, my dear Wilhelmina,"
she remarked. "Comes from your association with
Royalty, I suppose. Try one of your own caviare
sandwiches, if you want anything to eat. They're
ripping."

Wilhelmina — she was one of the few women of her set with whose Christian name no one had ever attempted to take any liberties — approached the tea-table and studied its burden. There were a dozen different sorts of sandwiches arranged in the most tempting form, hot-water dishes with delicately browned tea-cakes simmering gently, thick cream in silver jugs, tea and coffee, and in the background old China dishes piled with freshly gathered strawberries and peaches and grapes, on which the bloom still rested. On a smaller table were flasks of liqueurs and a spirit decanter.

"Anyhow," she remarked, pouring herself out some tea, "I do feed you people well. And as to being casual, I warned you that I never put in an appearance before five."

A man in the background, long and lantern-faced, a man whose age it would have been as impossible to guess as his character, opened and closed his watch with a clink.

"Twenty minutes past," he remarked. "To be exact, twenty-two minutes past."

His hostess turned and regarded him contemplatively.

"How painfully precise!" she remarked. "Somehow, it doesn't sound convincing, though. Your watch is probably like your morals."

"What a flattering simile!" he murmured.

"Flattering?"

"It presupposes, at any rate, their existence," he explained. "It is years since I was reminded of them."

Wilhelmina seated herself before an open card-table.

"No doubt," she answered. "You see I knew you when you were a boy. Seriously," she continued, "I have been engaged with my agent for the last half-hour — a most interesting person, I can assure you. There was an agreement with one Philip Crooks concerning a farm, which he felt compelled to read to me — every word of it! Come along and cut, all of you!"

The fourth person, slim, fair-haired, the typical army officer and country house habitué, came over to the table, followed by the lantern-jawed man. Lady Peggy also turned up a card.

"You and I, Gilbert," Wilhelmina remarked to the elder man. "Here's luck to us! What on earth is that you are drinking?"

"Absinthe," he answered calmly. "I have been trying to persuade Austin to join me, but it seems they don't drink absinthe in the Army."

"I should think not, indeed," his hostess answered. "And you my partner, too! Put the stuff away."

Gilbert Deyes raised his glass and looked thoughtfully into its opalescent depths.

"Ah! my dear lady," he said, "you make a great mistake when you number absinthe amongst the ordinary intoxicating beverages. I tell you that the man who invented it was an epicure in sensations and — er — gastronomy. If only De Quincey had realized the possibility of absinthe, he would have given us jewelled prose indeed."

Wilhelmina yawned.

"Bother De Quincey!" she declared. "It's your bridge I'm thinking of."

"Dear lady, you need have no anxiety," Deyes answered reassuringly. "One does not trifle with one's livelihood. You will find me capable of the most daring finesses, the most wonderful coups. I shall not revoke, I shall not lead out of the wrong hand. My declarations will be touched with genius. The rubber, in fact, is already won. Vive l'absinthe!"

"The rubber will never be begun if you go on talking nonsense much longer," Lady Peggy declared, tapping the table impatiently. "I believe I hear the motors outside. We shall have the whole crowd here directly."

"They won't find their way here," their hostess assured them calmly. "My deal, I believe."

They played the hand in silence. At its conclusion, Wilhelmina leaned back in her chair and listened.

"You were right, Peggy," she said, "they are all in the hall. I can hear your brother's voice."

Lady Peggy nodded.

"Sounds healthy, doesn't it?"

Gilbert Deyes leaned across to the side table and helped himself to a cigarette.

"Healthy! I call it boisterous," he declared. "Where have they all been?"

"Motoring somewhere," Wilhelmina answered. "They none of them have any idea how to pass the time away until the first run."

"Sport, my dear hostess," Deyes remarked, "is the one thing which makes life in a country house almost unendurable."

Wilhelmina shrugged her shoulders.

"That's all very well, Gilbert," she said, "but what should we do if we couldn't get rid of some of these lunatics for at least part of the day?"

"Reasonable, I admit," Deyes answered, "but think what an intolerable nuisance they make of themselves for the other part. I double No Trumps, Lady Peggy."

Lady Peggy laid down her cards.

"For goodness' sake, no more digressions," she implored. "Remember, please, that I play this game for the peace of mind of my tradespeople! I redouble!"

The hand was played almost in silence. Lady Peggy lost the odd trick and began to add up the score with a gentle sigh.

"After all," her partner remarked, returning to the subject which they had been discussing, "I don't think that we could get on very well in this country without sport, of some sort."

"Of course not," Deyes answered. "We are all sportsmen, every one of us. We were born so. Only, while some of us are content to wreak our instinct for destruction upon birds and animals, others choose the nobler game — our fellow-creatures! To hunt or trap a human being is finer sport than to shoot a rocketing pheasant, or to come in from hunting with mud all over our clothes, smelling of ploughed fields, steaming in front of the fire, telling lies about our exploits — all undertaken in pursuit of a miserable little animal, which as often as not outwits us, and which, in an ordinary way, we

wouldn't touch with gloves on! What do you say,
Lady Peggy?"

"You're getting beyond me," she declared. "It
sounds a little savage."

Deyes dealt the cards slowly, talking all the
while.

"Sport is savage," he declared. "No one can
deny it. Whether the quarry be human or animal,
the end is death. But of all its varieties, give
me the hunting of man by man, the brain of the
hunter coping with the wiles of the hunted, both
human, both of the same order. The game's even
then, for at any moment they may change places
— the hunter and his quarry. It's finer work than
slaughtering birds at the coverside. It gives your
sex a chance, Lady Peggy."

"It sounds exciting," she admitted.

"It is," he answered.

His hostess looked up at him languidly.

"You speak like one who knows!"

"Why not?" he murmured. "I have been both
quarry and hunter. Most of us have more or less!
I declare Hearts!"

Again there was an interval of silence, broken
only by the stock phrases of the game, and the soft
patter of the cards upon the table. Once more the
hand was played out and the cards gathered up.
Captain Austin delivered his quota to the general
discussion.

"After all," he said, "if it wasn't for sport, our
country houses would be useless."

"Not at all!" Deyes declared. "Country houses
should exist for —— "

"For what, Mr. Deyes? Do tell us," Lady Peggy
implored.

"For bridge!" he declared. "For giving weary
married people the opportunity for divorce, and as
an asylum from one's creditors."

Wilhelmina shook her head as she gathered up
her cards.

"You are not at your best to-day, Gilbert," she
said. "The allusion to creditors is prehistoric! No
one has them nowadays. Society is such a hop-
scotch affair that our coffers are never empty."

"What a Utopian sentiment!" Lady Peggy
murmured.

"We can't agree, can we?" Deyes whispered
in her ear.

"You! Why they say that you are worth a
million," she protested.

"If I am I remain poor, for I cannot spend it,"
he declared.

"Why not?" his hostess asked him from across
the table.

"Because," he answered, "I am cursed with a
single vice, trailing its way through a labyrinth of
virtues. I am a miser!"

Lady Peggy laughed incredulously.

"Rubbish!" she exclaimed.

"Dear lady, it is nothing of the sort," he answered, shaking his head sadly. "I have felt it
growing upon me for years. Besides, it is heredi-
tary. My mother opened a post-office savings bank
account for me. At an early age I engineered a
corner in marbles and sold out at a huge profit. I am
like the starving dyspeptic at the rich man's feast."

Captain Austin intervened.

"I declare Diamonds," he announced, and the hand proceeded.

Wilhelmina leaned back in her chair as the last trick fell. Her eyes were turned towards the window. She could just see the avenue of elms down which her agent had ridden a short while since. Deyes, through half closed eyes, watched her with some curiosity.

"If one dared offer a trifling coin of the realm——" he murmured.

"I was thinking of your theory," she interrupted. "According to you, I suppose the whole world is made up of hunters and their quarry. Can you tell, I wonder, by looking at people, to which order they belong?"

"It is easy," he answered. "Yet you must remember we are continually changing places. The man who cracks the whip to-day is the hunted beast to-morrow. The woman who mocks at her lover this afternoon is often the slave-bearer when dusk falls. Swift changes like this are like rain upon the earth. They keep us, at any rate, out of the asylums."

Wilhelmina was still looking out of the window. Up the great avenue, in and out amongst the tree trunks, but moving always with swift buoyant footsteps towards the house, came a slim, dark figure, soberly dressed in ill-fitting clothes. He walked with the swing of early manhood, his head was thrown back, and he carried his hat in his hand. She leaned forward to watch him more closely — he seemed to have associated himself in some mysteri-

ous manner with the mocking words of Gilbert
Deyes. Half maliciously, she drew his attention
to the swiftly approaching figure.

"Come, my friend of theories," she said mock-
ingly. "There is a stranger there, the young man
who walks so swiftly. To which of your two orders
does he belong?"

Deyes looked out of the window — a brief, careless glance.

"To neither," he answered. "His time has not
come yet. But he has the makings of both."

CHAPTER III

FIRST BLOOD

A FOOTMAN entered the room a few minutes later, and obedient, without a doubt, to some previously given command, waited behind his mistress' chair until a hand had been played. When it was over, she spoke to him without turning her head.

"What is it, Perkins? " she asked.

He bent forward respectfully.

"There is a young gentleman here, madam, who wishes to see you most particularly. He has no card, but he said that his name would not be known to you."

"Tell him that I am engaged," Wilhelmina said. "He must give you his name, and tell you what business he has come upon."

"Very good, madam! " the man answered, and withdrew.

He was back again before the next hand had been played. Once more he stood waiting in respectful silence.

"Well? " his mistress asked.

"His name, madam, is Mr. Victor Macheson. He said that he would wait as long as you liked, but he preferred telling you his business himself."

"I fancy that I know it," Wilhelmina answered.
"You can show him in here."

"Is it the young man, I wonder," Lady Peggy
remarked, "who came up the avenue as though he
were walking on air?"

"Doubtless," Wilhelmina answered. "He is
some sort of a missionary. I had him shown in here
because I thought his coming at all an impertinence,
and I want to make him understand it. You will
probably find him amusing, Mr. Deyes."

Gilbert Deyes shook his head quietly.

"There was a time," he murmured, "when the
very word missionary was a finger-post to the ridiculous. The comic papers rob us, however, of our
elementary sources of humour."

They all looked curiously towards the door as he
entered, all except Wilhelmina, who was the last to
turn her head, and found him hesitating in some
embarrassment as to whom to address. He was
somewhat above medium height, fair, with a mass
of wind-tossed hair, and had the smooth face of a
boy. His eyes were his most noticeable feature.
They were very bright and very restless. Lady
Peggy called them afterwards uncomfortable eyes,
and the others, without any explanation, understood
what she meant.

"I am Miss Thorpe-Hatton," Wilhelmina said
calmly. "I am told that you wished to see me."

She turned only her head towards him. Her
words were cold and unwelcoming. She saw that
he was nervous and she had no pity. It was unworthy of her. She knew that. Her eyes ques-
tioned him calmly. Sitting there in her light

muslin dress, with her deep-brown hair arranged
in the Madonna-like fashion, which chanced to be
the caprice of the moment, she herself — one of
London's most beautiful women — seemed little
more than a girl.

"I beg your pardon," he began hurriedly. "I
understood — I expected —— "

"Well? "

The monosyllable was like a drop of ice. A faint
spot of colour burned in his cheeks. He understood
now that for some reason this woman was inimical
to him. The knowledge seemed to have a bracing
effect. His eyes flashed with a sudden fire which
gave force to his face.

"I expected," he continued with more assurance,
"to have found Miss Thorpe-Hatton an older lady."

She said nothing. Only her eyebrows were very
slightly raised. She seemed to be asking him
silently what possible concern the age of the lady
of Thorpe-Hatton could be to him. He was to
understand that his remark was almost an impertinence.

"I wished," he said, "to hold a service in Thorpe
on Sunday afternoon, and also one during the week,
and I wrote to your agent asking for the loan of a
barn, which is generally, I believe, used for any
gathering of the villagers. Mr. Hurd found himself unable to grant my request. I have ventured
to appeal to you."

"Mr. Hurd," she said calmly, "decided, in my
opinion, quite rightly. I do not see what possible
need my villagers can have of further religious
services than the Church affords them."

"Madam," he answered, "I have not a word to say against your parish church, or against your excellent vicar. Yet I believe, and the body to which I am attached believes, that change is stimulating. We believe that the great truths of life cannot be presented to our fellow-creatures too often, or in too many different ways."

"And what," she asked, with a faint curl of her beautiful lips, "do you consider the great truths of life? "

"Madam," he answered, with slightly reddening cheeks, "they vary for every one of us, according to our capacity and our circumstances. What they may mean," he added, after a moment's hesitation, "to people of your social order, I do not know. It has not come within the orbit of my experience. It was your villagers to whom I was proposing to talk."

There was a moment's silence. Gilbert Deyes and Lady Peggy exchanged swift glances of amused understanding. Wilhelmina bit her lip, but she betrayed no other sign of annoyance.

"To what religious body do you belong? " she asked.

"My friends," he answered, "and I, are attached to none of the recognized denominations. Our only object is to try to keep alight in our fellow-creatures the flame of spirituality. We want to help them — not to forget."

"There is no name by which you call yourselves?" she asked.

"None," he answered.

"And your headquarters are where? " she asked.

"In Gloucestershire," he answered — "so far as we can be said to have any headquarters at all."

"You have no churches then?" she asked.

"Any building," he answered, "where the people are to whom we desire to speak, is our church. We look upon ourselves as missioners only."

"I am afraid," Wilhelmina said quietly, "that I am only wasting your time in asking these questions. Still, I should like to know what induced you to choose my village as an appropriate sphere for your labours."

"We each took a county," he answered. "Leicestershire fell to my lot. I selected Thorpe to begin with, because I have heard it spoken of as a model village."

Wilhelmina's forehead was gently wrinkled.

"I am afraid," she said, "that I am a somewhat dense person. Your reason seems to me scarcely an adequate one."

"Our belief is," he declared, "that where material prosperity is assured, especially amongst this class of people, the instincts towards spirituality are weakened."

"My people all attend church; we have no public-house; there are never any scandals," she said.

"All these things," he admitted, "are excellent. But they do not help you to see into the lives of these people. Church-going may become a habit, a respectable and praiseworthy thing — and a thing expected of them. Morality, too, may become a custom — until temptation comes. One must ask oneself what is the force which prompts these people to direct their lives in so praiseworthy a manner."

"You forget," she remarked, "that these are simple folk. Their religion with them is simply a matter of right or wrong. They need no further instruction in this."

"Madam," he said, "so long as they are living here, that may be so. Frankly, I do not consider it sufficient that their lives are seemly, so long as they live in the shadow of your patronage. What happens to those who pass outside its influence is another matter."

"What do you know about that?" she asked coldly.

"What I do know about it," he answered, "decided me to come to Thorpe."

There was a moment's silence. Any of the other three, Gilbert Deyes especially, perhaps, would have found it hard to explain, even to realize the interest with which they listened to the conversation between these two — the somewhat unkempt, ill-attired boy, with the nervous, forceful manner and burning eyes, and the woman, so sure of herself, so coldly and yet brutally ungracious. It was not so much the words themselves that passed between them that attracted as the undernote of hostility, more felt than apparent — the beginning of a duel, to all appearance so ludicrously onesided, yet destined to endure. Deyes turned in his chair uneasily. He was watching this intruder — a being outwardly so far removed from their world. The niceties of a correct toilet had certainly never troubled him, his clothes were rough in material and cut, he wore a flannel shirt, and a collar so low that his neck seemed ill-shaped. He had no special gifts of features or figure, his manner was nervous, his speech none too ready. Deyes found himself engaged in a swift analysis of the subtleties of personality. What did this young man possess that he should convey so strong a sense of power? There was something about him which told. They were all conscious of it, and, more than any of them, the woman who was regarding him with such studied ill-favour. To the others, her still beautiful face betrayed only some languid irritation. Deyes fancied that he saw more there — that underneath the mask which she knew so well how to wear there were traces of some deeper disturbance.

"Do you mind explaining yourself?" she asked. "That sounds rather an extraordinary statement of yours."

"A few months ago," he said, "I attended regularly one of the police courts in London. Day by day I came into contact with the lost souls who have drifted on to the great rubbish-heap. There was a girl, Martha Gullimore her name was, whose record for her age was as black as sin could make it. Her father, I believe, is the blacksmith in your model village! I spoke to him of his daughter yesterday, and he cursed me!"

"You mean Samuel Gullimore — my farrier?" she asked.

"That is the man," he answered.

"Have you any other — instances?" she asked.

"More than one, I am sorry to say," he replied. "There were two young men who left here only a year ago — one is the son of your gardener, the other was brought up by his uncle at your lodge gates. I was instrumental in saving them from prison a few months ago. One we have shipped to Canada — the other, I am sorry to say, has relapsed. We did what we could, but beyond a certain point we cannot go."

She leaned her head for a moment upon the slim, white fingers of her right hand, innocent of rings save for one great emerald, whose gleam of colour was almost barbaric in its momentary splendour. Her face had hardened a little, her tone was almost an offence.

"You would have me believe, then," she said, "that my peaceful village is a veritable den of iniquity? "

"Not I," he answered brusquely. "Only I would have you realize that roses and honeysuckle and regular wages, the appurtenances of material prosperity, are after all things of little consequence. They hear the song of the world, these people, in their leisure moments; their young men and girls are no stronger than their fellows when temptation comes."

Deyes leaned suddenly forward in his chair. He felt that his intervention dissipated a dramatic interest, of which he was keenly conscious, but he could not keep silence any longer.

"To follow out your argument, sir, to its logical conclusion," he said, "why not aim higher still? It is your contention, is it not, that the seeds of evil things are sown in indifference, that prosperity might even tend towards their propagation. Why not direct your energies, then, towards the men and women of Society? There is plenty of scope here for your labours."

The young man turned towards him. The lines of his mouth had relaxed into a smile of tolerant indifference.

"I have no sympathy, sir," he answered, "with the class you name. On a sinking ship, the cry is always, 'Save the women and children.' It is the less fortunate in the world's possessions who represent the women and children of shipwrecked morality. It is for their betterment that we work."

Deyes sighed gently.

"It is a pity," he declared. "I am convinced that there is a magnificent opening for mission work amongst the idle classes."

"No doubt," the young man agreed quickly. "The question is whether the game is worth the candle."

Deyes made no reply. Lady Peggy was laughing softly to herself.

"I have heard all that you have to say, Mr. Macheson," the mistress of Thorpe said calmly, "and I can only repeat that I think your presence here as a missioner most unnecessary. I consider it, in fact, an —— "

She hesitated. With a sudden flash of humour in his deep-set eyes, he supplied the word.

"An impertinence, perhaps! "

"The word is not mine," she answered, "but I accept it willingly. I cannot interfere with Mr. Hurd's decision as to the barn."

"I am sorry," he said slowly. "I must hold my meetings out of doors! That is all! "

There was a dangerous glitter in her beautiful eyes.

"There is no common land in the neighbourhood," she said, "and you will of course understand that I will consider you a trespasser at any time you are found upon my property."

He bowed slightly.

"I am here to speak to your people," he said, "and I will do so, if I have to stop in these lanes and talk to them one by one. You will pardon my reminding you, madam, that the days of feudalism are over."

Wilhelmina carefully shuffled the pack of cards which she had just taken up.

"We will finish our rubber, Peggy," she said. "Mr. Deyes, perhaps I may trouble you to ring the bell!"

The young man was across the room before Deyes could move.

"You will allow me," he said, with a delightfully humourous smile, "to facilitate my own dismissal. I shall doubtless meet your man in the hall. May I be allowed to wish you all good afternoon!"

They all returned his farewell save Wilhelmina, who had begun to deal. She seemed determined to remember his existence no more. Yet on the threshold, with the handle of the door between his fingers, he turned back. He said nothing, but his eyes were fixed upon her. Deyes leaned forward in his chair, immensely curious. Softly the cards fell into their places, there was no sign in her face of any consciousness of his presence. Deyes alone knew that she was fighting. He heard her breath come quicker, saw the fingers which gathered up her cards shake. Slowly, but with obvious unwillingness, she turned her head. She looked straight into the eyes of the man who still lingered.

"Good afternoon, Miss Thorpe-Hatton," he said pleasantly. "I am sorry to have troubled you."

Her lips moved, but she said nothing. She half inclined her head. The door was softly closed.

CHAPTER IV

BEATING HER WINGS

NEVER was a young man more pleased with himself than Stephen Hurd, on the night he dined at Thorpe-Hatton. He had shot well all day, and been accepted with the utmost cordiality by the rest of the party. At dinner time, his hostess had placed him on her left hand, and though it was true she had not much to say to him, it was equally obvious that her duties were sufficient to account for her divided attention. He was quite willing to be ignored by the lady on his other side — a little elderly, and noted throughout the country for her husband-hunting proclivities. He recognized the fact that, apart from the personal side of the question, he could scarcely hope to be of any interest to her. The novelty of the situation, Wilhelmina's occasional remarks, and a dinner such as he had never tasted before were sufficient to keep him interested. For the rest he was content to twirl his moustache, of which he was inordinately proud, and lean back in his chair with the comfortable reflection that he was the first of his family to be offered the complete hospitality of Thorpe-Hatton.

Towards the close of dinner, his hostess leaned towards him.

"Have you seen or heard anything of a young man named Macheson in the village?" she asked.

"I have seen him once or twice," he answered. "Here on a missionary expedition or something of the sort, I believe."

"Has he made any attempt to hold a meeting?" she asked.

"Not that I have heard of," he replied. "He has been talking to some of the people, though. I saw him with old Gullimore yesterday."

"That reminds me," she remarked, "is it true that Gullimore has had trouble with his daughter?"

"I believe so," young Hurd admitted, looking downwards at his plate.

"The man was to blame for letting her leave the place," Wilhelmina declared, in cold, measured tones. "A pretty girl, I remember, but very vain, and a fool, of course. But about this young fellow Macheson. Do you know who he is, and where he came from?"

Stephen Hurd shook his head.

"I'm afraid I don't," he said doubtfully. "He belongs to some sort of brotherhood, I believe. I can't exactly make out what he's at. Seems a queer sort of place for him to come missioning, this!"

"So I told him," she said. "By the bye, do you know where he is staying?"

"At Onetree farm," the young man answered. Wilhelmina frowned.

"Will you execute a commission for me to-morrow?" she asked.

"With pleasure!" he answered eagerly.

"You will go to the woman at Onetree farm, I forget her name, and say that I desire to take her rooms myself from to-morrow, or as soon as possible. I will pay her for them, but I do not wish that young man to be taken in by any of my tenants. You will perhaps make that known."

"I will do so," he declared. "I hope he will have the good sense to leave the neighbourhood."

"I trust so," Wilhelmina replied.

She turned away to speak once more to the man on her other side, and did not address Stephen Hurd again. He watched her covertly, with tingling pulses, as she devoted herself to her neighbour — the Lord-Lieutenant of the county. He considered himself a judge of the sex, but he had had few opportunities even of admiring such women as the mistress of Thorpe. He watched the curve of her white neck with its delicate, satin-like skin, the play of her features, the poise of her somewhat small, oval head. He admired the slightly wearied air with which she performed her duties and accepted the compliments of her neighbour. "A woman of mysteries" some one had once called her, and he realized that it was the mouth and the dark, tired eyes which puzzled those who attempted to classify her. What a triumph — to bring her down to the world of ordinary women, to drive the weariness away, to feel the soft touch, perhaps, of those wonderful arms! He was a young man of many conquests, and with a sufficiently good idea of himself. The thought was like wine in his blood. If only it were possible!

He relapsed into a day-dream, from which he was aroused only by the soft flutter of gowns and laces as the women rose to go. There was a momentary disarrangement of seats. Gilbert Deyes, who was on the other side of the table, rose, and carrying his glass in his hand, came deliberately round to the vacant seat by the young man's side. In his evening clothes, the length and gauntness of his face and figure seemed more noticeable than ever. His skin was dry, almost like parchment, and his eyes by contrast appeared unnaturally bright. His new neighbour noticed, too, that the glass which he carried so carefully contained nothing but water.

"I will come and talk to you for a few minutes, if I may," Deyes said. "I leave the Church and agriculture to hobnob. Somehow I don't fancy that as a buffer I should be a success."

Young Hurd smiled amiably. He was more than a little flattered.

"The Archdeacon," he remarked, "is not an inspiring neighbour."

Deyes lit one of his own cigarettes and passed his case.

"I have found the Archdeacon very dull," he admitted — "a privilege of his order, I suppose. By the bye, you are having a dose of religion from a new source hereabouts, are you not?"

"You mean this young missioner?" Hurd inquired doubtfully.

Deyes nodded.

"I was with our hostess when he came up to ask for the loan of a barn to hold services in. A very queer sort of person, I should think?"

"I haven't spoken to him," Hurd answered, "but I should think he's more or less mad. I can understand mission and Salvation Army work and all that sort of thing in the cities, but I'm hanged if I can understand any one coming to Thorpe with such notions."

"Our hostess is annoyed about it, I imagine," Deyes remarked.

"She seems to have taken a dislike to the fellow," Hurd admitted. "She was speaking to me about him just now. He is to be turned out of his lodgings here."

Gilbert Deyes smiled. The news interested him.

"Our hostess is practical in her dislikes," he remarked.

"Why not?" his neighbour answered. "The place belongs to her."

Deyes watched for a moment the smoke from his cigarette, curling upwards.

"The young man," he said thoughtfully, "impressed me as being a person of some determination. I wonder whether he will consent to accept defeat so easily."

The agent's son scarcely saw what else there was for him to do.

"There isn't anywhere round here," he remarked, "where they would take him in against Miss Thorpe-Hatton's wishes. Besides, he has nowhere to preach. His coming here at all was a huge mistake. If he's a sensible person he'll admit it."

Deyes nodded as he rose to his feet and lounged towards the door with the other men.

"Play bridge?" he asked his companion, as they crossed the hall.

"A little," the young man answered, "for moderate stakes."

They entered the drawing-room, and Deyes made his way to a secluded corner, where Lady Peggy sat scribbling alone in a note-book.

"My dear Lady Peggy," he inquired, "whence this exceptional industry?"

She closed the book and looked up at him with twinkling eyes.

"Well, I didn't mean to tell a soul until it was finished," she declared, "but you've just caught me. I've had such a brilliant idea. I'm going to write a Society Encyclopædia!"

Deyes looked at her solemnly.

"A Society Encyclopædia!" he repeated uncertainly. "'Pon my word, I'm not quite sure that I understand."

She motioned him to sit down by her side.

"I'll explain," she said. "You know we're all expected to know something about everything nowadays, and it's such a bore reading up things. I'm going to compile a little volume of definitions. I shall sell it at a guinea a copy, pay all my debts, and become quite respectable again."

Deyes shook his head. His attitude was scarcely sympathetic.

"My dear Lady Peggy, what nonsense!" he declared. "Respectable, indeed! I call it positively pandering to the middle classes!"

Lady Peggy looked doubtful.

"It is a horrid word, isn't it?" she admitted, "but it would be lovely to make some money. Of course, I haven't absolutely decided how to spend it yet. It does seem rather a waste, doesn't it, to pay one's debts, but think of the luxury of feeling one could do it if one wanted to!"

"There's something in that," Deyes admitted. "But an encyclopædia! My dear Lady Peggy, you don't know what you're talking about. I've got one somewhere, I know. It came in a van, and it took two of the men to unload it."

Lady Peggy laughed softly.

"Oh! I don't mean that sort, of course," she declared. "I mean just a little gilt-edged text book, bound in morocco, you know, with just those things in it we're likely to run up against. Radium, for instance. Now every one's talking about radium. Do you know what radium is?"

Deyes swung his eyeglass carefully by its black riband.

"Well," he admitted, "I've a sort of idea, but I'm not very good at definitions."

"Of course not," Lady Peggy declared triumphantly. "When it comes to the point, you see what a good idea mine is. You turn to my text-book," she added, turning the pages over rapidly, "and there you are. Radium! 'A hard, rare substance, invented by Mr. Gillette to give tone to his bachelor parties.' What do you think of that?"

"Wonderful!" Deyes declared solemnly. "Where do you get your information from?"

"Oh! I poke about in dictionaries and things, and ask every one questions," Lady Peggy declared airily. "Would you like to hear some more?"

"Our hostess is beckoning to me," Deyes answered, rising. "I expect she wants some bridge."

"I'm on," Lady Peggy declared cheerfully. "Whom shall we get for a fourth?"

"Wilhelmina has found him already," Deyes declared. "It's the new young man, I think."

Lady Peggy shrugged her shoulders.

"The agent's son?" she remarked. "I shouldn't have thought that he would have cared about our points."

"He can afford it for once in a way, I should imagine," Deyes answered. "I can't understand, though ——"

He stopped short. She looked at him curiously.

"Is it possible," she murmured, "that there exists anything which Gilbert Deyes does not understand?"

"Many things," he answered; "amongst them, why does Wilhelmina patronize this young man? He is well enough, of course, but ——" he shrugged his shoulders expressively; "the thing needs an explanation, doesn't it?"

"If Wilhelmina — were not Wilhelmina, it certainly would," Lady Peggy answered. "I call her craving for new things and new people positively morbid. All the time she beats her wings against the bars. There are no new things. There are no new experiences. The sooner one makes up one's mind to it the better."

Gilbert Deyes laughed softly.

"If my memory serves me," he said, "you are repeating a cry many thousand years old. Wasn't there a prophet —— "

"There was," she interrupted, "but they are beckoning us. I hope I don't cut with the young man. I don't believe he has a bridge face."

CHAPTER V

EVICTED

VICTOR MACHESON smoked his after-breakfast pipe with the lazy enjoyment of one who is thoroughly at peace with himself and his surroundings. The tiny strip of lawn on to which he had dragged his chair was surrounded with straggling bushes of cottage flowers, and flanked by a hedge thick with honeysuckle. Straight to heaven, as the flight of a bird, the thin line of blue smoke curled upwards to the summer sky; the very air seemed full of sweet scents and soothing sounds. A few yards away, a procession of lazy cows moved leisurely along the grass-bordered lane; from the other side of the hedge came the cheerful sound of a reaping-machine, driven slowly through the field of golden corn.

The man, through half closed eyes, looked out upon these things, and every line in his face spelt contentment. In repose, the artistic temperament with which he was deeply imbued, asserted itself more clearly — the almost fanatical light in his eyes was softened; one saw there was something of the wistfulness of those who seek to raise but a corner of the veil that hangs before the world of hidden

things — something, too, of the subdued joy which
even the effort brings. The lines of his forceful
mouth were less firm, more sensitive — a greater
sense of humanity seemed somehow to have descended upon him as he lounged there in the warmth
of the sun, with the full joy of his beautiful environ-
ment creeping through his blood.

"If you please, Mr. Macheson," some one said in
his ear.

He turned his head at once. A tall, fair girl had
stepped out of the room where he had been break-
fasting, and was standing by his elbow. She was
neatly dressed, pretty in a somewhat insipid fashion,
and her hands and hair showed signs of a refinement
superior to her station. Just now she was apparently nervous. Macheson smiled at her encourag-
ingly.

"Well, Letty," he said, "what is it?"

"I wanted — can I say something to you, Mr.
Macheson?" she began.

"Why not?" he answered kindly. "Is it anything very serious? Out with it!"

"I was thinking, Mr. Macheson," she said, "that
I should like to leave home — if I could — if there
was anything which I could do. I wanted to ask
your advice."

He laid down his pipe and looked at her seriously.

"Why, Letty," he said, "how long have you been
thinking of this?"

"Oh! ever so long, sir," she exclaimed, speaking
with more confidence. "You see there's nothing
for me to do here except when there's any one staying, like you, sir, and that's not often. Mother

won't let me help with the rough work, and Ruth's
growing up now, she's ever such a strong girl. And
I should like to go away if I could, and learn to be
a little more — more ladylike," she added, with
reddening cheeks.

Macheson was puzzled. The girl was not looking
him in the face. He felt there was something at
the back of it all.

"My dear girl," he said, "you can't learn to be
ladylike. That's one of the things that's born with
you or it isn't. You can be just as much a lady
helping your mother here as practising grimaces in
a London drawing-room."

"But I want to improve myself," she persisted.

"Go for a long walk every day, and look about
you," he said. "Read. I'll lend you some books
— the right sort. You'll do better here than away."

She was frankly dissatisfied.

"But I want to go away," she declared. "I want
to leave Thorpe for a time. I should like to go to
London. Couldn't I get a situation as lady's help
or companion or something of that sort? I shouldn't
want any money."

He was silent for a moment.

"Does your mother know of this, Letty?" he
asked.

"She wouldn't object," the girl answered eagerly.
"She lets me do what I like."

"Hadn't you better tell me — the rest?" Macheson asked quietly.

The girl looked away uneasily.

"There is no rest," she protested weakly.

Macheson shook his head.

"Letty," he said, "if you have formed any ideas of a definite future for yourself, different from any you see before you here, tell me what they are, and I will do my best to help you. But if you simply want to go away because you are dissatisfied with the life here, because you fancy yourself superior to it, well, I'm sorry, but I'd sooner prevent your going than help you."

Her eyes filled with tears.

"Oh! Mr. Macheson, it isn't that," she declared, "I — I don't want to tell any one, but I'm very — very fond of some one who's — quite different. I think he's fond of me, too," she added softly, "but he's always used to being with ladies, and I wanted to improve myself so much! I thought if I went to London," she added wistfully, "I might learn? "

Macheson laughed cheerfully. He laid his hand for a moment upon her arm.

"Oh! Letty, Letty," he declared, "you're a foolish little girl! Now, listen to me. If he's a good sort, and I'm sure he is, or you wouldn't be fond of him, he'll like you just exactly as you are. Do you know what it means to be a lady, the supreme test of good manners? It means to be natural. Take my advice! Go on helping your mother, enter into the village life, make friends with the other girls, don't imagine yourself a bit superior to anybody else. Read when you have time — I'll manage the books for you, and spend all the time you can out of doors. It's sound advice, Letty. Take my word for it. Hullo, who's this? "

A new sound in the lane made them both turn their heads. Young Hurd had just ridden up and

was fastening his pony to the fence. He looked
across at them curiously, and Letty retreated pre-
cipitately into the house. A moment or two later
he came up the narrow path, frowning at Macheson
over the low hedge of foxgloves and cottage roses,
and barely returning his courteous greeting. For
a moment he hesitated, however, as though about
to speak. Then, changing his mind, he passed on
and entered the farmhouse.

He met Mrs. Foulton herself in the passage, and
she welcomed him with a smiling face.

"Good morning, Mr. Hurd, sir!" she exclaimed,
plucking at her apron. "Won't you come inside,
sir, and sit down? The parlour's let to Mr. Macheson
there, but he's out in the garden, and he won't
mind your stepping in for a moment. And how's
your father, Mr. Hurd? Wonderful well he was
looking when I saw him last."

The young man followed her inside, but declined
a chair.

"Oh! the governor's all right, Mrs. Foulton," he
answered. "Never knew him anything else. Good
weather for the harvest, eh?"

"Beautiful, sir!" Mrs. Foulton answered.

"Were you wanting to speak to John, Mr. Stephen?
He's about the home meadow somewhere, or in the
orchard. I can send a boy for him, or perhaps
you'd step out."

"It's you I came to see, Mrs. Foulton," the young
man said, "and 'pon my word, I don't like my
errand much."

Mrs. Foulton was visibly anxious.

"There's no trouble like, I hope, sir?" she began.

"Oh! it's nothing serious," he declared reassuringly. "To tell you the truth, it's about your lodger."

"About Mr. Macheson, sir!" the woman exclaimed.

"Yes! Do you know how long he was proposing to stay with you?"

"He's just took the rooms for another week, sir," she answered, "and a nicer lodger, or one more quiet and regular in his habits, I never had or wish to have. There's nothing against him, sir — surely?"

"Nothing personal — that I know of," Hurd answered, tapping his boots with his riding-whip. "The fact of it is, he has offended Miss Thorpe-Hatton, and she wants him out of the place."

"Well, I never did!" Mrs. Foulton exclaimed in amazement. "Him offend Miss Thorpe-Hatton! So nice-spoken he is, too. I'm sure I can't imagine his saying a wry word to anybody."

"He has come to Thorpe," Hurd explained, "on an errand of which Miss Thorpe-Hatton disapproves, and she does not wish to have him in the place. She knows that he is staying here, and she wishes you to send him away at once."

Mrs. Foulton's face fell.

"Well, I'm fair sorry to hear this, sir," she declared. "It's only this morning that he spoke for the rooms for another week, and I was glad and willing enough to let them to him. Well I never did! It does sound all anyhow, don't it, sir, to be telling him to pack up and go sudden-like!"

"I will speak to him myself, if you like, Mrs.

Foulton," Stephen said. "Of course, Miss Thorpe-
Hatton does not wish you to lose anything, and I
am to pay you the rent of the rooms for the time he
engaged them. I will do so at once, if you will let
me know how much it is."

He thrust his hand into his pocket, but Mrs.
Foulton drew back. The corners of her mouth
were drawn tightly together.

"Thank you, Mr. Stephen," she said, "I ll obey
Miss Thorpe-Hatton's wishes, of course, as in duty
bound, but I'll not take any money for the rooms.
Thank you all the same."

"Don't be foolish, Mrs. Foulton," the young man
said pleasantly. "It will annoy Miss Thorpe-
Hatton if she knows you have refused, and you may
just as well have the money. Let me see. Shall
we say a couple of sovereigns for the week?"

Mrs. Foulton shook her head.

"I'll not take anything, sir, thank you all the
same, and if you'd say a word to Mr. Macheson, I'd
be much obliged. I'd rather any one spoke to him
than me."

Stephen Hurd pocketed the money with a shrug
of the shoulders.

"Just as you like, of course, Mrs. Foulton," he
said. "I'll go out and speak to the young gentleman at once."

He strolled out and looked over the hedge.

"Mr. Macheson, I believe?" he remarked interrogatively.

Macheson nodded as he rose from his chair.

"And you are Mr. Hurd's son, are you not?" he
said pleasantly. "Wonderful morning, isn't it?"

Young Hurd stepped over the rose bushes. The two men stood side by side, something of a height, only that the better cut of Hurd's clothes showed his figure to greater advantage.

"I'm sorry to say that I've come on rather a disagreeable errand," the agent's son began. "I've been talking to Mrs. Foulton about it."

"Indeed?" Macheson remarked interrogatively.

"The fact is you seem to have rubbed up against our great lady here," young Hurd continued. "She's very down on these services you were going to hold, and she wants to see you out of the place."

"I am sorry to hear this," Macheson said — and once more waited.

"It isn't a pleasant task," Stephen continued, liking his errand less as he proceeded; "but I've had to tell Mrs. Foulton that — that, in short, Miss Thorpe-Hatton does not wish her tenants to accept you as a lodger."

"Miss Thorpe-Hatton makes war on a wide scale," Macheson remarked, smiling faintly.

"Well, after all, you see," Hurd explained, "the whole place belongs to her, and there is no particular reason, is there, why she should tolerate any one in it of whom she disapproves?"

"None whatever," Macheson assented gravely.

"I promised Mrs. Foulton I would speak to you," Stephen continued, stepping backwards. "I'm sure, for her sake, you won't make any trouble. Good morning!"

Macheson bowed slightly.

"Good morning!" he answered.

Stephen Hurd lingered even then upon the garden path. Somehow he was not satisfied with his interview — with his own position at the end of it. He had an uncomfortable sense of belittlement, of having played a small part in a not altogether worthy game. The indifference of the other's manner nettled him. He tried a parting shaft.

"Mrs. Foulton said something about your having engaged the rooms for another week," he said, turning back. "Of course, if you insist upon staying, it will place the woman in a very awkward position."

Macheson had resumed his seat.

"I should not dream," he said coolly, "of resisting — your mistress' decree! I shall leave here in half an hour."

Young Hurd walked angrily down the path and slammed the gate. The sense of having been worsted was strong upon him. He recognized his own limitations too accurately not to be aware that he had been in conflict with a stronger personality.

"D—— the fellow!" he muttered, as he cantered down the lane. "I wish he were out of the place."

A genuine wish, and one which betrayed at least a glimmering of a prophetic instinct. In some dim way he seemed to understand, even before the first move on the board, that the coming of Victor Macheson to Thorpe was inimical to himself. He was conscious of his weakness, of a marked inferiority, and the consciousness was galling. The fellow had no right to be a gentleman, he told himself angrily — a gentleman and a missioner!

Macheson re-lit his pipe and called to Mrs. Foulton.

"Mrs. Foulton," he said pleasantly, "I'll have to

go! Your great lady doesn't like me on the estate.
I dare say she's right."

"I'm sure I'm very sorry, sir," Mrs. Foulton declared shamefacedly. "You've seen young Mr.
Hurd?"

"He was kind enough to explain the situation to
me," Macheson answered. "I'm afraid I am rather
a nuisance to everybody. If I am, it's because they
don't quite understand!"

"I'm sure, sir," Mrs. Foulton affirmed, "a nicer
lodger no one ever had. And as for them services,
and the Vicar objecting to them, I can't see what
harm they'd do! We're none of us so good but
we might be a bit better!"

"A very sound remark, Mrs. Foulton," Macheson
said, smiling. "And now you must make out my
bill, please, and what about a few sandwiches? You
could manage that? I'm going to play in a cricket
match this afternoon."

"Why you've just paid the bill, sir! There's only
breakfast, and the sandwiches you're welcome to,
and very sorry I am to part with you, sir."

"Better luck another time, I hope, Mrs. Foulton,"
he answered, smiling. "I must go upstairs and pack
my bag. I shan't forget your garden with its
delicious flowers."

"It's a shame as you've got to leave it, sir," Mrs.
Foulton said heartily. "If my Richard were alive
he'd never have let you go for all the Miss Thorpe-
Hattons in the world. But John — he's little more
than a lad — he'd be frightened to death for fear of
losing the farm, if I so much as said a word to him."

Macheson laughed softly.

"John's a good son," he said. "Don't you worry him."

He went up to his tiny bedroom and changed his clothes for a suit of flannels. Then he packed his few belongings and walked out into the world. He lit a pipe and shouldered his portmanteau.

"There is a flavour of martyrdom about this affair," he said to himself, as he strolled along, "which appeals to me. I don't think that young man has any sense of humour."

He paused every now and then to listen to the birds and admire the view. He had the air of one thoroughly enjoying his walk. Presently he turned off the main road, and wandered along a steep green lane, which was little more than a cart-track. Here he met no one. The country on either side was common land, sown with rocks and the poorest soil, picturesque, but almost impossible of cultivation. A few sheep were grazing upon the hills, but other sign of life there was none. Not a farm-house — scarcely a keeper's cottage in sight! It was a forgotten corner of a not unpopulous county — the farthest portion of a belt of primeval forest land, older than history itself. Macheson laughed softly as he reached the spot he had had in his mind, and threw his bag over the grey stone wall into the cool shade of a dense fragment of wood.

"So much," he murmured softly, "for the lady of Thorpe!"

CHAPTER VI

CRICKET AND PHILOSOPHY

"THE instinct for games," Wilhelmina remarked, "is one which I never possessed. Let us see whether we can learn something."

In obedience to her gesture, the horses were checked, and the footman clambered down and stood at their heads. Deyes, from his somewhat uncomfortable back seat in the victoria, leaned forward, and, adjusting his eyeglass, studied the scene with interest.

"Here," he remarked, "we have the 'flannelled fool' upon his native heath. They are playing a game which my memory tells me is cricket. Everyone seems very hot and very excited."

Wilhelmina beckoned to the footman to come round to the side of the carriage.

"James," she said, "do you know what all this means? "

She waved her hand towards the cricket pitch, the umpires with their white coats, the tent and the crowd of spectators. The man touched his hat.

"It is a cricket match, madam," he answered, "between Thorpe and Nesborough."

Wilhelmina looked once more towards the field,

and recognized Mr. Hurd upon his stout little cob.

"Go and tell Mr. Hurd to come and speak to me," she ordered.

The man hastened off. Mr. Hurd had not once turned his head. His eyes were riveted upon the game. The groom found it necessary to touch him on the arm before he could attract his attention. Even when he had delivered his message, the agent waited until the finish of the over before he moved. Then he cantered his pony up to the waiting carriage. Wilhelmina greeted him graciously.

"I want to know about the cricket match, Mr. Hurd," she asked, smiling.

Mr. Hurd wheeled his pony round so that he could still watch the game.

"I am afraid that we are going to be beaten, madam," he said dolefully. "Nesborough made a hundred and ninety-eight, and we have six wickets down for fifty."

Wilhelmina seemed scarcely to realize the tragedy which his words unfolded.

"I suppose they are the stronger team, aren't they?" she remarked. "They ought to be. Nesborough is quite a large town."

"We have beaten them regularly until the last two years," Mr. Hurd answered. "We should beat them now but for their fast bowler, Mills. I don't know how it is, but our men will not stand up to him."

"Perhaps they are afraid of being hurt," Wilhelmina suggested innocently. "If that is he bowling now, I'm sure I don't wonder at it."

Mr. Hurd frowned.

"We don't have men in the eleven who are afraid of getting hurt," he remarked stiffly.

A shout of dismay from the onlookers, a smothered exclamation from Mr. Hurd, and a man was seen on his way to the pavilion. His wickets were spreadeagled, and the ball was being tossed about the field.

"Another wicket!" the agent exclaimed testily. "Crooks played all round that ball!"

"Isn't that your son going in, Mr. Hurd?" Wilhelmina asked.

"Yes! Stephen is in now," his father answered. "If he gets out, the match is over."

"Who is the other batsman?" Deyes asked.

"Antill, the second bailiff," Mr. Hurd answered. "He's captain, and he can stay in all day, but he can't make runs."

They all leaned forward to witness the continuation of the match. Stephen Hurd's career was brief and inglorious. He took guard and looked carefully round the field with the air of a man who is going to give trouble. Then he saw the victoria, with its vision of parasols and fluttering laces, and the sight was fatal to him. He slogged wildly at the first ball, missed it, and paid the penalty. The lady in the carriage frowned, and Mr. Hurd muttered something under his breath as he watched his son on the way back to the tent.

"I'm afraid it's all up with us now," he remarked. "We have only three more men to go in."

"Then we are going to be beaten," Wilhelmina remarked.

"I'm afraid so," Mr. Hurd assented gloomily.

The next batsman had issued from the tent and was on his way to the wicket. Wilhelmina, who had been about to give an order to the footman, watched him curiously.

"Who is that going in? " she asked abruptly.

Mr. Hurd was looking not altogether comfortable.

"It is the young man who wanted to preach," he answered.

Wilhelmina frowned.

"Why is he playing? " she asked. "He has nothing to do with Thorpe."

"He came down to see them practise a few evenings ago, and Antill asked him," the agent answered. "If I had known earlier I would have stopped it."

Wilhelmina did not immediately reply. She was watching the young man who stood now at the wicket, bat in hand. In his flannels, he seemed a very different person from the missioner whose request a few days ago had so much offended her. Nevertheless, her lip curled as she saw the terrible Mills prepare to deliver his first ball.

"That sort of person," she remarked, "is scarcely likely to be much good at games. Oh!"

Her exclamation was repeated in various forms from all over the field. Macheson had hit his first ball high over their heads, and a storm of applause broke from the bystanders. The batsman made no attempt to run.

"What is that?" Wilhelmina asked.

"A boundary — magnificent drive," Mr. Hurd answered excitedly. "By Jove, another!"

The agent dropped his reins and led the applause. Along the ground this time the ball had come at such a pace that the fieldsman made a very half-hearted attempt to stop it. It passed the horses' feet by only a few yards. The coachman turned round and touched his hat.

"Shall I move farther back, madam?" he asked.

"Stay where you are," Wilhelmina answered shortly. Her eyes were fixed upon the tall, lithe figure once more facing the bowler. The next ball was the last of the over. Macheson played it carefully for a single, and stood prepared for the bowling at the other end. He began by a graceful cut for two, and followed it up by a square leg hit clean out of the ground. For the next half an hour, the Thorpe villagers thoroughly enjoyed themselves. Never since the days of one Foulds, a former blacksmith, had they seen such an exhibition of hurricane hitting. The fast bowler, knocked clean off his length, became wild and erratic. Once he only missed Macheson's head by an inch, but his next ball was driven fair and square out of the ground for six. The applause became frantic.

Wilhelmina was leaning back amongst the cushions of her carriage, watching the game through half closed eyes, and with some apparent return of her usual graceful languor. Nevertheless, she remained there, and her eyes seldom wandered for a moment from the scene of play. Beneath her apparent indifference, she was watching this young man with an interest for which she would have found it hard to account, and which instinct alone prompted her to conceal. It was a very ordinary scene, after all, of which he was the dominant figure. She had seen so much of life on a larger scale — of men playing heroic parts in the limelight of a stage as mighty as this was insignificant. Yet, without stopping to reason about it, she was conscious of a curious sense of pleasure in watching the doings of this forceful young giant. With an easy good-humoured smile, replaced every now and then with a grim look of determination as he jumped out from the crease to hit, he continued his victorious career, until a more frantic burst of applause than usual announced that the match was won. Then Wilhelmina turned towards Stephen Hurd, who was standing by the side of the carriage.

"You executed my commission," she asked, "respecting that young man?"

"The first thing this morning," he answered. "I went up to see Mrs. Foulton, and I also spoke to him."

"Did he make any difficulty?"

"None at all!" the young man answered.

"What did he say?"

Stephen hesitated, but Wilhelmina waited for his reply. She had the air of one remotely interested, yet she waited obviously to hear what this young man had said.

"I think he said something about your making war upon a large scale," Stephen explained diffidently.

She sat still for a moment. She was looking towards the deserted cricket pitch.

"Where is he staying now?" she asked.

"I do not know," he answered. "I have warned

all the likely people not to receive him, and I have told him, too, that he will only get your tenants into trouble if he tries to get lodgings here."

"I should like," she said, "to speak to him. Perhaps you would be so good as to ask him to step this way for a moment."

Stephen departed, wondering. Deyes was watching his hostess with an air of covert amusement.

"Do you continue the warfare," he asked, "or has the young man's prowess softened your heart?"

Wilhelmina raised her parasol and looked steadily at her questioner.

"Warfare is scarcely the word, is it?" she remarked carelessly. "I have no personal objection to the young man."

They watched him crossing the field towards them. Notwithstanding his recent exertions, he walked lightly, and without any sign of fatigue. Deyes looked curiously at the crest upon the cap which he was carrying in his hand.

"Magdalen," he muttered. "Your missioner grows more interesting."

Wilhelmina leaned forwards. Her face was inscrutable, and her greeting devoid of cordiality.

"So you have decided to teach my people cricket instead of morals, Mr. Macheson," she remarked.

"The two," he answered pleasantly, "are not incompatible."

Wilhelmina frowned.

"I hope," she said, "that you have abandoned your idea of holding meetings in the village."

"Certainly not," he answered. "I will begin next week."

"So you have decided to teach my people cricket instead of morals, Mr. Macheson," she remarked.   Page 68

"You understand," she said calmly, "that I con-sider you — as a missioner — an intruder — here! Those of my people who attend your services will incur my displeasure!"

"Madam," he answered, "I do not believe that you will visit it upon them."

"But I will," she interrupted ruthlessly. "You are young and know little of the world. You have not yet learnt the truth of one of the oldest of pro-verbs — that it is well to let well alone!"

"It is a sop for the idle, that proverb," he an-swered. "It is the motto for the great army of those who drift."

"I have been making inquiries," she said. "I find that my villagers are contented and prosperous. There are no signs of vice in the place."

"There is such a thing," he answered, "as being too prosperous, over-contented. The person in such a state takes life for granted. Religion is a thing he hears about, but fails to realize. He has no need of it. He becomes like the prize cattle in your park! He has a mind, but has forgotten how to use it."

She looked at him steadily, perhaps a trifle inso-lently.

"How old are you, Mr. Macheson?" she asked.

"Twenty-eight," he answered, with a slight flush.

"Twenty-eight! You are young to make yourself the judge of such things as these. You will do a great deal of mischief, I am afraid, before you are old enough to realize it."

"To awaken those who sleep in the daytime — is that mischief?" he asked.

"It is," she answered deliberately. "When you are older you will realize it. Sleep is the best."

He bent towards her. The light in his eyes had blazed out.

"You know in your heart," he said, "that it is not true. You have brains, and you are as much of an artist as your fettered life permits you to be. You know very well that knowledge is best."

"Do you believe," she answered, "that I — I take myself not personally but as a type — am as happy as they are?"

She moved her parasol to where the village lay beyond the trees. He hesitated.

"Madam," he answered gravely, "I know too little of your life to answer your question."

She shrugged her shoulders. For a moment her parasol hid her face.

"We are quite à la mode, are we not, my dear Peggy?" she remarked, with a curious little laugh. "Philosophy upon the village green. Gilbert, tell them to drive on."

She turned deliberately to Macheson.

"Come and convert us instead," she said. "We need it more."

"I do not doubt it, madam," he answered. "Good afternoon!"

The carriage drove off. Macheson, obeying an impulse which he did not recognize, watched it till it was out of sight. At the bend, Wilhelmina deliberately turned in her seat and saw him standing there. She waved her parasol in ironical farewell, and Macheson walked back to the tent with burning cheeks.

CHAPTER VII

AN UNDERNOTE OF MUSIC

A GREAT dinner party had come to an end, and the Lord-Lieutenant of the county bowed low over the cold hand of his departing guest, in whose honour it had been given. A distant relationship gave Lord Westerdean privileges upon which he would willingly have improved.

"You are leaving us early, Wilhelmina," he murmured reproachfully. "How can I expect to keep my other guests if you desert us?"

Wilhelmina withdrew the hand and nodded her other farewells. The heat of the summer evening had brought every one out from the drawing-room. The hall doors stood open. Those of the guests who were not playing bridge or billiards were outside upon the terrace — some had wandered into the gardens.

"My dear Leslie," she said, as she stood upon the broad steps, "you are losing your habit of gallantry. A year ago you would not have ventured to suggest that in my absence the coming or going of your other guests could matter a straw."

"You know very well that it doesn't," he answered, dropping his voice. "You know very well ——"

"To-night," she interrupted calmly, "I will not be made love to! I am not in the humour for it."

He looked down at her curiously. He was a man of exceptional height, thin, grey, still handsome, an ex-diplomat, whose career, had he chosen to follow it, would have been a brilliant one. Wealth and immense estates had thrust their burdens upon him, however, and he was content to be the most popular man in his county.

"There is nothing the matter?" he asked anxiously.

She shook her head.

"You are well?" he persisted, dropping his voice.

"Absolutely," she answered. "It is not that. It is a mood. I used to welcome moods as an escape from the ruts. I suppose I am getting too old for them now."

He shook his head.

"I wonder," he said, "if the world really knows how young you are."

"Don't," she interrupted, with a shudder, "I have outlived my years."

A motor omnibus and a small victoria came round from the stables. The party from Thorpe began slowly to assemble upon the steps.

"I am going in the victoria — alone," she said, resting her fingers upon his arm. "Don't you envy me?"

"I envy the vacant place," he answered sadly. "Isn't this desire for solitude somewhat of a new departure, though?"

"Perhaps," she admitted. "I am rather looking forward to my drive. To-night, as we came here, the whole country seemed like a great garden of perfumes and beautiful places. That is why I had them telephone for a carriage. There are times when I hate motoring!"

He broke off a cluster of pink roses and placed them in her hands.

"If your thoughts must needs fill the empty seat," he whispered, as he bent over her for his final adieux, "remember my claims, I beg. Perhaps my thoughts might even meet yours!"

She laughed under her breath, but the light in his eyes was unanswered.

"Perhaps!" she answered. "It is a night for thoughts and dreams, this. Even I may drift into sentiment. Good night! Such a charming evening."

The carriage rolled smoothly down the avenue from the great house, over which she might so easily have reigned, and turned into the road. A few minutes later the motor-car flashed by. Afterwards there was solitude, for it was already past midnight. Gilbert Deyes looked thoughtfully out at the carriage from his place in the car. He had begged — very hard for him — for that empty seat.

"Of what is it a sign," he asked, "when a woman seeks solitude?"

Lady Peggy shrugged her shoulders.

"Wilhelmina is tired of us all, I suppose," she remarked. "She gets like that sometimes."

"Then of what is it a sign," he persisted, "when a woman tires of people — like us?"

Lady Peggy yawned.

"In a woman of more primitive instincts," she

said, "it would mean an affair. But Wilhelmina
has outgrown all that. She is the only woman of our
acquaintance of whom one would dare to say it, but
I honestly believe that to Wilhelmina men are like
puppets. Was she born, I wonder, with ice in her
veins?"

"One wonders," Deyes remarked softly. "A
woman like that is always something of a mystery.
By the bye, wasn't there a whisper of something the
year she lived in Florence?"

"People have talked of her, of course," Lady
Peggy answered. "In Florence, a woman without
a lover is like a child without toys. To be virtuous
there is the one offence which Society does not
pardon."

"I believe," Deyes said, "that a lover would
bore Wilhelmina terribly."

"Why the dickens doesn't she marry Leslie?"
Austin asked, opening his eyes for a moment.

"Too obvious," Deyes murmured. "Some day I
can't help fancying that she will give us all a shock."

A mile or more behind, the lady with ice in her
veins, leaned back amongst the cushions of her carriage, drinking in, with a keenness of appreciation
which surprised even herself, the beauties of the
still, hot night. The moon was as yet barely risen.
In the half light, the country and the hills beyond,
with their tumbled masses of rock, seemed unreal —
of strange and mysterious outline. More than anything, she was conscious of a sense of softness.
The angles were gone from all the crude places, it
was peace itself which had settled upon the land.
Peace, and a wonderful silence! The birds had long

ago ceased to sing, no breath of wind was abroad to
stir the leaves of the trees.   All the cheerful chorus
of country sounds which make music throughout
the long summer day had ceased.   Once, when a
watch-dog barked in the valley far below, she started.
The sound seemed unreal — as though, indeed, it
came from a different world!

The woman in the carriage looked out with steady
tireless eyes upon this visionary land.   The breath
of the honeysuckle and the pleasant odour of warm
hay seemed to give life to the sensuous joy of the
wonderful night.   She herself was a strange being
to be abroad in these quiet lanes.   Her only wrap
was a long robe of filmy lace, which she had thrown
back, so that her shoulders and neck, with its collar
of lustrous pearls, were bare to the faint breeze,
which only their own progress made.   Her gleaming
dress of white satin, undecorated, unadorned, fell
in delicate lines about her limbs.   No wonder that
the only person whom they passed, a belated farmer,
rubbed his eyes and stared at her as at a ghost!

It seemed to her that something of the confusion
of this delightful, half-seen world, had stolen, too,
into her thoughts.   All day long she had been conscious of it.   There was something alien there,
something wholly unrecognizable.   She felt a new
light falling upon her life.   From where?   She
could not tell.   Only she knew that its pitiless
routine, its littleness, its frantic struggle for the
front place in the great pleasure-house, seemed suddenly to stand revealed in pitiful colours.   Surely
it belonged to some other woman!   It could not
be she who did those things and called them life.

She, who scarcely knew what nerves were, was suddenly afraid. Some change was coming upon her; she felt herself caught in a silent, swift-flowing current. She was being carried away, and she had not strength to resist. And all the time there was an undernote of music. That was what made it so strange. The light that was falling was like summer rain upon the bare, dry places. She was conscious of a new vitality, a new life, and she feared it. Fancy being endowed with a new sense, in the midst of an ordinary work-a-day existence! She felt like that. It was unbelievable, and yet its tumult was stirring in her heart, was rushing through her veins. Often before, her tired eyes had rested unmoved upon a country as beautiful as this, even the mystery of this half light was no new thing. To-night she saw farther — she felt the throbbing, half-mad delight of the wanderer in the enchanted land, the pilgrim who hears suddenly the Angelus bell from the shrine he has journeyed so far to visit. What it meant she could not, she dared not ask herself. She was content to sit there, her eyes wide open now, the tired lines smoothed from her forehead, her face like the face of an eager and beautiful child. No one of her world would have recognized her, as she travelled that night through the perfumed lanes.

It was when they were within a mile or two of home that an awakening came. They had turned into a lonely lane leading to one of the back entrances to Thorpe, and were climbing a somewhat steep hill. Suddenly the horses plunged and almost stopped. She leaned forward.

"What is it, Johnson?" she asked.

The man touched his hat.

"The 'osses shied, madam, at the light in the trees there. Enough to frighten 'em, too."

Her eyes followed his pointing finger. A few yards back from the roadside, a small, steady light was burning amongst the trees.

"What is it?" she asked quickly.

"I can't say, madam," the man answered. "It looks like a lantern or a candle, or something of that sort."

"There is no cottage there?" she asked.

The man shook his head.

"There's none nearer than the first lodge, madam," he answered. "There's a bit of a shelter there — Higgs, the keeper, built it for a watchman."

"Can I take care of the horses for a moment, while you go and see what it is?" she asked.

"They take a bit of holding, madam," the man answered doubtfully. "We got your message so late at the stables, or I should have had a second man."

Wilhelmina stepped softly out into the road.

"I will go myself," she said. "I daresay it is nothing. If I call, though, you must leave the horses and come to me."

She opened the gate, and raising her skirts with both hands, stepped into the plantation. Her small, white-shod feet fell noiselessly upon the thick undergrowth; she reached the entrance of the shelter without making any sound. Cautiously she peeped in. Her eyes grew round with surprise, her bosom began rapidly to rise and fall. It was Macheson who lay there, fast asleep! He had fallen asleep

evidently whilst reading. A book was lying by his
side, and a covered lantern was burning by his left
shoulder. He was dressed in trousers and shirt; the
latter was open at the throat, showing its outline
firm and white, and his regular breathing. She
drew a step nearer, and leaned over him. Curiously
enough, in sleep the boyishness of his face was less
apparent. The straight, firm mouth, rigidly closed,
was the mouth of a man; his limbs, in repose, seemed
heavy, even massive, especially the bare arm upon
which his head was resting. His shirt was old, but
spotlessly clean; his socks were neatly darned in
many places. He occupied nearly the whole of
the shelter, in fact one foot was protruding through
the opening. In the corner a looking-glass was
hanging from a stick, and a few simple toilet articles
were spread upon the ground.

She bent more closely over him, holding her
breath, although he showed no signs of waking.
Her senses were in confusion, and there was a mist
before her eyes. An unaccountable impulse was
urging her on, driving her, as it seemed, into incredible folly. Lower and lower she bent, till her
hot breath fell almost upon his cheek. Suddenly
he stirred. She started back. After all he did not
open his eyes, but the moment was gone. She
moved backwards towards the opening. She was
seized now with sudden fright. She desired to
escape. She was breathless with fear, the fear of
what she might not have escaped. Yet in the
midst of it, with hot trembling fingers she loosened
the roses from her dress and dropped them by his
side. Then she fled into the semi-darkness.

The habits of a lifetime die hard. They are proof, as a rule, against these fits of temporary madness.

Wilhelmina stepped languidly into her carriage, and commanded her coachman's attention.

"Johnson," she said, "I found a poor man sleeping there. There is no necessity for him to be disturbed. It is my wish that you do not mention the occurrence to any one — to any one at all. You understand?"

The man touched his hat. He would have been dull-witted, indeed, if he had not appreciated the note of finality in his mistress' tone. His horses sprang forward, and a few minutes later turned into the dark avenue which led to the house.

CHAPTER VIII

MACHESON woke with the daylight, stiff, a little tired, and haunted with the consciousness of disturbing dreams. He sprang to his feet and stretched himself. Then he saw the roses.

For a moment or two he stared at them incredulously. Then his thoughts flashed backwards — where or how had he become possessed of them? A few seconds were sufficient. Some one had been there in the night — most likely a woman.

His cheeks burned at the thought. He stooped and took them hesitatingly, reverently, into his hand. To him they represented part of the mystery of life, the mystery of which he knew so little. Soft and fragrant, the touch of the drooping blossoms was like fire to his fingers. Had he been like those predecessors of his in the days of the Puritans, he would have cast them away, trampled them underfoot; he would have seen in them only the snare of the Evil One. But to Macheson this would have seemed almost like sacrilege. They were beautiful and he loved beautiful things.

He made his way farther into the plantation, to where the trees, suddenly opening, disclosed a small,

disused slate quarry, the water in which was kept
fresh by many streams. Stripping off his clothes,
he plunged into the deep cool depths, swimming
round for several minutes on his back, his face
upturned to the dim blue sky. Then he dressed —
in the ugly black suit, for it was Sunday, and made
a frugal breakfast, boiling the water for his coffee
over a small spirit-lamp. And all the time he
kept looking at the roses, now fresh with the water
which he had carefully sprinkled over them. Their
coming seemed to him to whisper of beautiful things,
they turned his thoughts so easily into that world
of poetry and sentiment in which he was a habitual
wanderer. Yet, every now and then, their direct
significance startled, almost alarmed. Some one
had actually been in the place while he slept, and
had retreated without disturbing him. Roses do
not drop from the sky, and of gardens there were
none close at hand. Was it one of the village girls,
who had seen him that afternoon? His cheeks
reddened at the thought. Perhaps he had better
leave his shelter. Another time if she came she
might not steal away so quietly. Scandal would
injure his work. He must run no risks. Deep
down in his heart he thrust that other, that impossi-
bly sweet thought. He would not suffer his mind
to dwell upon it.

After breakfast he walked for an hour or so across
the hills, watching the early mists roll away in the
valleys, and the sunlight settle down upon the land.
It was a morning of silence, this — that peculiar,
mysterious silence which only the first day of the
week seems to bring. The fields were empty of

toilers, the harvest was stayed. From its far-away nest amongst the hills, he could just hear, carried on the bosom of a favouring breeze, the single note of a monastery bell, whose harshness not even distance, or its pleasant journey across the open country, could modify. Macheson listened to it for a moment, and sat down upon a rock on the topmost pinnacle of the hills he was climbing.

Below him, the country stretched like a piece of brilliant patchwork. Thorpe, with its many chimneys and stately avenues, and the village hidden by a grove of elms, was like a cool oasis in the midst of the landscape. Behind, the hills ran rockier and wilder, culminating in a bleak stretch of country, in the middle of which was the monastery. Macheson looked downwards at Thorpe, with the faint clang of that single bell in his ears. The frown on his forehead deepened as the rush of thoughts took insistent hold of him.

For a young man blessed with vigorous health, free from all material anxieties, and with the world before him, Macheson found life an uncommonly serious matter. Only a few years ago, he had left the University with a brilliant degree, a splendid athletic record, and a host of friends. What to do with his life! That was the problem which pressingly confronted him. He recognized in himself certain gifts inevitably to be considered in this choice. He was possessed of a deep religious sense, an immense sympathy for his fellows, and a passion for the beautiful in life, from which the physical side was by no means absent.

How to find a career which would satisfy such

varying qualities! A life of pleasure, unless it were shared by his fellows, did not appeal to him at all; personal ambition he was destitute of; his religion, he was very well aware, was not the sort which would enable him to enter with any prospect of happiness any of the established churches. For a time he had travelled, and had come back with only one definite idea in his mind. Chance had brought him, on his return, into contact with two young men of somewhat similar tastes. A conversation between them one night had given a certain definiteness to his aims. He recalled it to himself as he sat looking down at the thin blue line of smoke rising from the chimneys of Thorpe.

"To use one's life for others," he had repeated thoughtfully — it was the enthusiast of the party who had spoken — "but how?"

"Teach them to avoid like filth the ugly things of life — help them in their search for the things beautiful."

"What are the things beautiful?" he had asked. "Don't they mean something different to every man?"

Holderness had lifted his beautiful head — the boy with whom he had played at school — the friend of his younger life.

"The Christian morality," he had answered.

Macheson had been surprised.

"But you —— " he said, "you don't believe anything."

"It is not necessary," Holderness had answered. "It is a matter of the intelligence. As an artist, if I might dare to call myself one, I say that the

Christian life, if honestly lived, is the most beautiful
thing of all the ages.''

Macheson walked down to the village with the
memory of those words still in his brain. The bell
was ringing for service from the queer, ivy-covered
church, the villagers were coming down the lane in
little groups. Macheson found himself one of a
small knot of people, who stood reverently on one
side, with doffed hats, just by the wooden porch.
He looked up, suddenly realizing the cause.

A small vehicle, something between a bath-chair
and a miniature carriage, drawn by a fat, sleek
pony, was turning into the lane from one of the
splendid avenues which led to the house. A boy
led the pony, a footman marched behind. Wilhelmina, in a plain white muslin dress and a black hat,
was slowly preparing to descend. She smiled
languidly, but pleasantly enough, at the line of
curtseying women and men with doffed hats. The
note of feudalism which their almost reverential
attitudes suggested appealed irresistibly to Macheson's sense of humour. He, too, formed one of
them; he, too, doffed his hat. His greeting, however, was different. Her eyes swept by him unsee-
ing, his pleasant "Good morning" was unheeded.
She even touched her skirt with her fingers, as
though afraid lest it might brush against him in
passing. With tired, graceful footsteps, she passed
into the cool church, leaving him to admire against
his will the slim perfection of her figure, the wonderful carriage of her small but perfect head.

He followed with the others presently, and found
a single seat close to the door. The service began

almost at once, a very beautiful service in its way, for the organ, a present from the lady of the manor, was perfectly played, and the preacher's voice was clear and as sweet as a boy's. Macheson, however, was nervous and ill at ease. From the open door he heard the soft whispering of the west wind — for the first time in his life he found the simple but dignified ritual unconvincing. He was haunted by the sense of some impending disaster. When the prayers came, he fell on his knees and remained there! Even then he could not collect himself! He was praying to an unknown God for protection against some nameless evil! He knew quite well that the words he muttered were vain words. Through the stained glass windows, the sunlight fell in a subdued golden stream upon the glowing hair, the gracefully bent head of the woman who sat alone in the deep square pew. She, too, seemed to be praying. Macheson got up and softly, but abruptly, stole from the church.

Up into the hills, as far away, as high up as possible! A day of sabbath calm, this! Macheson, with the fire in his veins and a sharp pain in his side, climbed as a man possessed. He, too, was fleeing from the unknown. He was many miles away when down in the valley at Thorpe some one spoke of him.

"By the bye," Gilbert Deyes remarked, looking across the luncheon table at his hostess, "when does this athletic young missioner of yours begin his work of regeneration?"

Wilhelmina raised her eyebrows.

"To-morrow evening, I believe," she answered. "He is going to speak at the cross-roads. I fancy that his audience will consist chiefly of the children, and Mrs. Adnith's chickens."

"Can't understand," Austin remarked, "why a chap who can play cricket like that — he did lay on to 'em, too — can be such a crank!"

"He is very young," Wilhelmina remarked composedly, "and I fancy that he must be a little mad. I hope that Thorpe will teach him a lesson. He needs it."

"You do not anticipate then," Deyes remarked, "that his labours here will be crowned with success?"

"He won't get a soul to hear him," Stephen Hurd replied confidently. "The villagers all know what Miss Thorpe-Hatton thinks of his coming here. It will be quite sufficient."

Wilhelmina lit a cigarette and rose to her feet.

"Let us hope so," she remarked drily. "Please remember, all of you, that this is the Palace of Ease! Do exactly what you like, all of you, till five o'clock. I shall be ready for bridge then."

Lady Peggy rose briskly.

"No doubt about what I shall do," she remarked. "I'm going to bed."

Deyes smiled.

"I," he said, "shall spend the afternoon in the rose garden. I need — development."

Wilhelmina looked at him questioningly.

"Please don't be inexplicable," she begged. "It is too hot."

"Roses and sentiment," he declared, "are supposed to go together. I want to grow into accord with my surroundings."

Wilhelmina was silent for a moment.

"If you have found sentiment here, she said carelessly, "you must have dug deep."

"On the contrary," he answered, "I have scarcely scratched the surface!"

Stephen Hurd looked uneasily from Deyes to his hostess. Never altogether comfortable, although eager to accept the most casually offered invitation to Thorpe, he had always the idea that the most commonplace remark contained an innuendo purposely concealed from him.

"Mr. Deyes," he remarked, "looks mysterious."

Deyes glanced at him through his eyeglass.

"It is a subtle neighbourhood," he said. "By the bye, Mr. Hurd, have you ever seen the rose gardens at Carrow?"

"Never," Hurd replied enviously. "I have heard that they are very beautiful."

Wilhelmina passed out.

"The gardens are beautiful," she said, looking back, "but the roses are like all other roses, they fade quickly. Till five o'clock, all of you!"

CHAPTER IX

STEPHEN HURD walked into the room which he and his father shared as a sanctum, half office, half study. Mr. Hurd, senior, was attired in his conventional Sabbath garb, the same black coat of hard, dull material, and dark grey trousers, in which he had attended church for more years than many of the villagers could remember. Stephen, on the other hand, was attired in evening clothes of the latest cut. His white waistcoat had come from a London tailor, and his white tie had cost him considerable pains. His father looked him over with expressionless face.

"You are going to the House again, Stephen?" he asked calmly.

"I am asked to dine there, father," he answered.

"Sorry to leave you alone."

"I have no objection to being alone," Mr. Hurd answered. "I think that you know that. You lunched there, didn't you?"

Stephen nodded.

"Miss Thorpe-Hatton asked me as we came out of church," he answered.

"You play cards?"

The directness of the question allowed of no evasion. Stephen flushed as he answered.

"They play bridge. I may be asked to join. It — is a sort of whist, you know."

"So I understand," the older man remarked. "I have no remark to make concerning that. Manners change, I suppose, with the generations. You are young and I am old. I have never sought to impose my prejudices upon you. You have seen more of the world than I ever did. Perhaps you have found wisdom there."

Stephen was not at his ease.

"I don't know about that, sir," he answered. "Of course, Sunday isn't kept so strictly as it used to be. I like a quiet day myself, but it's pretty dull here usually, and I didn't think it would be wise to refuse an invitation from Miss Thorpe-Hatton."

"Perhaps not," Mr. Hurd answered. "On the other hand, I might remind you that during the forty years during which I have been agent to this estate I have never accepted — beyond a glass of wine — the hospitality offered to me by Miss Thorpe-Hatton's father and grandfather, and by the young lady herself. It is not according to my idea of the fitness of things. I am a servant of the owner of these estates. I prefer to discharge my duties honestly and capably — as a servant."

Stephen frowned at his reflection in the glass. He did not feel in the least like a servant.

"That's rather an old-fashioned view, dad," he declared.

"It may be," his father answered. "In any case, I do not seek to impose it upon you. You are

free to come and go according to your judgment.
But you are young, and I cannot see you expose
yourself to trouble without some warning. Miss
Thorpe-Hatton is not a lady whom it is wise for you
to see too much of."

The directness of this speech took the young man
aback.

"I — she seems very pleasant and gracious," he
faltered.

"Not even to you," his father continued gravely,
"can I betray the knowledge of such things as have
come under my notice as the servant of these estates
and this young lady. Her father was a fine, self-
respecting gentleman, as all the Thorpe-Hattons
have been; her mother came from a noble, but
degenerate, French family. I, who live here a life
without change, who mark time for the years and
watch the striplings become old men, see many
things, and see them truthfully. The evil seed of
her mother's family is in this young woman's blood.
She lives without a chaperon, without compan-
ionship, as she pleases — and to please herself
only."

Stephen frowned irritably. His father's cold,
measured words were like drops of ice.

"But, father," he protested, "she is a leader of
Society, she goes to Court and you see her name at
the very best places. If there was anything wrong
about her, she wouldn't be received like that."

"I know nothing about Society or its require-
ments," his father answered. "She has brains and
wealth, and she is a woman. Therefore, I suppose
the world is on her side. I have said all that I wish

to say. You can perhaps conjecture the reason of
my speaking at all."

"She wouldn't take the trouble to make a fool of
me," Stephen answered bitterly. "I just happen
to make up a number, that's all."

"I am glad that you understand the young lady
so well," his father answered. "Before you go, will
you be good enough to pass me the Bible and my
spectacles, and let Mary know that Mr. Stuart will
be in to supper with me."

Stephen obeyed in silence. He remembered the
time, not so long ago, when he would have been
required to seat himself on the opposite side of the
fireplace, with a smaller Bible in his hand, and read
word for word with his father. His mind went back
to those days as he walked slowly up the great grass-
grown avenue to the house, picking his steps carefully, lest he should mar the brilliancy of his well-
polished patent-leather boots. He compared that
old time curiously with the evening which was now
before him; the round table drawn into the midst
of the splendid dining-room, an oasis of exquisitely
shaded light and colour; Lady Peggy with her daring toilette and beautiful white shoulders; Deyes
with his world-worn face and flippant tongue; the
mistress of Thorpe herself, more subdued, perhaps,
in dress and speech, and yet with the ever-present
mystery of eyes and lips wherein was always the
fascination of the unknown. More than ever that
night Stephen Hurd felt himself to be her helpless
slave. All his former amours seemed suddenly
empty and vulgar things. She came late into the
drawing-room, her greeting was as carelessly kind

as usual, there was no perceptible difference in her manner of speech. Yet his observation of her was so intense that he found readily the signs of some subtle, indefinable change, a change which began with her toilette, and ended — ah! as yet there was no ending. Her gown of soft white silk was daring as a French modiste could make it, but its simplicity was almost nun-like. She wore a string of pearls, no earrings, no rings, and her hair was arranged low down, almost like a schoolgirl's. She had more colour than usual, a temporary restlessness seemed to have taken the place of her customary easy languor. What did it mean? he asked himself breathlessly. Was it Deyes? Impossible, for Deyes himself was a watcher, a thin smile parting sometimes the close set lips of his white, mask-like face. After all, how hopelessly at sea he was! He knew nothing of her life, of which these few days atThorpe were merely an interlude. She might have lovers by the score of whom he knew nothing. He was vain, but he was not wholly a fool.

She talked more than usual at dinner-time, but afterwards she spoke of a headache, and sat on the window-seat of the library, a cigarette between her lips, her eyes half closed. When the bridge table was laid out, she turned her head languidly.

"I will come in in the next rubber," she said. "You four can start."

They obeyed her, of course, but Lady Peggy shrugged her shoulders slightly. She had no fancy for Stephen's bridge, and they cut together. Wilhelmina waited until the soft fall of the cards had ceased, and the hands were being examined.

Then, with a graceful movement, she slipped out
of the window and away into the shadows. No
signs of her headache were left. She passed swiftly
along a narrow path, bordered by gigantic shrubs,
until she reached a small iron gate. Here for the
first time she paused.

For several moments she listened. There was no
sound from the great house, whose outline she could
barely see but whose long row of lights stretched
out behind her. She turned her head and looked
along the grass-grown lane beyond the gate. There
was no one in sight — no sound. She lifted the
latch and passed through.

For a summer night it was unusually dark. All
day the heat had been almost tropical, and now the
sky was clouded over, and a south wind, dry and
unrefreshing, was moving against the tall elms.
Every few seconds the heavens were ablaze with
summer lightning; once the breathless silence
was broken by a low rumble of distant thunder.

She reached the end of the lane. Before her,
another gate led out on to a grass-covered hill,
strewn with fragments of rocks. She paused for a
moment and looked backwards. She was suddenly
conscious that her heart was beating fast: the
piquant sense of adventure with which she had
started had given place to a rarer and more exciting
turmoil of the senses. Her breath was coming
short, as though she had been running.

The silence seemed more complete than ever. She
lifted her foot and felt the white satin slipper. It
was perfectly dry, there was no dew, and as yet no

rain had fallen. She lifted the latch of the gate and passed through.

The footpath skirted the side of a plantation, and she followed it closely, keeping under the shelter of the hedge. Every now and then a rabbit started up almost from under her feet, and rushed into the hedge. The spinney itself seemed alive with birds and animals, startled by her light footsteps in the shelter which they had sought, disturbed too by their instinct of the coming storm. Her footsteps grew swifter. She was committed now to her enterprise, vague though it had seemed to her. She passed through a second gate into a ragged wood, and along a winding path into a country road. She turned slowly up the hill. Her breath was coming faster than ever now. What folly! — transcendental! — exquisite! Her footsteps grew slower. She kept to the side of the hedge, raising her skirts a little, for the grass was long. A few yards farther was the gate. The soft swish of her silken draperies as she stole along, became a clearly recognizable sound against the background of intense silence. Macheson had been leaning against a tree just inside. He opened the gate. She stepped almost into his arms. Her white face was suddenly illuminated by the soft blaze of summer lightning which poured from the sky. He had no time to move, to realize. He felt her hands upon his cheek, his face drawn downwards, her lips, soft and burning, pressed against his for one long, exquisite second. And then — the darkness once more and his arms were empty.

HE FELT HER HANDS UPON HIS CHEEK. Page 84

CHAPTER X

THE STILL FIGURE IN THE CHAIR

WITH upraised skirts, and feet that flashed like silver across the turf and amongst the bracken, Wilhelmina flew homewards. Once more her heart was like the heart of a girl. Her breath came in little sobs mingled with laughter, the ground beneath her feet was buoyant as the clouds. She had no fear of being pursued — least of anything in the world did she desire it. The passion of a woman is controlled always by her sentiment. It seemed to her that that breathless episode was in itself an epic, she would not for worlds have added to it, have altered it in any shape or form. A moment's lingering might so easily have spoilt everything. Had he attempted to play either the prude or the Lothario, the delicate flavour would have passed away from the adventure, which had set her heart beating once more, and sent the blood singing so sweetly through her veins. So she sped through the darkness, leaving fragments of lace upon the thorns, like some beautiful bird, escaped from long captivity, rushing through a strange world.

Before she reached the grounds the storm came.

There was a crash of thunder, which seemed to tear apart the heavens above, and then the big rain-drops began to fall upon her bare shoulders and her clothes as light and airy as butterfly's wings. She abandoned herself to the ruin of a Paquin gown without a thought of regret; she even laughed softly with pleasure as she lifted her burning face to the cool sweet deluge, and lessened her pace in the avenue, walking with her hands behind her and her head still upraised. It was a wonderful night, this. She had found something of her lost girl-hood.

She reached the house at last, and stole through the hall like a truant schoolgirl. Her shoes were nothing but pulp; her dress clung to her limbs like a grey, sea-soaked bathing-costume; every-where on the oak floor and splendid rugs she left a trail of wet. On tiptoe she stole up the stairs, looking guiltily around, yet with demure laughter in her glowing eyes. She met only one amazed servant, whom she dispatched at once for her own maid. In the bath-room she began to strip off her clothes, even before Hortense, who loved her, could effect a breathless entrance.

"Eh! Madame, Madame!" the girl exclaimed, with uplifted hands.

Wilhelmina stopped her, laughing.

"It's all right, Hortense," she exclaimed gaily. "I was out in the grounds, and got caught in the storm. Turn on the hot water and cut these laces — so!"

To Hortense the affair was a tragedy. Her mis-tress' indifference could not lessen it.

"Madame," she declared, "the gown is ruined —
a divine creation. Madame has never looked so
well in anything else."

"Then I am glad I wore it to-night," was the
astonishing reply. "Quick, quick, quick, Hortense!
Get me into the bath, and bring me some wine and
biscuits. I am hungry. I don't think I could have
eaten any dinner."

Hortense worked with nimble fingers, but her
eyes at every opportunity were studying her mistress' face. Was it the English rain which could
soften and beautify like this? Madame was brilliant — and so young! Such a colour! Such a
fire in the eyes! Madame laughed as she thrust her
from the room.

"The wine, Hortense, and the biscuits — no sandwiches! I die of hunger. And send word to the
library that I have been caught in the storm, and
must change my clothes, but shall be down presently. So!"

She found them, an hour later, just finishing a
rubber. Their languid post-mortem upon a curiously played hand was broken off upon her entrance.
They made remarks about the storm and her ill-
luck — had she been far from shelter? was she
not terrified by the lightning? Lady Peggy remembered her gown. Deyes alone was silent. She
felt him watching her all the time, taking cold
note of her brilliant colour, the softer light in her
eyes. She felt that he saw her as she was — a
woman suddenly set free, even though for a few

short hours. She had broken away from them all, and she gloried in it.

She played bridge later — brilliantly as usual, and with success. Then she leaned back in her chair and faced them all.

"Dear guests," she murmured, "you remember the condition, the only condition upon which we bestowed our company upon one another in this benighted place. You remember it was agreed that when you were bored, you left without excuse or any foolish apologies. The same to apply to your hostess."

"My dear Wilhelmina," Lady Peggy exclaimed, "I know what you're going to say, and I won't go! I'm not due anywhere till the thirteenth. I won't be stranded."

Wilhelmina laughed.

"You foolish woman!" she exclaimed. "Who wants you to go? You shall be chatelaine — play hostess and fill the place if you like. Only you mustn't have Leslie over more than twice a week."

"You are going to desert us?" Deyes asked coolly.

"It was in the bond, wasn't it?" she answered. "Peggy will look after you all, I am sure."

"You mean that you are going away, to leave Thorpe?" Stephen Hurd asked abruptly.

She turned her head to look at him. He was sitting a little outside the circle — an attitude typical, perhaps, of his position there. The change in her tone was slight indeed, but it was sufficient.

"I am thinking of it," she answered. "You, Gilbert, and Captain Austin can find some men to

shoot, no doubt. Ask any one you like. Peggy will
see about some women for you. I draw the line at
that red-haired Egremont woman. Anybody else!"

"This is a blow," Deyes remarked, "but it was
in the bond. Nothing will move me from here till
the seventeenth— unless your *chef* should leave.
Do we meet in Marienbad?"

"I am not sure," Wilhelmina answered, playing
idly with the cards. "I feel that my system re-
quires something more soothing."

"I hate them all — those German baths," Lady
Peggy declared. "Ridiculous places every one of
them."

"After all, you see," Wilhelmina declared, "ill-
ness of any sort is a species of uncleanliness. I think
I should like to go somewhere where people are
healthy, or at least not so disgustingly frank about
their livers."

"Why not stay here?" Stephen ventured to
suggest. "I doubt whether any one in Thorpe
knows what a liver is."

" 'Inutile!' " Lady Peggy exclaimed. "Wilhelmina has the 'wander fever.' I can see it in her
face. Is it the thunder, I wonder?"

Deyes walked to the window and threw it open.
The storm was over, but the rain was still falling,
a soft steady downpour. The cooler air which swept
into the room was almost faint with the delicious
perfume of flowers and shrubs bathed in the refresh-
ing downpour.

"I think," he said, "that there is some magic
abroad to-night. Did you meet Lucifer walking
in the rose garden?" he asked, turning slightly

towards his hostess. "The storm may have brought him — even here!"

"Neither Lucifer nor any other of his princely fellows," she answered. "The only demon is here," — she touched her bosom lightly — "the demon of unrest. It is not I alone who am born with the wanderer's curse! There are many of us, you know."

He shook his head.

"You have not the writing in your face," he said. "I do not believe that you are one of the accursed at all. To-night —— "

She was standing by his side now, looking out into the velvety darkness. Her eyes challenged his.

"Well! To-night?"

"To-night you have the look of one who has found what she has sought for for a long time. This sounds bald, but it is as near to truth as I can get."

She was silent for a moment. She stood by his side listening to the soft constant patter of the rain, the far-away rumblings of the dying storm.

"One has moods," she murmured.

"Heaven forbid that a woman should be without them!" he answered.

"Do you ever feel as though something were going to happen?" she asked suddenly.

"Often," he answered; "but nothing ever does!"

Lady Peggy came yawning over to them.

"My dear," she said, "I feel it in my very bones. I firmly believe that something is going to happen to every one of us. I have a most mysterious pricking about my left elbow!"

"To every one of us?" Stephen Hurd asked, idly enough.

"To every one of us!" she answered. "To you, even, who live in Thorpe. Remember my words when you get home to-night, or when you wake in the morning. As for you, Wilhelmina, I am not at all sure that you have not already met with your adventure."

Deyes lit a cigarette.

"Let us remember this," he declared. "In a week's time we will compare notes."

Stephen Hurd stood up to take his leave.

"You are really going — soon?" he asked, as he bent over her carelessly offered hand.

"As soon as I can decide where to go to," she answered.

"Can I give my father any message? Would you care to see him to-morrow morning?" he asked.

She shook her head.

"It is not necessary," she answered.

He made his adieux reluctantly. Somehow he felt that the night had not been a success. She was going away. Very likely he would not see her again. The great house and all its glories would be closed to him. To do him justice, he thought of that less than the casual manner of her farewell. His vanity was deeply wounded. She had begun by being so gracious — no wonder that he had lost his head a little. He thought over the events of the last few days. Something had occurred to alter her. Could he have offended in any way?

He walked dejectedly home, heedless of the sodden path and wet grass. A light was still burning in the study. He hesitated for a moment, and then, turning the handle, entered.

"You're late, father," he remarked, going towards the cupboard to select a pipe.

There was no answer. The still figure in the chair never moved. Something in the silence struck Stephen as ominous. He turned abruptly round, and for the first time noticed the condition of the room. A chair was overturned, a vase of flowers spilt upon the table, the low window, from which one stepped almost into the village street, was wide open. The desk in front of the motionless figure was littered all over with papers in wild confusion. Stephen, with a low cry of horror, crossed the room and laid his hand upon his father's shoulder. He tried to speak to him, but the words stuck in his throat. He knew very well that there could be no reply. His father was sitting dead in his chair.

CHAPTER XI

THE BAYING OF THE HOUNDS

OUT amongst the broken fragments of the storm, on the hill-top and down the rain-drenched lane, Macheson sought in vain by physical exertion to still the fever which burned in his veins. Nothing he could do was able to disturb that wonderful memory, to lessen for an instant the significance of those few amazing seconds. The world of women, all the lighter and quieter joys of life, he had, with the fierce asceticism of the young reformer, thrust so resolutely behind him. But he had never imagined anything like this! Its unexpectedness had swept him off his feet. The memory of it was most delicious torture!

Sleep? — he dared not think of it. Who could sleep with such a fire in his blood as this? He heard the storm die away, thunder and wind and rain melted into the deep stillness of midnight. A dim moon shone behind a veil of mist. The dripping of rain from the trees alone remained. Then he heard a footstep coming down the lane. His first wild thought was that she had returned. His eyes burned their way through the darkness. Soon he saw that it was a man who came unsteadily, but swiftly, down the roadway.

Macheson leaned over the gate. He would have preferred not to disclose himself, but as the man passed, he was stricken with a sudden consciousness that for him the events of the night were not yet over. This was no villager; he had not even the appearance of an Englishman. He was short and inclined to be thick-set, his coat collar was turned up, and a tweed cap was drawn down to his eyes. He walked with uneven footsteps and muttered to himself words that sounded like words of prayer, only they were in some foreign language. Macheson accosted him.

"Hullo!" he said. "Have you lost your way?"

The man cried out and then stood still, trembling on the roadside. He turned a white, scared face to where Macheson was leaning against the gate.

"Who is that?" he cried. "What do you want with me?"

Macheson stepped into the lane.

"Nothing at all," he answered reassuringly. "I simply thought that you might have lost your way. These are lonely parts."

The newcomer drew a step nearer. He displayed a small ragged beard, a terror-stricken face, and narrow, very bright eyes. His black clothes were soaked and splashed with mud.

"I want a railway station," he said rapidly. "Where is the nearest?"

Macheson pointed into the valley.

"Just where you see that light burning," he

answered, "but there will be no trains till the morning."

"Then I must walk," the man declared feverishly. "How far is it to Nottingham?"

"Twenty-five miles," Macheson answered.

"Too far! And Leicester?"

"Twelve, perhaps! But you are walking in the wrong direction."

The man turned swiftly round.

"Point towards Leicester," he said. "I shall find my way."

Macheson pointed across the trees.

"You can't miss it," he declared. "Climb the hill till you get to a road with telegraph wires. Turn to the left, and you will walk into Leicester."

For some reason the stranger seemed to be occupied in looking earnestly into Macheson's face.

"What are you doing here?" he asked abruptly.

"I am close to where I am staying," Macheson answered. "Just in the wood there."

The man took a quick step forwards and then reeled. His hand flew to his side. He was attacked by sudden faintness and would have fallen, but for Macheson's outstretched arm.

"God!" he muttered, "it is finished."

He was obviously on the verge of a collapse. Macheson dragged him into the shelter and poured brandy between his teeth. He revived a little and tried to rise.

"I must go on," he cried. "I dare not stay here."

The terror in his face was unmistakable. Macheson looked at him gravely.

"You had better stay where you are till morning," he said. "You are not in a fit state to travel."

The man had raised himself upon one arm. He looked wildly about him.

"Where am I?" he demanded. "What is this place?"

"It is a gamekeeper's shelter," Macheson answered, "which I am making use of for a few days. You are welcome to stay here until the morning."

"I must go on," the man moaned. "I am afraid."

Almost as he uttered the words he fell back, and went off immediately into an uneasy doze. Macheson threw his remaining rug over the prostrate figure, and, lighting his pipe, strolled out into the spinney. The man's coming filled him with a vague sense of trouble. He seemed so utterly out of keeping with the place, he represented an alien and undesirable note — a note almost of tragedy. All the time in his broken sleep he was muttering to himself. Once or twice he cried out in terror, once especially — Macheson turned round to find him sitting up on the rug, his brown eyes full of wild fear, and the perspiration running down his face. A stream of broken words flowed from his lips. Macheson thrust him back on the rug.

"Go to sleep," he said. "There is nothing to be afraid of."

After that the man slept more soundly. Macheson himself dozed for an hour until he was awakened by the calling of the birds. Directly he opened his eyes he knew that something had happened to him. It was not only the music of the birds — there was a strange new music stirring in his heart. The pearly light in the eastern sky had never seemed so beautiful; never, surely, had the sunlight streamed down upon so perfect a corner of the earth. And then, with a quick rush of blood to his cheeks, he remembered what it was that had so changed the world. He lived again through that bewildering moment, again he felt the delicious warmth of her presence, the touch of her hair as it had brushed his cheek, the soft passionate pressure of her lips against his. It was like an episode from a fairy story, there was something so delicate, so altogether fanciful in that flying visit. Something, too, so unbelievable when he thought of her as the mistress of Thorpe, the languid, insolent woman of the world who had treated him so coldly.

Then a movement behind reminded him of his strange visitor. He turned round. The man was already on his feet. He looked better for his sleep, but the wild look was still in his eyes.

"I must go," he said. "I ought to have started before. Thank you for your shelter."

Macheson reached out for his spirit lamp.

"Wait a few minutes," he said, "and I will have some coffee ready."

The man hesitated. He looked sorely in need of something of the sort. As he came to the opening of the shelter, the trembling seized him again. He looked furtively out as though he feared the daylight. The sunshine and the bright open day seemed to terrify him.

"I ought to have gone on last night," he muttered. "I must —— "

He broke off his sentence. Macheson, too, had turned his head to listen.

"What is that?" he asked sharply.

"The baying of dogs," Macheson answered.

"Dogs! What dogs?" he demanded.

"Colonel Harvey's bloodhounds!"

The man's face was ashen now to the lips. He clutched Macheson's arm frantically.

"They are after me!" he exclaimed. "Where can I hide? Tell me quick!"

Macheson looked at him gravely.

"What have you been doing?" he asked. "They do not bring bloodhounds out for nothing."

"I have hurt a man down in the village," was the terrified answer. "I didn't mean to — no! I swear that I did not mean to. I went to his house and I asked him for money. I had a right to it! And I asked him to tell me where — but oh! you would not understand. Listen! I swear to you that I did not mean to hurt him. Why should I? He was old, and I think he fainted. God! do you hear that?"

He clung to Macheson in a frenzy. The deep baying of the dogs was coming nearer and nearer.

"Listen," Macheson said, "the dogs will not be allowed to hurt you, but if you are loose I promise that I will protect you from them. You had better wait here with me."

The man fell upon his knees.

"Sir," he begged, "I am innocent of everything except a blow struck in anger. Help me to escape, I implore you. There are others who will suffer — if anything happens to me."

"Help me to escape, I implore you." Page 98

"The law is just," Macheson answered. "You will suffer nothing except justice."

"I want mercy, not justice," the man sobbed. "For the love of God, help me!"

Macheson hesitated. Again the early morning stillness was broken by that hoarse, terrifying sound. His sporting instincts were aroused. He had small sympathy with the use of such means against human beings.

"I will give you a chance," he said. "Remember it is nothing more. Follow me!"

He led the way to the slate pit.

"Can you swim?" he asked.

"Yes!" the man answered.

"This is where I take my morning bath," Macheson said. "You will see that though you can scramble down and dive in, it is too precipitous to get out. Therefore, I have fixed up a rope on the other side — it goes through those bushes, and is attached to the trunk of a tree beneath the bracken. If you swim across, you can pull yourself out of the water and hide just above the water in the bushes. There is just a chance that you may escape observation."

Already he was on his way down, but Macheson stopped him.

"I shall leave a suit of dry clothes in the shelter," he said. "If they should give up the chase you are welcome to them. Now you had better dive. They are in the spinney."

The man went in, after the fashion of a practised diver. Macheson turned round and retraced his steps towards his temporary dwelling-house.

CHAPTER XII

RETREAT

OUT in the lane a motley little group of men were standing. Stephen Hurd was in the act of springing off his brown cob. The dogs were already in the shelter.

"What the devil are you doing here?" Hurd asked, as Macheson strode through the undergrowth.

Macheson pointed to the shelter.

"I could find no other lodging," he answered, "thanks to circumstances of which you are aware."

Stephen Hurd kicked the gate open. He was pale and there were deep lines under his eyes. He was still in his evening clothes, except for a rough tweed coat, but his white tie was hanging loose, and his patent-leather shoes were splashed with mud.

"We are chasing a man," he said. "Have you seen him."

"I have," Macheson answered. "What has he done?"

There was a momentary silence. Hurd spoke with a sob.

"Murdered — my father!"

Macheson was shocked.

"You mean — that Mr. Hurd is dead?" he asked, in an awe-stricken tone.

"Dead!" the young man answered with a sob. "Killed in his chair!"

The dogs came out of the shelter. They turned towards the interior of the spinney. The little crowd came streaming through the gate.

"I gave shelter to a man who admitted that he was in trouble," he said gravely. "He heard the dogs and he was terrified. He has jumped into the slate quarry."

The dogs were on the trail now. They followed them to the edge of the quarry. Here the bushes were trodden down, a man's cap was hanging on one close to the bottom. They all peered over into the still water, unnaturally black. Amies, the head keeper, raised his head.

"It's twenty-five feet deep — some say forty, and a sheer drop," he declared impressively. "We'll have to drag it for the body."

"Best take the dogs round the other side, and make sure he ain't got out again," one of the crowd suggested.

Amies pointed scornfully to the precipitous side. Such a feat was clearly impossible. Nevertheless the dogs were taken round. For a few minutes they were uneasy, but eventually they returned to the spot from which their intended victim had dived. Every one was peering down into the dark water as though fascinated.

"I thought as they come up once or twice before they were drownded," somebody remarked.

"Not unless they want to," another answered. "This chap wasn't too anxious. He knew his goose was cooked."

The dogs were muzzled and led away. One by one the labourers and servants dispersed. Two of them started off to telegraph for a drag. Stephen Hurd was one of the last to depart.

"I hope you will allow me to say how sorry I am for you," Macheson declared earnestly. "Such a tragedy in a village like Thorpe seems almost incredible. I suppose it was a case of attempted robbery?"

"I don't know, I'm sure," Hurd answered. "There was plenty of money left untouched, and I can't find that there is any short. The man arrived after the maids had gone to bed, but they heard him knock at the door, and heard my father let him in."

"They didn't hear any struggle then?" Macheson asked.

Hurd shook his head.

"There was only one blow upon his head," he answered. "Graikson says that death was probably through shock."

Macheson felt curiously relieved.

"The man did not go there as a murderer then," he remarked. "Perhaps not even as a thief. There may have been a quarrel."

"He killed him, anyhow," Hurd said brokenly. "What time was it when you first saw him?"

"About midnight, I should think," Macheson answered. "He came down the lane like a drunken man."

"What was he like?" Hurd asked.

"Small, and I should say a foreigner," Macheson answered. "He spoke English perfectly, but there was an accent, and when he was asleep he talked to himself in a language which, to the best of my belief, I have never heard before in my life."

"A foreigner?" Hurd muttered. "You are sure of that?"

"Quite," Macheson answered. "There could be no mistake about it."

Stephen Hurd mounted his cob and turned its head towards home. He asked no more questions; he seemed, if possible, graver than ever. Before he started, however, he pointed with his whip towards the shelter.

"You've no right there, you know," he said. "We can't allow it. You must clear out at once."

"Very well," Macheson answered. "I'm trespassing, of course, but one must sleep somewhere."

"There is no necessity for you to remain in Thorpe at all," Hurd said. "I think, in the circumstances, the best thing you can do is to go."

"In the circumstances!" The irony of the phrase struck home. What did this young man know of the circumstances? There were reasons now, indeed, why he should fly from Thorpe as from a place stricken with the pestilence. But no other soul in this world could know of those reasons save himself — and she.

"I should not, of course, think of holding my services at present," Macheson said gravely. "If you think it would be better, I will go away."

Stephen Hurd nodded as he cantered off.

"I am glad to hear you say so," he declared shortly. "Go and preach in the towns where this scum is reared. There's plenty of work for missioners there."

Macheson stood still until the young man on his

pony had disappeared. Then he turned round and walked slowly back towards the slate quarry. The black waters remained smooth and unrippled; there was no sound of human movement anywhere. In the adjoining field a harvesting-machine was at work; in the spinney itself the rabbits, disturbed last night by the storm, were scurrying about more frolicsome than usual; a solitary thrush was whistling in the background. The sunlight lay in crooked beams about the undergrowth, a gentle west breeze was just stirring the foliage overhead. There was nothing in the air to suggest in any way the strange note of tragedy which the coming of this hunted man had nevertheless brought.

Macheson was turning away when a slight disturbance in the undergrowth on the other side of the quarry attracted his notice. He stood still and watched the spot. The bracken was shaking slightly — then the sound of a dry twig, suddenly snapped! For a moment he hesitated. Then he turned on his heel and walked abruptly away. With almost feverish haste, he flung his few belongings into his portmanteau, leaving in the shelter his flask, a suit of clothes, and several trifles. Five minutes later he was on his way down the hill, with his bag upon his shoulder and his face set southwards.

CHAPTER XIII

A CREATURE OF IMPULSE

UP the broad avenue to the great house of Thorpe, Stephen Hurd slowly made his way, his hands clasped behind him, his eyes fixed upon the ground. But his appearance was not altogether the appearance of a man overcome with grief. The events of the last few days had told upon him, and his deep mourning had a sombre look. Yet there were thoughts working even then in his brain which battled hard with his natural depression. Strange things had happened — stranger things than he was able all at once to digest. He could not see the end, but there were possibilities upon which he scarcely dared to brood.

He was shown into the library and left alone for nearly twenty minutes. Then Wilhelmina came, languid, and moving as though with tired feet. Yet her manner was gentler and kinder than usual. She leaned back in one of the vast easy-chairs, and murmured a few graceful words of sympathy.

"We were all so sorry for you, Mr. Hurd," she said. "It was a most shocking affair."

"I thank you very much — madam," he replied, after a moment's pause. It was better, perhaps, for the present, to assume that their relations were to continue those of employer and employed.

"I do not know," she continued, "whether you care to speak about this shocking affair. Perhaps you would prefer that we did not allude to it for the present."

He shook his head.

"I am not sure," he answered, "that it is not rather a relief to have it spoken of. One can't get it out of one's mind, of course."

"There is no news of the man — no fresh capture?"

"None," he answered. "They are dragging the slate quarry again to-day. I believe there are some very deep holes where the body may have drifted."

"Do you believe that that is the case?" she asked; "or do you think that he got clean away?"

"I cannot tell," he answered. "It seems impossible that he should have escaped altogether without help."

"And that he could not have had, could he?" she asked.

He looked across at her thoughtfully, watching her face, curious to see whether his words might have any effect.

"Only from one person," he said.

"Yes?"

"From Macheson, the fellow who came here to convert us all," he said deliberately.

Beyond a slight elevation of the eyebrows, his scrutiny was in vain, for she made no sign.

"He scarcely seems a likely person, does he, to aid a criminal?" she asked in measured tones.

Stephen Hurd shrugged his shoulders.

"Perhaps not," he admitted, "but at any rate he sheltered him."

"As he doubtless would have done any passer-by on such a night," she remarked. "By the bye, what has become of that young man?"

"He has left the neighbourhood," Hurd answered shortly.

"Left altogether?" she inquired.

"I imagine so," Hurd answered. "I had the shelter destroyed, and I gave him to understand pretty clearly what your wishes were. There really wasn't much else for him to do."

Her eyelids drooped over her half closed eyes. For a moment she was silent.

"If you hear of him again," she said quietly, "be so good as to let me know."

Her indifference seemed too complete to be assumed. Yet somehow or other Hurd felt that she was displeased with him.

"I will do so," he said, "if I hear anything about him. It scarcely seems likely."

Wilhelmina sat quite still. Her head, resting slightly upon the long delicate fingers of her right hand, was turned away from the young man who was daring to watch her. She was apparently gazing across the park, down the magnificent avenue of elms which led to the village. So he was gone — without a word! How else? On the whole she could not but approve! And yet! — and yet!

She turned once more to Hurd.

"I read the account of the inquest on your father's death," she said, speaking very slowly, with her usual drawl, yet with a softer note in her voice, as though out of respect for the dead man. "Does it not seem very strange that the money was left untouched?"

"Yes!" he answered. "Yet, after all, I don't know. You see, the governor must have closed with the fellow and shown fight before he got that knock on the head. If the thief was really only an ordinary tramp, he'd be scared to death at what he'd done, and probably bolt for his life without stopping to take anything with him."

"Isn't it rather surprising to have tramps — in Thorpe?" she asked.

"I have scarcely ever seen one," he answered.

Wilhelmina turned her head slightly, so that she was now directly facing him. She looked him steadily in the eyes.

"Has it occurred to you, Mr. Hurd," she asked, "that this young man may not have been a tramp at all, and that his visit to your father may have been on other business than that of robbery?"

He hesitated for a moment.

"My father's connexions with the outside world," he said slowly, "were so slight."

"Yet it has occurred to you?"

"Yes!" he admitted.

"And have you come to any conclusion?"

"None," he declared.

"You carried out my instructions with regard to the papers and documents belonging to the estate?"

"Certainly, madam," he answered. "Within five minutes of receiving your message, they were all locked up in the safe and the key handed to your messenger."

"You did not go through them yourself?" she asked.

"I did not," he answered, lying with admirable steadiness. "I scarcely felt that I was entitled to do so."

" So that you could not tell if any were missing?" she continued.

"I could not," he admitted.

"Your father never spoke, then, of any connexions with people — outside Thorpe — likely to prove of a dangerous character?"

The young man smiled. "My father," he said, "had not been farther than Loughborough for twenty years."

There was a short silence. Wilhelmina, deliberately, and without any attempt at concealment, was meditatively watching the young man, studying his features with a half-contemptuous and yet searching interest. Perhaps the slightly curving lips, the hard intentness of her gaze, suggested that he was disbelieved. He lost colour and fidgeted about. It was a scrutiny not easy to bear, and he felt that it was going against him. Already she had written him down a liar.

She spoke to him at last. If the silence had not ended soon, he would have made some blundering attempt to retrieve his position. She spoke just in time to avert such ignominy.

"Mr. Hurd," she said, "the question of your father's successor is one that has doubtless occurred to you as it has to me. I trust that you will, at any rate, remain here. As to whether I can offer

you your father's position in its entirety, I am not
for the present assured."

He glanced up at her furtively. He was certain
now that he had played his cards ill. She had read
through him easily. He cursed himself for a lout.

"You see," she continued, "the post is one of
great responsibility, because it entails the manage-
ment of the whole estates. It is necessary for me to
feel absolute confidence in the person who undertakes
it. I have not known you very long, Mr. Hurd."

He bowed. He could not trust himself to words.

"I have instructed them to send some one down
from my solicitor's office for a week or so," she
continued, "to assist you. In the meantime, I
must think the matter over."

"I am very much obliged to you, madam," he
said. "You will find me, I think, quite as trust-
worthy and devoted to your interests as my father."

She smiled slightly. She recognized exactly his
quandary, and it amused her. The slightest suggestion of menace in his manner would be to give
the lie to himself.

"I am coming down this afternoon," she said,
"to go through the safes. Please be there in case
I want you. You will not forget, in case you should
hear anything of Mr. Macheson, that I desire to
be informed."

He took his leave humiliated and angry. He
had started the game with a wrong move — retriev-
able, perhaps, but annoying. Wilhelmina passed
into the library, where Lady Peggy, in a wonderful morning robe, was leaning back in an easy-chair
dictating letters to Captain Austin.

"You dear woman!" she exclaimed, "don't interrupt us, will you? I have found an ideal secretary, writes everything I tell him, and spells quite decently considering his profession. My conscience is getting lighter every moment."

"And my heart heavier," Austin grumbled. "A most flirtatious correspondence yours."

She laughed softly.

"My next shall be to my dressmaker," she declared. "Such a charming woman, and so trustful. Behave yourself nicely, and you shall go with me to call on her next week, and see her mannikins. By the bye, Wilhelmina, am I hostess or are you?"

"You, by all means," Wilhelmina answered. "I shall go to-morrow or the next day. Is any one coming to lunch?"

"His Grace, I fancy — no one else."

Wilhelmina yawned.

"Where is Gilbert?" she asked.

"Asleep on the lawn last time I saw him."

"No one shooting, then?"

"We're going to beat up the home turnips after lunch," Captain Austin answered. "It's rather an off day with us. Gilbert is nursing his leg — fancies he has rheumatism coming."

She strolled out into the garden, but she avoided the spot where Gilbert Deyes lounged in an easy-chair, reading the paper and smoking cigarettes, with his leg carefully arranged on a garden chair in front of him. She took the winding path which skirted the kitchen gardens and led to the green lane, along which the carts passed to the home farm. She felt that what she was doing was in the nature of an experiment, she was yielding again to that most astonishing impulse which once before had taken her so completely by surprise. She passed out of the gate and along the lane. She began to climb the hill. About the success of her experiment she no longer had any doubt. Her heart was beating with pleasant insistence, a feeling of suppressed excitement sent the blood gliding through her veins with delicious softness. All the time she mocked at herself — that this should be Wilhelmina Thorpe-Hatton, to whom the most distinguished men, not only in one capital, but in Europe, had paid court, whom the most ardent wooer had failed to move, who had found, indeed, in all the professions of love-making something insufferably tedious. She was at once amused and annoyed at herself, but an instinctive habit of truthfulness forbade even self-deception. Her cheeks were aflame, and her heart was beating like a girl's as she reached the spinney. She recognized the fact that she was experiencing a new and delightful pleasure, an emotion as unexpected and ridiculous as it was inexplicable. But she hugged it to herself. It pleased her immensely to feel that the impossible had happened. What all this army of men, experienced in the wiles of love-making, had failed to do, a crazy boy had accomplished without an effort. Absolutely bizarre, of course, but not so wonderful after all! She was so secure against any ordinary assault. She felt herself like the heroine of one of Gautier's novels. If he had been there himself, she would have taken him into her arms with all the passionate simplicity of a child.

But he was not there.   On the contrary, the place was looking forlorn and deserted.   The shelter had been razed to the ground — she felt that she hated Stephen Hurd as she contemplated its ruin — the hedge was broken down by the inrush of people a few days ago.   In the absence of any sunshine, the country around seemed bleak and colourless. She leaned over the gate and half closed her eyes. Memory came more easily like that!

CHAPTER XIV

SEARCHING THE PAPERS

THE late Stephen Hurd had been a methodical man. Every one of those many packets of foolscap and parchment bore in the left-hand corner near the top a few carefully written words summarizing their contents. It was clear from the first that Wilhelmina had undertaken not an examination but a search. Mortgages, leases, agreements, she left unopened and untouched. One by one she passed them back to the young man who handed them out to her, for replacement. In the end she had retained one small packet of letters only, on the outside of which were simply the initials P. N. These she held for a moment thoughtfully in her hand.

"Do you happen to remember, Mr. Hurd," she said, "whether this small packet which I have here was amongst the papers which you found had been disturbed after the attack upon your father?"

"I am sorry," the young man answered, "but it is quite impossible for me to say. I do not remember it particularly."

Wilhelmina turned it over thoughtfully. It was an insignificant packet to hold the tragedy of a woman's life.

"You see," she continued, "that it has the appearance of having been tampered with. There are marks of sealing wax upon the tape and upon the paper here. Then, too," she continued, turning it over, "it has been tied up hastily, unlike any of the other packets. The tape, too, is much too long. It looks almost as though some letters or papers had been withdrawn."

"I am afraid I cannot help you at all," he admitted regretfully. "My father never allowed any one but himself to open that safe. Mine was the out-of-door share of the work — and the rent-book, of course. I kept that."

She slowly undid the tape. The contents of the packet consisted of several letters, which she smoothed out with her fingers before beginning to read. Stephen Hurd stood with his back towards her, rearranging the bundles of documents in the safe.

"You have no idea then," she asked softly, "of the contents of this packet?"

He turned deliberately round. He was not in the least comfortable. It was almost as though she could see through his tweed shooting-jacket into that inner pocket.

"May I see which packet you refer to?" he asked.

She showed it to him without placing it in his hand. He shook his head.

"No!" he said, "I have not noticed them before."

She sighed — or was it a yawn? At any rate, her eyes left his face, for which he was immediately grateful. She began to read the papers, and, having finished his task, he walked towards the window and stood there looking out. He stood there minute after minute, hearing only the sound of rustling paper behind. When at last it ceased he turned around.

She had risen to her feet and was slowly drawing on her gloves. The letters had disappeared, presumably into her pocket, but she made no reference to them. When she spoke, her voice was smooth and deliberate as usual. Somehow or other he was at once conscious, however, that she had received a shock.

"I presume, Mr. Hurd," she said quietly, "that amongst your father's private papers you did not discover anything — unexpected?"

"I am afraid I scarcely follow you, madam," he answered.

"I am asking you," she repeated deliberately, "whether amongst your father's private papers, which I presume you have looked through, you found anything of a surprising nature?"

He shook his head.

"I found scarcely any," he answered, "only his will and a memorandum of a few investments. May I ask —— "

She turned towards the door.

"No!" she said, "do not ask me any questions. To tell you the truth, I am not yet fully persuaded that the necessity exists."

"I do not understand," he protested.

She shrugged her shoulders. She did not trouble to explain her words. He followed her along the cool, white-flagged hall, hung with old prints and trophies of sport, into the few yards of garden out-

" Forgive me," he said, with his hand upon the gate.   Page 117

side, brilliant with cottage flowers. Beyond the little iron gate her carriage was waiting — a low victoria, drawn by a pair of great horses, whose sleek coats and dark crimson rosettes suggested rather a turn in the Park than these country lanes. The young man was becoming desperate. She was leaving him altogether mystified. Somewhere or other he had missed his cue: he had meant to have conducted the interview so differently. And never had she looked so provokingly well! He recognized, with hopeless admiration, the perfection of her toilette — the trim white flannel dress, shaped by the hand of an artist to reveal in its simple lines the peculiar grace of her slim figure; the patent shoes with their suggestion of open-work silk stockings; the black picture hat and veil a delicate recognition of her visit to a house of mourning, yet light and gossamer-like, with no suggestion of gloom. Never had she seemed so desirable to him, so fascinating and yet so unattainable. He made a last and clumsy effort to re-establish himself.

"Forgive me," he said, with his hand upon the gate, "but I must ask you what you mean by that last question. My father had no secrets that I know of. How could he, when for the last forty years his life was practically spent in this village street?"

She nodded her head slowly.

"Sometimes," she murmured, "events come to those even who sit and wait, those whose lives are absolutely secluded. No one is safe from fate, you know."

"But my father!" he answered. "He had no

tastes, no interests outside the boundary of your estates."

She motioned to him to open the gate.

"Perhaps not," she assented, "yet I suppose that there is not one of us who knows as much of his neighbour's life as he imagines he does. Good afternoon, Mr. Hurd! My visit has given me something to think about. I may send for you to come to the house before I go away."

She drove away, leaning back amongst the cushions with half closed eyes, as though tired. The country scenery with its pastoral landscape, its Watteau-like perfections, was wholly unseen. Her memory had travelled back, she was away amongst the days when the roar of life had been in her ears, when for a short while, indeed, the waves had seemed likely to break over her head. An unpleasant echo, this! No more than an echo — and yet! The thought of old Stephen Hurd lying in his grave suddenly chilled her. She shivered as she left the carriage, and instead of entering the house, crossed the lawn to where Gilbert Deyes was lounging. He struggled to his feet at her approach, but she waved him back again.

"Sybarite," she murmured, glancing around at his arrangements for complete comfort. "You have sent Austin out alone."

"Dear lady, I confess it," he answered. "What would you have? It is too fine an afternoon to kill anything."

She sank into a chair by his side. A slight smile parted her lips as she glanced around. On a table by his side, a table drawn back into the shade of the cedar tree, were several vellum-bound volumes, a tall glass, and a crystal jug half full of some delicate amber beverage, mixed with fruit and ice, a box of cigarettes, an ivory paper-cutter, and a fan.

"Your capacity for making yourself comfortable," she remarked, "amounts almost to genius."

"Let it go at that," he answered. "I like the sound of the word."

"I want you to go to Paris for me," she said abruptly.

He flicked the ash off the end of his cigarette and looked at her thoughtfully. Not a line of his face betrayed the least sign of surprise.

"To-morrow?" he asked.

"Yes!"

"I can get up in time for the two-twenty," he remarked thoughtfully. "I wonder whether it will be too late for the Armenonville!"

She laughed quietly.

"You are a 'poseur,' " she declared.

"Naturally," he admitted. "We all are, even when the audience consists of ourselves alone. I fancy I'm rather better than most, though."

She nodded.

"You won't mind admitting — to me — that you are surprised?"

"Astonished," he said. "To descend to the commonplace, what on earth do you want me to go to Paris for?"

"I will tell you," she answered. "Forget for a moment the Paris that you know, and remember the Paris of the tourist."

"Painful," he answered; "but it is done."

"The *Hotel de Luxe!* "

"I know it well."

"There are a race of creatures there, small, parasitical insects, who hang about the hall and the boulevard outside — guides they call themselves."

" 'Show you something altogether new this evening, Captain,' " he quoted. "Yes; I know them."

"There is, or was, one," she continued, "who goes by the name of Thomas Johnson. He is undersized; he has red cheeks, and puffy brown eyes. He used to wear a glazed black hat, and he speaks every language without an accent."

"I should know the beast anywhere," he declared.

"Find out if he is there still. Let him take you out. Don't lose sight of him — and write to me."

"To-morrow night," he said, "I will renew my youth. I will search for him on the boulevards, and see the sights which make a gay dog of the travelling Briton."

She nodded.

"You're a good sort, Gilbert," she said simply.

"Thanks!"

CHAPTER XV

ON THE SPREE

HIGH up on the seventh floor of one of London's newest and loftiest buildings, a young man sat writing in a somewhat barely furnished office. He wrote deliberately, and with the air of one who thoroughly enjoyed his occupation. The place had a bookish aspect — the table was strewn with magazines and books of reference; piles of literature of a varied order stood, in the absence of bookshelves, against the wall. The young man himself, however, was the most interesting object in the room. He was big and dark and rugged. There was strength in his square-set shoulders, in the compression of his lips, even in the way his finger guided the pen across the paper. He was thoroughly absorbed in his task. Nevertheless he raised his head at a somewhat unusual sound. The lift had swung up to his floor, he heard the metal gate thrown open. There was a knock at the door, and Matheson walked in.

"Victor, by glory!"

Down went the pen, and Richard Holderness stood up at his desk with outstretched hands. Matheson grasped them heartily and_seated himself on the edge of the table.

"It's good to see you, Dick," he declared, "like coming back to the primitive forces of nature, unchanged, unchanging. The sight of you's enough to stop a revolution."

"You're feeling like that, are you?" his friend answered, his eyes fixed upon Macheson's face. "Yes, I see you are. Go ahead! Or will you smoke first?"

Macheson produced his pipe, and his host a great tin of honeydew. Macheson helped himself slowly. He seemed to be trying to gain time.

"Blessed compact, ours," the giant remarked, leaning back in his chair. "No probing for confidences, no silly questions. Out with it!"

"I've started wrong," Macheson said. "I'll have to go back on my tracks a bit anyway."

Holderness grunted affably.

"Nothing like mistakes," he remarked. "Best discipline in the world."

"I started on a theory," Macheson continued thoughtfully. "It didn't pan out. The people I have been trying to get at are better left alone."

"Exactly why?" Holderness asked.

"I'll tell you," Macheson answered. "You know I've seen a bit of what we call village life. Their standard isn't high enough, of course. Things come too easily, their noses are too close to the ground. They are moderately sober, moderately industrious, but the sameness of life is at work all the time. It makes machines of the factory hands, animals of the country folk. I knew that before I started. I

thought I could lift their heads a little. It's too
big a task for me, Dick."

"Of course," Holderness assented. "You can't
graft on to dead wood."

"They live decent lives — most of them," Macheson continued thoughtfully. "They can't understand
that any change is needed, no more can their land-
lords, or their clergy. A mechanical performance
of the Christian code seems all that any one expects
from them. Dick, it's all they're capable of. You
can't alter laws. You can't create intelligence.
You can't teach these people spirituality."

"As well try to teach 'em to fly," Holderness
answered. "I could have told you so before, if it
had been of any use. What about these Welshmen,
though?"

"It's hysteria," Macheson declared. "If you can
get through the hide, you can make the emotions
run riot, stir them into a frenzy. It's a debauch.
I've been there to see. The true spiritual life is
partly intellectual."

"What are you going to do now?" Holderness
asked.

"I don't know," Macheson answered. "I haven't
finished yet. Dick, curse all women!"

The giant looked thoughtful.

"I'm sorry," he said simply.

Macheson swung himself from the table. He
walked up and down the room.

"It isn't serious," he declared. "It isn't even
definite. But it's like a perfume, or a wonderful
chord of music, or the call of the sea to an inland-
bred viking! It's under my heel, Dick, but I can't

crush it. I came away from Leicestershire because
I was afraid."

"Does she — exist?" Holderness asked.

"Not for me," Macheson declared hurriedly.
"Don't think that. I shouldn't have mentioned it,
but for our compact."

Holderness nodded.

"Bad luck," he said. "This craving for something we haven't got — can't have — I wish I
could find the germ. The world should go free of
it for a generation. We'd build empires, we'd
reconstruct society. It's a deadly germ, though,
Victor, and it's the princes of the world who suffer
most. There's only one antidote — work!"

"Give me some," Macheson begged.

The giant looked at him thoughtfully.

"Right," he answered, "but not to-day. Clothes
up in town?"

Macheson nodded.

"We'll go on the bust," Holderness declared.
"I've been dying for a spree! We'll have it.
Where are you staying?"

"My old rooms," Macheson answered. "I looked
in on my way from the station and found them
empty."

"Capital! We're close together. Come on! We'll
do the West End like two gay young bucks. Five
o'clock, isn't it? We'll walk up Regent Street and
have an 'apéritif' at Biflore's. Wait till I brush
my hat."

Macheson made no difficulties, but he was puzzled.
Holderness he knew well enough had no leanings
towards the things which he proposed with so much

enthusiasm. Was it a pilgrimage they were to start upon — or what? After all, why need he worry? He was content to go his friend's way.

So they walked up Regent Street, bright with the late afternoon sunshine, threading their way through the throngs of sauntering men and women gazing into the shops — and at one another! At Biflore's Macheson would have felt out of his element but for Holderness' self-possession. He had the air of going through what might have been an everyday performance, ordered vermouth mixed, lit a cigarette, leaned back at his ease upon the cushioned seat, and told with zest and point a humorous story. There were women there, a dozen or more, some alone, some in little groups, women smartly enough dressed, good-looking, too, and prosperous, with gold purses and Paris hats, yet — lacking something. Macheson did not ask himself what it was. He felt it; he knew, too, that Holderness meant him to feel it. The shadow of tragedy was there — the world's tragedy. . . .

They went back to their rooms to dress and met at a popular restaurant — one of the smartest. Here Macheson began to recover his spirits. The music was soft yet inspiring, the women — there were none alone here — were well dressed, and pleasant to look at, the sound of their laughter and the gay murmur of conversation was like a delightful undernote. The dinner and wine were good. Holderness seemed to know very well how to choose both. Macheson began to feel the depression of a few hours ago slipping away from him. Once or twice he laughed softly to himself. Holderness looked at him questioningly,

"You should have been with me for the last fortnight, Dick," he remarked, smiling. "The lady of the manor at Thorpe didn't approve of me, and I had to sleep for two nights in a gamekeeper's shelter."

"Didn't approve of you to such an extent?" Holderness remarked. "Was she one of those old country frumps — all starch and prejudice?"

Then for a moment the heel was lifted, and a rush of memory kept him dumb. He felt the tearing of the blood in his veins, the burning of his cheeks, the wild, delicious sense of an exaltation, indefinable, mysterious. He was tongue-tied, suddenly apprehensive of himself and his surroundings. He felt somehow nearer to her — it was her atmosphere, this. Was he weaker than his friend — had he, indeed, more to fear? He raised his glass mechanically to his lips, and the soft fire of the amber wine soothed whilst it disquieted him. Again he wondered at his friend's whim in choosing this manner of spending their evening.

"No!" he said at last, and he was surprised to find his voice composed and natural, "the mistress of Thorpe is not in the least that sort. Thorpe is almost a model village, and of course there is the church, and a very decent fellow for vicar. I am not at all sure that she was not right. I must have seemed a fearful interloper."

Holderness stretched his long limbs under the table and laughed softly.

"Well," he declared, "it was a hare-brained scheme. Theoretically, I believe you were right. There's nothing more dangerous than content. Sort

of armour you can't get through. . . .Come, we
mustn't miss the ballet."

They threaded their way down the room. Suddenly Macheson stopped short. He was passing a
table set back in a recess, and occupied by two per-
sons. The girl, who wore a hat and veil, and whose
simple country clothes were conspicuous, was staring
at him with something like fear in her eyes. Her
cheeks were flushed; her lips parted, she was leaning
forward as though to call her companion's attention
to Macheson's approach. Macheson glanced towards
him with a sudden impulse of indignant apprehen-
sion. It was Stephen Hurd, in irreproachable
evening clothes save only for his black tie, and his
companion was Letty.

Macheson stopped before the table. He scarcely
knew what to say or how to say it, but he was determined not to be intimidated by Hurd's curt nod.

"So you are up in town, Letty," he said gravely.
"Is your mother with you?"

The girl giggled hysterically.

"Oh, no!" she declared. "Mother can't bear
travelling. A lot of us came up this morning at
six o'clock on a day excursion, six shillings each."

"And what time does the train go back?" Macheson asked quickly.

"At twelve o'clock," the girl answered, "or as
soon afterwards as they can get it off. It was
terribly full coming up."

Macheson was to some extent relieved. At any
rate there was nothing further that he could do.
He bent over the girl kindly.

"I hope you have had a nice day," he said, "and

won't be too tired when you get home. These excursions are rather hard work. Remember me to your mother."

He exchanged a civil word with the girl's companion, who was taciturn almost to insolence. Then he passed on and joined Holderness, who was waiting near the door.

"An oddly assorted couple, your friends," he remarked, as they struggled into their coats.

Macheson nodded.

"The girl was my landlady's daughter at Thorpe, and the young man's the son of the agent there," he said.

"Engaged?" Holderness asked.

"I'm — afraid not," Macheson answered. "She's up on an excursion — for the day — goes back at twelve."

"I suppose he's a decent fellow — the agent's son?" Holderness remarked. "She seems such a child."

"I suppose he is," Macheson repeated. "I don't care for him very much, Dick; I suppose I'm an evil-minded person, but I hate leaving them."

Holderness looked back into the restaurant.

"You can't interfere," he said. "It's probably a harmless frolic enough. Come on!"

CHAPTER XVI

THE NIGHT SIDE OF LONDON

"NO stalls left," Holderness declared, turning away from the box office at the Alhambra. "We'll go in the promenade. We can find a chair there if we want to sit down."

Macheson followed him up the stairs and into the heavily carpeted promenade. His memory of the evening, a memory which clung to him for long afterwards, seemed like a phantasmagoria of thrilling music, a stage packed with marvellously dressed women, whose movements were blended with the music into one voluptuous chorus — a blaze of colour not wholly without its artistic significance, and about him an air heavy with tobacco smoke and perfumes, a throng of moving people, more women — many more women. A girl spoke to Holderness, — a girl heavily rouged but not ill-looking, dressed in a blue muslin gown and large black hat. Holderness bent towards her deferentially. His voice seemed to take to itself its utmost note of courtesy, he answered her inquiry pleasantly, and accepted a glance at her programme. The girl looked puzzled, but they talked together for several moments of casual things. Then Holderness lifted his hat.

"My friend and I are tired," he said. "We are going to look for a seat."

She bowed and they strolled on down the promenade, finding some chairs at the further end. The dresses of the women brushed their feet and the perfume from the clothes was stronger even than the odour from the clouds of tobacco smoke which hung about the place. Macheson, in whom were generations of puritanical impulses, found himself shrinking back in his corner. Holderness turned towards him frowning.

"No superiority, Victor," he said. "These are your fellow-creatures. Don't look at them as though you'd come down from the clouds."

"It isn't that," Macheson answered, "it's a matter of taste."

"Taste! Rot!" Holderness answered. "The factory girl's hat offends my taste, but I don't shrink away from her."

A girl, in passing, stumbled against his foot. Holderness stood up as he apologized.

"I am really very sorry," he said. "No one with feet like mine ought to sit down in a public place. I hope you haven't torn your dress?"

"It really doesn't matter," the girl answered. "I ought to have looked where I was going."

"In which case," Holderness remarked, with a laugh, "you could not have failed to see my feet."

There were two empty chairs at their table. The girl glanced towards them and hesitated.

"Do you mind if we sit down here for a minute," she asked, "my friend and I? We are rather tired."

He drew the chairs towards them.

"By all means," he answered courteously. "Your friend does look tired."

The party arranged itself. Holderness called to a waiter and gave an order.

"My friend and I," he remarked, indicating Macheson, who was fiercely uncomfortable and struggling hard not to show it, "are disappointed that we could not get stalls. We wanted to see La Guerrero and this wonderful conjurer."

"The place is full every night," the girl answered listlessly. "La Guerrero comes on at ten o'clock, you can see her from the front of the promenade easily. You don't often come here, do you?"

"Not very often," Holderness answered. "And you?"

"Every night," the girl answered in a dull tone.

"That must be monotonous," he said kindly.

"It is," she admitted.

They talked for a few minutes longer, or rather it was Holderness who mostly talked, and the others who listened. It struck Macheson as curious that his friend should find it so easy to strike the note of their conversation and keep it there, as though without any definite effort he could assume control over even the thoughts of these girls, to whom he talked with such easy courtesy. He told a funny story and they all laughed naturally and heartily. Macheson had an idea that the girls had forgotten for the moment exactly where they were. Something in their faces, something which had almost terrified him at their first coming, had relaxed, if it had not passed wholly away. At the sound of a few bars of music one of them leaned almost eagerly forward.

"There," she said, "if you want to see La Guerrero you must hurry. She is coming on now."

The two young men rose to their feet. One of the girls looked wistfully at Holderness, but nothing was said beyond the ordinary farewells.

"Thank you so much for telling us," Holderness said. "Come along, Victor. It is La Guerrero."

Macheson breathed more freely when once they were in the throng. They watched the Spanish dancer with her exquisite movements, sinuous, full of grace. Holderness especially applauded loudly. Afterwards they found seats in the front and remained there for the rest of the performance.

Out in the street they hesitated. Holderness passed his arm through his companion's.

"Supper!" he declared. "This way! Did you know what a man about town I was, Victor? Ah! but one must learn, and life isn't all roses and honey. One must learn!"

They threaded their way through the streets, crowded with hansoms, electric broughams, and streams of foot passengers. Holderness led the way to a sombre-looking building, and into a room barely lit save for the rose-shaded lamps upon the tables. Macheson gasped as he entered. Nearly every table was occupied by women in evening dress, women alone — waiting. Holderness glanced around quite unconcernedly as he gave up his coat and hat to a waiter.

"Feeling shy, Victor?" he asked, smiling. "Never mind. We'll find a table to ourselves all right."

They sat in a corner. The girls chattered and
talked across them — often at them. A Frenchwoman, superbly gowned in white lace, and with a
long rope of pearls around her neck, paused as she
passed their table. She carried a Pomeranian under
her arm and held it out towards them.

"See! My little dog!" she exclaimed. "He bite
you. Messieurs are lonely?"

"Alas! Of necessity," Holderness answered in
French. "Madame is too kind."

She passed on, laughing. Macheson looked across
the table almost fiercely.

"What are you doing it for, Dick?" he exclaimed.
"What does it mean?"

His friend looked across at him steadfastly.

"Victor," he said, "I want you to understand.
You are an enthusiast, a reformer, a prophet of lost
causes. I want you to know the truth if you can
see it. There are many sides to life."

"What am I to learn of this?" Macheson asked,
almost passionately.

"If I told you," Holderness answered, "the lesson
would only be half learnt. Sit tight and don't be a
fool. Drink your wine. Mademoiselle in violet
there wants to flirt with you."

"Shall I ask her to join us?" Macheson demanded
with wasted satire.

"You might do worse," Holderness answered
calmly. "She could probably teach you something."

It was a dull evening, and many of the tables remained unoccupied — save for the one waiting figure.
The women, tired of looking towards the door,
were smoking cigarettes, twirling their bracelets,

yawning, and looking around the room. Many a mute invitation reached the two young men, but Holderness seemed to have lost his sociability. His face had grown harder and he seemed glad when their meal was over and they were free to depart. In the hall below they had to wait for their overcoats. Macheson strolled idly towards the entrance of another supper room on the ground floor, and looked in. An exclamation broke from his lips. He turned towards Holderness.

"You see the time," he exclaimed, "and they are here! Those two!"

Holderness nodded gravely.

"The girl has been crying," he said, "and there is an A B C on the table. It's up to you, Victor. We may both have to take a hand in the game. No! I wouldn't go in. Wait till they come out!".

They stood in the throng, jostled, cajoled, besought. At last the two rose and came towards the door. Letty had dried her eyes, but she looked still pale and terrified. Hurd, on the contrary, was flushed as though with wine. Macheson took her by the arm as she passed.

"Letty," he said gravely, "have you missed your train?"

She gave a stifled cry and shrank back, when she saw who it was. However, she recovered herself quickly.

"Mr. Macheson!" she exclaimed. "How you startled me! I didn't expect — to see you again."

"About this train, Letty?" he repeated.

"Mr. Hurd's watch stopped," she declared, her eyes filling once more with tears. "He thought it was eleven o'clock,— and it was ten minutes past twelve. I don't know what mother will say, I am sure."

"What are you going to do?" he asked.

She looked round nervously.

"Mr. Hurd is going to take me to some friends of his," she answered. "You see it was his fault, so he has promised to see mother and explain."

Hurd pushed angrily forward.

"Look here," he said to Macheson, "have you been following us about?"

"I have not," Macheson answered calmly. "I am very glad to have come across you, though."

"Sorry I can't return the compliment," Hurd remarked. "Come, Letty."

A girl who was passing tapped him on the arm. She was dressed in blue silk, with a large picture hat, and she was smoking a cigarette.

"Hullo, Stephen!" she exclaimed. "Edith wants to see you. Are you coming round to-night?"

Hurd muttered something under his breath and moved away. Letty looked at him with horror.

"Stephen!" she exclaimed. "You can't — you don't mean to say that you know — any of these?"

She was trembling in every limb. He tried to pass his arm through hers.

"Don't be a fool, Letty," he said. "It's time we went, or my friends will have gone to bed."

She looked at him with wide-open eyes. Her lips were quivering. It was as though she saw some new thing in his face.

"Your friends," she murmured, "are they — that sort? Oh! I am afraid."

She clung to Macheson. People were beginning to notice them. He led her out into the street. Hurd followed, angrily protesting. Holderness was close behind.

"I say, you know," Hurd began, with his arm on Macheson's shoulder. Macheson shook it off.

"Mr. Hurd," he said, "at the risk of seeming impertinent, I must ask you precisely where you intend taking this girl to-night?"

"What the devil business is it of yours?" Hurd answered angrily.

"Tell me, all the same," Macheson persisted.

Hurd passed his arm through Letty's.

"Come, Letty," he said, "we will take this hansom."

The girl was only half willing. Macheson declined to let them go.

"No!" he said, "I will have my question answered."

Hurd turned as though to strike him, but Holderness intervened, head and shoulders taller than the other.

"I think," he said, "that we will have my friend's question answered."

Hurd was almost shaking with rage, but he answered.

"To some friends in Cambridge Terrace," he said sullenly. "Number eighteen."

"You will not object," Macheson said, "if I accompany you there?"

"I'll see you damned first," Hurd answered savagely. "Get in, Letty."

The girl hesitated. She turned to Macheson.

" WHAT . . . BUSINESS IS IT OF YOURS ? " Page 156

"I should like to go to the station and wait," she declared.

"I think," Macheson said, "that you had better trust yourself to me and my friend."

"I am sure of it," Holderness added calmy.

She put her hand in Macheson's. She was as pale as death and avoided looking at Hurd. He took a quick step towards her.

"Very well, young lady," he said. "If you go now, you understand that I shall never see you again."

She began to cry again.

"I wish," she murmured, "that I had never seen you at all — never!"

He turned on his heel. A row was impossible. It occurred to him that a man of the world would face such a position calmly.

"Very good," he said, "we will leave it at that."

He paused to light a cigarette, and strolled back down the street towards the restaurant which they had just left. Letty was crying now in good earnest. The two young men looked at one another in something like dismay. Then Holderness began to laugh quietly.

"You're a nice sort of Don Quixote to spend an evening with," he remarked softly.

CHAPTER XVII

THE VICTIMS OF SOCIETY

THE girl was still crying, softly but persistently. She caught hold of Macheson's arm.

"If you please, I think I had better go back to Stephen," she said. "Do you think I could find him?"

"I think you had much better not, Letty," he answered. "He ought not to have let you miss your train. My friend here and I are going to look after you."

"It's very kind of you," the girl said listlessly, "but it doesn't matter much what becomes of me now. Mother will never forgive me — and the others will all know — that I missed the train."

"We must think of some way of putting that all right," Macheson declared. "I only wish that I had some relations in London. Can you suggest anything, Dick?"

"I can take the young lady to some decent rooms," Holderness answered. "The landlady's an old friend of mine. She'll be as right as rain there."

The girl shook her head.

"I'd as soon walk about the streets," she said

pathetically. "Mother'll never listen to me — or the others. Some of them saw me with Stephen, and they said things. I think I'll go to the station and wait till the five o'clock train."

They were walking slowly up towards Piccadilly. A fine rain had begun to fall, and already the pavements were shining. Neither of them had an umbrella, and Letty's hat, with its cheap flowers and ribbon, showed signs of collapse. Suddenly Macheson had an idea.

"Look here," he said, "supposing you spent the night at Miss Thorpe-Hatton's house in Berkeley Square — no one could say anything then, could they?"

The girl looked up with a sudden gleam of hope.

"No! I don't suppose they could," she admitted; "but I don't know where it is, and I don't suppose they'd take me in anyway."

"I know where it is," Macheson declared, "and we'll see about their taking you in. I believe Miss Thorpe-Hatton may be there herself. Stop that fourwheeler, Dick."

They climbed into a passing cab, and Macheson directed the driver. The girl was beginning to lose confidence again.

"The house is sure to be shut up," she said.

"There will be a caretaker." Macheson declared hopefully. "We'll manage it, never fear. I believe Miss Thorpe-Hatton is there herself."

Letty was trembling with excitement and fear.

"I'm scared to death of her," she admitted. "She's so beautiful, and she looks at you always as though you were something a long way off."

Macheson was suddenly silent. A rush of memories surged into his brain. He had sworn to keep away! This was a different matter, an errand of mercy. Nevertheless he would see her, if only for a moment. His heart leaped like a boy's. He looked eagerly out of the window. Already they were entering Berkeley Square. The cab stopped.

Macheson looked upwards. There were lights in many of the windows, and a small electric brougham, with a tall footman by the side of the driver, was waiting opposite the door.

"The house is open," he declared. "Don't be afraid, Letty."

The girl descended and clung to his arm as they crossed the pavement.

"I shall wait here for you," Holderness said. "Good luck to you, and good night, young lady!"

Macheson rang the bell. The door was opened at once by a footman, who eyed them in cold surprise.

"We wish to see Miss Thorpe-Hatton for two minutes," Macheson said, producing his card. "It is really an important matter, or we would not disturb her at such an hour. She is at home, is she not?"

The footman looked exceedingly dubious. He looked from the card to Macheson, and from Macheson to the girl, and he didn't seem to like either of them.

"Miss Thorpe-Hatton has just returned from the opera," he said, "and she is going on to the Countess of Annesley's ball directly. Can't you come again in the morning?"

"Quite impossible," Macheson declared briskly. "I am sure that Miss Thorpe-Hatton will see me for a moment if you take that card up."

The footman studied Macheson again, and was forced to admit that he was a gentleman. He led the way into a small morning-room.

"Miss Thorpe-Hatton shall have your card, sir," he said. "Kindly take a seat."

He left the room. Macheson drew up a chair for Letty, but she refused it, trembling.

"Oh! I daren't sit down, Mr. Macheson," she declared. "And please — don't say that I was with Mr. Hurd. I know he wouldn't like it."

"Probably not," Macheson answered, "but what am I to say?"

"Anything — anything but that," she begged.

Macheson nodded his promise. Then the door opened, and his heart seemed to stand still. She entered the room in all the glory of a wonderful toilette; she wore her famous ropes of pearls, the spotless white of her gown was the last word from the subtlest Parisian workshop of the day. But it was not these things that counted. Had he been dreaming, he wondered a moment later, or had that strange smile indeed curved her lips, that marvellous light indeed flowed from her eyes? It was the lady of his dreams who had entered — it was a very different woman who, with a slight frown upon her smooth forehead, was looking at the girl who stood trembling by Macheson's side.

"It is Mr. Macheson, is it not?" she said calmly, "the young man who wanted to convert my villagers."

And you — who are you?" she asked, turning to the girl.

"Letty Foulton, if you please, ma'am," the girl answered.

"Foulton! Letty Foulton!" Wilhelmina repeated.

"Yes, ma'am! My brother has Onetree farm," the girl continued.

Wilhelmina inclined her head.

"Ah, yes!" she remarked, "I remember now. And what do you two want of me at this hour of the night?" she asked frigidly.

"If you will allow me, I will explain," Macheson interrupted eagerly. "Letty came up from Thorpe this morning on an excursion train which returned at midnight."

Wilhelmina glanced at the clock. It was five minutes to one.

"Well?"

"She missed it," Macheson continued. "It was very careless and very wrong, of course, but the fact remains that she missed it. I found her in great distress. She had lost her friends, and there is no train back to Thorpe till the morning. Her brother and mother are very strict, and all her friends who came from Thorpe will, of course, know that — she remained in London. The position, as you will doubtless realize, is a serious one for her."

Wilhelmina made no sign. Nothing in her face answered in any way the silent appeal in his.

"I happened to know," he continued, "that you were in London, so I ventured to bring her at once to you. You are the mistress of Thorpe, and in our recent conversation I remember you admitted a certain amount of responsibility as regards your people there. If she passes the night under your roof, no one can have a word to say. It will save her at once from her parent's anger and the undesirable comments of her neighbours."

Wilhelmina glanced once more towards the clock.

"It seems to me," she remarked, "that a considerable portion of the night has already passed."

Both Macheson and the girl were silent. Wilhelmina for the first time addressed the latter.

"Where have you been spending the evening?" she asked.

"We had dinner and went to a place of entertainment," she faltered. "Then we had supper, and I found out how late it was."

"Who is we?"

The girl's face was scarlet. She did not answer. Wilhelmina waited for a moment and then shrugged her shoulders.

"You are to be congratulated," she said, with cold irony, "upon your fortunate meeting with Mr. Macheson."

She had touched the bell, and a footman entered.

"Reynolds," she said, "show this young person into the housekeeper's room, and ask Mrs. Brown to take charge of her for the night."

The girl moved forward impulsively, but something in Wilhelmina's expression checked her little speech of gratitude. She followed the man from the room without a word. Wilhelmina also turned towards the door.

"You will excuse me," she said coldly to Macheson. "I am already later than I intended to be."

"I can only apologize for disturbing you at such an hour," he answered, taking up his hat. "I could think of nothing else."

She looked at him coldly.

"The girl's parents," she said, "are respectable people, and I am sheltering her for their sake. But I am bound to say that I consider her story most unsatisfactory."

They were standing in the hall — she had paused on her way out to conclude her sentence. Her maid, holding out a wonderful rose-lined opera cloak, was standing a few yards away; a man-servant was waiting at the door with the handle in his hand. She raised her eyes to his, and Macheson felt the challenge which flashed out from them. She imagined, then, that he had been the girl's companion; the cold disdain of her manner was in itself an accusation.

His cheeks burned with a sort of shame. She had dared to think this of him — and that afterwards he should have brought the girl to her to beg for shelter! There were a dozen things which he ought to have said, which came flashing from his brain to find themselves somehow imprisoned behind his tightly locked lips. He said nothing. She passed slowly, almost unwillingly, down the hall. The maid wrapped her coat around her — still he stood like a statue. He watched her pass through the opened door and enter the electric brougham. He watched it even glide away. Then he, too, went and joined Holderness, who was waiting outside.

"Hail, succourer of damsels in distress!" Holder-

"I AM BOUND TO SAY THAT I CONSIDER HER STORY MOST
UNSATISFACTORY." Page 144

ness called out, producing his cigar-case. "Jolly glad you got rid of her! It would have meant the waiting-room at St. Pancras and an all-night sitting. Smoke, my son, and we will walk home — unless you mind this bit of rain. Was her ladyship gracious?"

"She was not," Macheson answered grimly, "but she is keeping the girl. I'd like to walk," he added, lighting a cigar.

"A very elegant lady," Holderness remarked, "but I thought she looked a bit up in the air. Did you notice her pearls, Victor?"

Macheson nodded.

"Wonderful, weren't they?"

"Yes. She wears them round her neck, and these — these wear always their shame," he added, pushing gently away a woman who clutched at his arm. "Funny thing, isn't it? What are they worth? Ten thousand pounds, very likely. A lot of money for gewgaws — to hang upon a woman's body. Shall we ever have a revolution in London, do you think, Victor?"

"Who knows?" Macheson answered wearily. "Not a political one, perhaps, but the other might come. The sewers underneath are pretty full."

They passed along in silence for a few minutes. Neither the drizzling rain nor the lateness of the hour could keep away that weary procession of sad, staring-eyed women, who seemed to come from every shadow, and vanish Heaven knows where. Macheson gripped his companion by the arm.

"Holderness," he cried, "for God's sake let's

get out of it. I shall choke presently. We'll take a side street."

But Holderness held his arm in a grip of iron.

"No," he said, "these are the things which you must feel. I want you to feel them. I mean you to."

"It's heart-breaking, Dick."

Holderness smiled faintly.

"I know how you feel," he declared. "I've gone through it myself. You are a Christian, aren't you — almost an orthodox Christian?"

"I am not sure!"

"Don't waste your pity, then," Holderness declared. "God will look after these. It's the women with the pearl necklaces and the scorn in their eyes who're looking for hell. Your friend in the electric brougham, for instance. Can't you see her close her eyes and draw away her skirts if she should brush up against one of these?"

"It's hard to blame her," Macheson declared.

Holderness looked down at him pityingly.

"Man," he said, "you're a long way down in the valley. You'll have to climb. Vice and virtue are little else save relative terms. They number their adherents by accident rather than choice."

"You mean that it is all a matter of temptation?"

Holderness laughed. They had passed into the land of silent streets. Their own rooms were close at hand.

"Wait a little time," he said. "Some day you'll understand."

CHAPTER XVIII

"YOU are quite sure," the girl said anxiously, "that Miss Thorpe-Hatton wants to see me? You see there's a train at ten o'clock I could catch."

The housekeeper looked up from the menu she was writing, and tapped the table impatiently with her pencil.

"My dear child," she said, "is it likely I should keep you here without orders? We have sent a telegram to your mother, and you are to wait until the mistress is ready to see you."

"What time does she generally get down?" Letty asked.

"Any time," Mrs. Brown answered, resuming her task. "She was back early last night, only stayed an hour at the ball, so she may send for you at any moment. Don't fidget about so, there's a good girl. I'm nervous this morning. We've twenty-four people dining, and I haven't an idea in my head. I'm afraid I shall have to send for François."

"Is François the man-cook who comes down to Thorpe?" Letty asked.

Mrs. Brown nodded.

"The *chef* you should call him," she answered. "A very clever man, no doubt, in his way, but takes a lot of keeping in order."

"Do you have to look after all the servants?" Letty asked. "Doesn't Miss Thorpe-Hatton ever order anything?"

Mrs. Brown looked pityingly at her guest.

"My dear child," she said, "I doubt if she could tell you to three or four how many servants there are in the house, and as to ordering anything, I don't suppose such a thought's ever entered into her head. Here's James coming. Perhaps it's a message for you."

A footman entered and greeted Letty kindly.

"Good morning, young lady!" he said. "You are to go into the morning-room at once."

Letty rose with alacrity.

"Is — is she there?" she asked nervously.

"She is," the man answered, "and if I were you, miss, I wouldn't do much more than just answer her questions and skedaddle. I haven't had any conversation with her myself, but mademoiselle says she's more than a bit off it this morning. Slept badly or something."

"Don't frighten the child, James," Mrs. Brown said reprovingly. "She's not likely to say much to you, my dear. You hurry along, and come back and have a glass of wine and a biscuit before you go. Show her the way, James."

"If you please, miss," the man answered, becoming once more an automaton.

Letty was ushered into a small room, full, it seemed to her as she entered, of sunshine and flowers.

Wilhelmina, in a plain white-serge gown, with a string of beads around her neck of some strange-coloured shade of blue, was sitting in a high-backed easy-chair. A small wood fire was burning in the grate, filling the room with a pleasant aromatic odour, and the window leading into the square was thrown wide open.

On a table by her side were a pile of letters, an ivory letter-opener, several newspapers, and a silver box of cigarettes. For the moment, however, none of these things claimed her attention. The lady of the house was leaning back in her chair, and her eyes were half closed. If she had not been sitting with her back to the light, Letty might have noticed the dark rings under her eyes. It was true that she had not slept well.

Letty advanced doubtfully into the room. Wilhelmina turned her head.

"Oh, it is you," she remarked. "Come up to the table where I can see you."

"Mrs. Brown told me that you wished to see me before I went," the girl said hesitatingly.

Wilhelmina was silent for a moment. She was looking at the girl. Yes! she was pretty in a rustic, uncultured way. Her figure was unformed, her hands and feet what might have been expected, and it was obvious that she lacked taste. Were men really attracted by this sort of thing?

"Yes!" Wilhelmina said, "I wish to speak to you. I am not altogether satisfied about last night."

Letty said nothing. She went red and then white. Wilhelmina's examination of her was merciless.

"I wish to know," Wilhelmina said, "who your companion was — with whom you had dinner and supper. I look upon that person as being responsible for your lost train."

Letty prayed that she might sink into the ground. Her worst imaginings had not been so bad as this. She remained silent, tongue-tied.

"I'm waiting," Wilhelmina said mercilessly. "I suppose it is obvious enough, but I wish to hear from your own lips."

"I — he — I don't think that he would like me to tell you, ma'am," she faltered.

Wilhelmina smiled — unpleasantly.

"Probably not," she answered. "That, however, is beside the question. I wish to know."

The girl was desperate. It was indeed a quandary with her. To offend the mistress of Thorpe was something like sacrilege, but she knew very well what Stephen would have had her do.

"If you please, ma'am," she said at last, "I can't."

Wilhelmina said nothing for a moment, only her eyebrows were slowly lifted.

"If you do not," she said, calmly, "I must write to your mother and tell her what I think of your behaviour last night. I do not care to have people near me who are disobedient, or — foolish."

The girl burst into tears. Wilhelmina watched her with cold patience.

"I presume," she said, "that it was Mr. Macheson. You do not need to mention his name. You need only say 'Yes!'"

The girl said nothing.

"Mr. Macheson lodged with your mother, I believe?" Wilhelmina continued.

"Yes!" the girl whispered.

"And you waited upon him?"

"Yes!"

The girl lifted her head.

"Mr. Macheson always behaved like a gentleman to me," she said.

Wilhelmina regarded her contemptuously.

"Your ideas of what constitutes gentlemanly behaviour are probably primitive," she said. "I do not think that I need trouble you for any direct answer. Still, it would be better for you to give it."

The girl was again silent. There was a knock at the door. The footman ushered in Stephen Hurd.

He entered confident and smiling. He was wearing a new grey tweed suit, and he was pleased with himself and the summons which had brought him to London. But the sight of the girl took his breath away. She, too, was utterly taken by surprise, and forgot herself.

"Stephen!" she exclaimed, taking a quick step towards him.

"You! You here!" he answered.

It was quite enough! But what puzzled Letty was that Wilhelmina did not seem in the least angry. There was a strange look on her face as she looked from one to the other. Something had sprung into her eyes which seemed to transform her. Her voice, too, had lost all its hardness.

"How do you do, Mr. Hurd?" she said. "I hope

you have come to explain how you dared let this child lose her train last night."

"I — really I — it was quite a mistake," he faltered, darting an angry glance at Letty.

"You had supper with her," Wilhelmina said, "and you knew what time the train went."

"She met some other friends," Stephen answered. "She left me."

Wilhelmina smiled. She had found out all that she wanted to know.

"Well," she said, "I won't inquire too closely into it this time, only I hope that nothing of the sort will occur again. You had better have lunch with Mrs. Brown in the housekeeper's room, Letty, and I'll send you over to St. Pancras for the four o'clock train. I'll give you a letter to your mother this time, but mind, no more foolishness of this sort."

The girl tried to stammer out her thanks, but she was almost incoherent. Wilhelmina dismissed her with a smile. Her manner was distinctly colder when she turned to Hurd.

"Mr. Hurd," she said, "I hope you will understand me when I say that I do not care to have my agent, or any one connected with the estate, play the Don Juan amongst my tenants' daughters."

He flushed up to the eyes.

"It was idiotic of me," he admitted frankly. "I simply meant to give the child a good time."

"She is quite pretty in her way," Wilhelmina said, "and her parents, I believe, are most respectable people. You were perhaps thinking of settling down?"

He looked at her in amazement.

"What, with Letty Foulton!" he exclaimed.

"Why not?" she asked.

He drew a breath through his teeth. He could scarcely trust himself to speak for anger.

"You — are not serious?" he permitted himself to ask.

"Why not?" she demanded.

Hurd struggled to express himself with dignity.

"I should not consider such a marriage a suitable one, even if I were thinking of marrying at all," he said.

She raised her eyebrows.

"No? Well, I suppose you know best," she said carelessly. "Is there anything fresh down at Thorpe?"

She was angry about that fool of a girl, he told himself. A good sign. But what an actress! His conceit barely kept him up.

"There really isn't anything I couldn't arrange with Mr. Fields," he admitted. "I thought, perhaps, as I was up, you might have some special instructions. That is why I sent to ask if you would see me."

He looked at her almost eagerly. After all, she was the same woman who had been kind to him at Thorpe? And yet, was she? A sudden thought startled him. She was changed. Had she guessed that he knew her secret?

"No!" she said deliberately. "I do not think that there is anything. If you could find out Mr. Macheson's address I should be much obliged."

Hurd was puzzled. This was the second time. What could she have to say to Macheson?

"He was here last night, but I forgot to ask him," she continued equably.

"Macheson, here!" he exclaimed.

"It was he who brought the girl, Letty," she said.

He was silent for a moment.

"He's a queer lot," he said. "Came to Thorpe, of all places, as a sort of missioner, and he was about town last night most immaculately got up; nothing of the parson about him, I can assure you."

"No!" she answered quietly. "Well, if you can discover his address, remember I should be glad to hear it."

He took up his hat reluctantly. He had hoped at least that he might have been asked to luncheon. It was obvious, however, that he was expected to depart, and he did so. On the whole, although he had escaped from an exceedingly awkward situation, he could scarcely consider his visit a success. On his way out he passed Deyes, stepping out of a cab piled up with luggage. He nodded to Hurd in a friendly manner.

"Miss Thorpe-Hatton in?" he asked.

"Just left her," Hurd answered.

Deyes passed on, and was received by the butler as a favoured guest. He was shown at once into the morning-room.

CHAPTER XIX

A REPORT FROM PARIS

"FOR the first time in my life," Deyes declared, accepting the cigarette and the easy-chair, "I have appreciated Paris. I have gone there as a tourist. I have drunk strange drinks at the Café de la Paix. I have sat upon the boulevards and ogled the obvious lady."

"And my little guide?" she asked.

"Has disappeared!" he answered.

"Since when?"

"A month ago! It is reported that he came to England."

Wilhelmina sat still for several moments. To a casual observer she might have seemed unmoved. Deyes, however, was watching her closely, and he understood.

"I am sorry," he said, "to have so little to tell you. But that is the beginning and the end of it. The man had gone away."

"That is precisely what I desired to ascertain," she said. "It seemed to me possible that the man had come to England. I wished to know for certain whether it was true or not."

"I think," Deyes said, withdrawing his cigarette and looking at it thoughtfully, "that it is true."

"You have any further reason for thinking so," she asked, "beyond your casual inquiries?"

"Well, yes!" he admitted. "I went a little farther than those casual inquiries. It seemed such a meagre report to bring you."

"Go on!"

"The ordinary person," he continued smoothly, "would never believe the extreme difficulty with which one collects any particulars as to the home life of a guide. More than once I felt inclined to give up the task in despair. It seemed to me that a guide could have no home, that he must sleep in odd moments on a bench at the *Hôtel de Luxe*. I tried to fancy a guide in the bosom of his family, carving a Sunday joint, and surrounded by Mrs. Guide and the little Guides. I couldn't do it. It seemed to me somehow grotesque. Just as I was giving it up in despair, the commissionaire at a night café in Montmartre told me exactly what I wanted to know. He showed me the house where Johnny, as they called him, had a room."

"You went there?" she asked.

"I did," he answered.

"It was locked up?"

"On the contrary," he declared, "Mrs. or Miss Guide was at home, and very pleased to see me."

"There was a woman there?"

"Assuredly. Whether she is there now or not I cannot say, for it is three days ago, and to me she seemed nearer than that to death!"

"And about this woman! What was she like? Was she his wife or his daughter?"

"He called her his daughter. I am not sure

about the relationship.   She had been good-looking,
I should say, but she was very ill."

"What did she tell you—about the man Johnson?"

"That he had gone to England to try to get
some money.   They were almost destitute!   He was
a good guide, she said, but people came so often to
Paris, and they liked some one fresh.   Then she
coughed — how she coughed!"

"Did she tell you to what part of England the man
Johnson had gone?"

"I asked her, but she was not sure.   I do not
believe that she knew.   She said that there was
some one in England who was very rich, and from
whom he hoped to be able to get money."

"Anything else?"

"No!   I spoke of myself as an old client of
Johnny's, and I left money.   Afterwards, at the
café where I lunched, I found a commissionaire
who told me more about our friend."

"Ah!   What was the name of the café?"

"The Café de Paris!"

She took up a screen and held it before her face.
There seemed to be little need of it, however, for her
cheeks were as pale as the white roses by her side.

"This man Johnny, as they call him," Deyes
continued, "seems to have had his ups and downs.
One big stroke of luck he had, however, which seems
to have kept him going for several years.   The
commissionaire was able to tell me something about
it.   Shall I go on?" he asked, dropping his voice a
little.

"I should like to know what the commissionaire
told you," she answered.

"Somehow or other this fellow, Johnny or Johnson as some of them called him, was recommended to a young lady, a very young lady, who was in Paris with an invalid chaperon."

"Stop!" she cried.

He looked at her fixedly.

"You were that young lady," he said softly. "Of course, I know that!"

"I was," she admitted. "Don't speak to me for a few moments. It was years ago — but —— "

She bent the screen which she held in her hand until the handle snapped.

"You seem," she said, "to have rather exceeded your instructions. I simply wanted to know whether the man was in Paris or not."

He bowed.

"The man is in England," he said. "Don't you think it might be helpful if you gave me more of your confidence, and told me why you wanted to hear about him?"

She shook her head.

"I would sooner tell you than any one, Gilbert," she said, "but I do not want to talk about it."

"It must be as you will, of course," he answered, "but I hope you will always remember that you could do me no greater kindness — at any time — than to make use of my services. I do not know everything of what happened in Paris—about that time. I do not wish to know. I am content to serve you — blindly."

"I will not forget that," she said softly. "If ever the necessity comes I will remind you. There! Let that be the end of it."

She changed the subject, giving him to understand that she did not wish to discuss it further.

"You are for Marienbad, as usual?" she asked.

"Next week," he answered. "One goes from habit, I suppose. No waters upon the earth or under it will ever cure me!"

"Liver?" she asked.

"Heart!" he declared.

"You shouldn't smoke so many cigarettes."

"Harmless," he assured her. "I don't inhale."

"I think," she said, "that I shall come over next month."

"Do!" he begged. "I'll answer for the bridge. May I come and lunch to-morrow?"

She turned to a red morocco book by her side.

"A bishop and Lady Sarah," she said. "Several more parsons, and I think the duchess."

"I'll face 'em," he declared.

"I think I shall send for Peggy," Wilhelmina said. "She is always so sweet to the Church."

Deyes grinned.

"I shall go round and look her up," he declared. "Perhaps she'll come and have lunch with me somewhere."

She held out her hand.

"You're a good sort to have gone over for me," she said. "The things you tumbled up against you'd better forget."

"Until you remind me of them," he said. "Very well, I'll do that. Sorry I didn't run Johnny to earth."

He went off, and Wilhelmina after a few minutes went to her desk and wrote a letter to Stephen Hurd.

"As usual," she wrote, "when you were here this morning I forgot to mention several matters upon which I meant to speak to you. The first is with regard to the man whose brutal assault upon your father caused his death. I understand that the police have never traced him, have never even found the slightest clue to his whereabouts. The more I think of this, the more strange it seems to me, and I am inclined to believe that he never, after all, escaped from the wood in which he first took shelter. I know that the slate quarry was dragged at the time, but I have been told that this was hastily done, and that there are several very deep holes into which the man's body may have drifted. I wish you, therefore, to send over to Nottingham to get some experienced men to bring back the drags and make an exhaustive search. Please have this done without delay.

"Further, I wish to communicate with the young man Macheson, who was in Thorpe at the time. They may know his address at the post-office, but if you are unable to procure it in any other way, you must advertise in your own name. Please carry out my instructions in these two matters immediately."

Wilhelmina laid down her pen and looked thoughtfully through the window into the square. A policeman was coming slowly along the pavement. She watched him approach and pass the house, his eyes still fixed in front of him, his whole appearance stolid and matter-of-fact to the last degree. She watched him disappear with fascinated eyes. After all, he represented great things; behind him was a whole national code; the machinery of which he was so small a part drove the wheels of life or death. She turned away from the window with a shrug of the shoulders.   Humming a tune, she threw herself back in her chair, and began the leisurely perusal of her letters.

CHAPTER XX

LIKE A TRAPPED ANIMAL

MACHESON in those days felt himself rapidly growing older. An immeasurable gap seemed to lie between him and the eager young apostle who had plunged so light-heartedly into the stress of life. All that wonderful enthusiasm, that undaunted courage with which he had faced coldness and ridicule in the earlier days of his self-chosen vocation seemed to have left him. Some way, somehow, he seemed to have suffered shipwreck! There was poison in his system! Fight against it as he might — and he did fight — there were moments when memory turned the life which he had taken up so solemnly into the maddest, most fantastic fairy story. At such times his blood ran riot, the sweetness of a strange, unknown world seemed to be calling to him across the forbidden borders. Inaction wearied him horribly — and, after all, it was inaction which Holderness had recommended as the best means of re-establishing himself in a saner and more normal attitude towards life!

"Look round a bit, old chap," he advised, "and think. Don't do anything in a hurry. You're young, shockingly young for any effective work. You can't teach before you understand. Life

"So you are still in London, Mr. Macheson," she said. Page 163

isn't such a sink of iniquity as you young prigs at Oxford professed to find it.   See the best of it and the worst.   You'll be able to put your finger on the weak spots quick enough."

But the process of looking around wearied Macheson excessively — or was it something else which had crept into his blood to his immense unsettlement?   There were several philanthropic schemes started by himself and his college friends in full swing now, in or about London.   To each of them he paid some attention, studying its workings, listening to the enthusiastic outpourings of his quondam friends and doing his best to catch at least some spark of their interest.   But it was all very unsatisfactory.   Deep down in his heart he felt the insistent craving for some fiercer excitement, some mode of life which should make larger and deeper demands upon his emotional temperament.   A heroic war would have appealed to him instantly — for that, he realized with a sigh, he was born many centuries too late.   For weeks he wandered about London in a highly unsatisfied condition.   Then one afternoon, in the waning of a misty October day, he came face to face with Wilhelmina in Bond Street.

She was stepping into her motor brougham when she saw him.   He had no opportunity for escape, even if he had desired it.   Her tired lips were suddenly curved into a most bewildering smile. She withdrew her hand from her muff and offered it to him — for the first time.

"So you are still in London, Mr. Macheson," she said.   "I am very glad to see you."

The words were unlike her, the tone was such as he had never heard her use. Do what he could, he could not help the answering light which sprang into his own eyes.

"I am still in London," he said. "I thought you were to go to Marienbad?"

"I left it until it was too late," she answered. "Walk a little way with me," she added abruptly. "I should like to talk to you."

"If I may," he answered simply.

She dismissed the brougham, and they moved on.

"I am sorry," she began, "that I was rude to you when you brought that girl to me. You did exactly what was nice and kind, and I was hateful. Please forgive me."

"Of course," he answered simply. "I felt sure that when you thought it over you would understand."

"You are not going back — to Thorpe?" she asked.

"Not at present, at any rate," he answered.

She looked up at him with a faint smile.

"You can have the barn," she said.

His eyes answered her smile, but his tone was grave.

"I have given that up — for a little time, at any rate," he said. "I mean that particular sort of work."

"My villagers must content themselves with Mr. Vardon, then," she remarked.

He nodded.

"Perhaps," he said, "ours was a mistaken enterprise. I am not sure. But at any rate, so far as

Thorpe is concerned, I have abandoned it for the present."

She was walking close to his side, so close that the hand which raised her skirt as they crossed the street touched his, and her soft breath as she leaned over and spoke fell upon his cheek.

"Why?"

He felt the insidious meaning of her whispered monosyllable, he felt her eyes striving to make him look at her. His cheeks were flushed, but he looked steadily ahead.

"There were several reasons," he said.

"Do tell me," she begged; "I am curious."

"For one," he said steadily, "I did an unjust thing at Thorpe. I sheltered a criminal and helped him to escape."

"So it was you who did that," she remarked. "You mean, of course, the man who killed Mr. Hurd?"

"Yes!" he answered. "I showed him where to hide. He either got clean away, or he is lying at the bottom of the slate quarry. In either case, I am responsible for him."

"Well," she said, "he is not at the bottom of the slate quarry. I can at least assure you of that. I have had the place dragged, and every foot of it gone over by experienced men from Nottingham."

"Really," he said, surprised. "Well, I am glad of it."

She sighed.

"I want you, if you can," she said, "to describe the man to me. It is not altogether curiosity. I have a reason for wishing to know what he was like."

"He was in such a state of panic," Macheson said doubtfully, "that I am afraid I have only an imperfect impression of him. He was not very tall, he had a round face, cheeks that were generally, I should think, rather high-coloured, brown eyes and dark hair, almost black. He wore a thick gold ring on the finger of one hand, and although he spoke good English, I got the idea somehow that he was either a foreigner or had lived abroad. He was in a terrible state of fear, and from what I could gather, I should say that he struck old Mr. Hurd in a scuffle, and not with any deliberate intention of hurting him."

She nodded.

"I have heard all that I want to," she declared.

They walked on in silence for several minutes. Then she turned to him with a shrug of the shoulders.

"The subject," she declared, "is dismissed. I did not ask you to walk with me to discuss such unpleasant things. I should like to know about yourself."

He sighed.

"About myself," he answered, "there is nothing to tell. There isn't in the whole of London a more unsatisfactory person."

She laughed softly.

"Such delightful humility," she murmured, "especially amongst the young, is too touching. Nevertheless, go on. It amuses me to hear."

The note of imperiousness in her tone was pleasantly reminiscent. It was the first reminder he had received of the great lady of Thorpe.

"Well," he said, "what do you want to know?"

"Everything," she answered. "I am possessed by a most unholy curiosity. Your relatives for instance, and where you were born."

He shook his head.

"I have no relatives," he answered. "I was born in Australia. I am an orphan, twenty-eight years old, and feel forty-eight, no profession, no settled purpose in life. I am Japhet in search of a career."

She glanced at his shabby clothes. He had been to a mission-house in the East End.

"You are poor?" she asked softly.

"I have enough, more than enough," he answered, "to live on."

Her eyes lingered upon his clothes, but he offered no explanation. Enough to live on, she reflected, might mean anything!

"You say that you have no profession," she remarked. "I suppose you would call it a vocation. But why did you want to come and preach to my villagers at Thorpe? Why didn't you go into the Church if you cared for that sort of thing?"

"There was a certain amount of dogma in the way," he answered. "I should make but a poor Churchman. They would probably call me a freethinker. Besides, I wanted my independence."

She nodded.

"I am beginning to understand a little better," she said. "Now you must tell me this. Why did you entertain the idea of mission work in a place like Thorpe, when the whole of that awful East End was there waiting for you?"

"All the world of reformers," he answered, "rushes

to the East End. We fancied there was as important work to be done in less obvious places."

"And you started your work," she asked, "directly you left college?"

"Before, I think," he answered. "You see, I wasn't alone. There were several of us who felt the same way — Holderness, for instance, the man who came to your house with me the other night. He works altogether upon the political side. He's a Socialist — of a sort. Two of the others went into the Church, one became a medical missionary. I joined in with a few who thought that we might do more effective work without tying ourselves down to anything, or subscribing to any religious denomination."

She looked at him curiously. He was tall, broad-shouldered and muscular. He wore even his shabby clothes with an air of distinction.

"I suppose," she said calmly, "that I must belong to a very different world. But what I cannot understand is why you should choose a career which you intend to pursue apparently for the benefit of other people. All the young men whom I have known who have taken life seriously enough to embrace a career at all, have at least studied their individual tastes."

"Well," he answered, smiling, "it isn't that I fancy myself any better than my fellows. I was at Magdalen, you know, under Heysey. I think that it was his influence which shaped our ideas."

"Yes! I have heard of him," she said thoughtfully. "He was a good man. At least every one says so. I'm afraid I don't know much about good

men myself.   Most of those whom I have met have
been the other sort."

The faint bitterness of her tone troubled him.
There was deliberation, too, in her words.   In-
stinctively he knew that this was no idle speech.

"You have asked me," he reminded her, "a good
many questions.   I wonder if I might be permitted
to ask you one?"

"Why not?   I can reserve the privilege of not
answering it," she remarked.

"People call you a fortunate woman," he said.
"You are very rich, you have a splendid home, the
choice of your own friends, a certain reputation —
forgive me if I quote from a society paper — as a
brilliant and popular woman of the world.   Yours
is rather a unique position, isn't it?   I wonder,"
he added, "whether you are satisfied with what you
get out of life!"

"I get all that there is to be got," she answered,
a slight hardness creeping into her tone.   "It
mayn't be much, but it amuses me — sometimes."

He shook his head.

"There is more to be got out of life," he said,
"than a little amusement."

She shrugged her shoulders.

"How about yourself?   You haven't exactly the
appearance of a perfectly contented being."

"I'm hideously dissatisfied," he admitted
promptly.   "Something seems to have gone wrong
with me — I seem to have become a looker-on at life.
I want to take a hand, and I can't.   There doesn't
seem to be any place for me.   Of course, it's only
a phase," he continued.   "I shall settle down into

something presently. But it's rather beastly while it lasts."

She looked at him, her eyes soft with laughter. Somehow his confession seemed to have delighted her.

"I'm glad you are human enough to have phases," she declared. "I was beginning to be afraid that you might turn out to be just an ordinary superior person. Perhaps you are also human enough to drink tea and eat muffins. Try, won't you?"

They were in front of her door, which flew immediately open. She either took his consent for granted, or chose not to risk his refusal, for she went on ahead, and his faint protests were unheard. His hat and stick passed into the care of an elderly person in plain black clothes; with scarcely an effort at resistance, he found himself following her down the hall. She stopped before a small wrought-iron gate, which a footman at once threw open.

"It makes one feel as though one were in a hotel, doesn't it?" she remarked, "but I hate stairs. Besides, I am going to take you a long, long way up. . . . I am not at home this afternoon, Groves."

"Very good, madam," the man answered.

They stepped out into a smaller hall. A dark-featured young woman came hurrying forward to meet them.

"I shall not need you, Annette," Wilhelmina said. "Go down and see that they send up tea for two, and telephone to Lady Margaret — say I'm sorry that I cannot call for her this afternoon."

"Parfaitement, madame," the girl murmured, and hurried away. Wilhelmina opened the door of a sitting-room — the most wonderful apartment Macheson had ever seen. A sudden nervousness seized him. He felt his knees shaking, his heart began to thump, his brain to swim. All at once he realized where he was! It was not the lady of Thorpe, this! It was the woman who had come to him with the storm, the woman who had set burning the flame which had driven him into a new world. He looked around half wildly! He felt suddenly like a trapped animal. It was no place for him, this bower of roses and cushions, and all the voluptuous appurtenances of a chamber subtly and irresistibly feminine! He was bereft of words, awkward, embarrassed. He longed passionately to escape.

Wilhelmina closed the door and raised her veil. She laid her two hands upon his shoulders, and looked up at him with a faint but very tender smile. Her forehead was slightly wrinkled, her fingers seemed to cling to him, so that her very touch was like a caress! His heart began to beat madly. The perfume of her clothes, her hair, the violets at her bosom, were like a new and delicious form of intoxication. The touch of her fingers became more insistent. She was drawing his face down to hers.

"I wonder," she murmured, "whether you remember!"

BOOK II

CHAPTER I

RATHER A GHASTLY PART

MADEMOISELLE ROSINE raised her glass.
Her big black eyes flashed unutterable
things across the pink roses.

"I think," she said, "that we drink the good
health of our host, Meester Macheson, Meester
Victor, is it not?"

"Bravo!" declared a pallid-looking youth, her
neighbour at the round supper table. "By Jove, if
we were at the *Côte d'Or* instead of the *Warwick*,
we'd give him musical honours."

"I drink," Macheson declared, "to all of us who
know how to live! Jules, another magnum, and
look sharp."

"Certainly, sir," the man answered.

There flashed a quick look of intelligence between
the waiter and a maître d'hôtel who was lingering
near. The latter hesitated for a moment, and then
nodded. It was a noisy party and none too repu-
table, but a magnum of champagne was an order.
They were likely to make more noise still if they
didn't get it. So the wine was brought, and more
toasts were drunk. Mademoiselle Rosine's eyes

flashed softer things than ever across the table, but
she had the disadvantage of distance.   Ella Merriam, the latest American importation, held the place
of honour next Macheson, and she was now en-
deavouring to possess herself of his hand under
the table.

"I say, Macheson, how is it none of us ever ran
up against you before?" young Davenant demanded,
leaning back in his chair.   "Never set eyes on you
myself, from the day you left Magdalen till I ran
up against you at the Alhambra the other evening.
Awfully studious chap Macheson was at college,"
he added to the American girl.   "Thought us chaps
no end of rotters because we used to go the pace a
bit.   That's so, isn't it, Macheson?"

Macheson nodded.

"It is only the young who are really wise," he
declared coolly.   "As we grow older we make fools
of ourselves inevitably, either fools or beasts, according to our proclivities.   Then we begin to enjoy
ourselves."

The girl by his side laughed.

"I guess you don't mean that," she said.   "It
sounds smart, but it's real horrid.   How old are
you, Mr. Macheson?"

"Older than I look and younger than I feel," he
answered, gazing into his empty glass.

"Have you found what you call your proclivities?"
she asked.

"I am searching for them," Macheson answered.
"The trouble is one doesn't know whether to dig
or to climb."

"Why should one search at all?" the other man

asked, drawing out a gold cigarette case from his trousers pocket, and carefully selecting a cigarette. "Life comes easiest to those who go blindfold. I've got a brother, private secretary to a Member of Parliament. He's got views about things, and he makes an awful fag of life. What's the good of it! He'll be an old man before he's made up his mind which way he wants to go. This sort of thing's good enough for me!"

The magnum had arrived, and Macheson lifted a foaming glass.

"Davenant," he declared, "you are a philosopher. We will drink to life as it comes! To life — as it comes!"

They none of them noticed the little break in his voice. A party of newcomers claimed their attention. Macheson, too, had seen them. He had seen her. Like a ghost at the feast, he sat quite motionless, his glass half raised in the air, the colour gone from his cheeks, his eyes set in a hard fast stare. Wilhelmina, in a plain black velvet gown, with a rope of pearls about her neck, her dark hair simply arranged about her pallid, distinguished face, was passing down the room, followed closely by the Earl of Westerdean, Deyes, and Lady Peggy. Her first impulse had been to stop; a light sprang into her eyes, and a delicate spot of colour burned in her cheeks. Then her eyes fell upon his companions; she realized his surroundings. The colour went: the momentary hesitation was gone. She passed on without recognition; Lady Peggy, after a curious glance, did the same. She whispered and laughed in Deyes' ear as they seated themselves at an adjacent table. He looked round behind her back and nodded, but Macheson did not appear to see him.

A momentary constraint fell upon the little party. The American young lady leaned over to ask Davenant who the newcomers were.

"The elder man," he said, "is the Earl of Westerdean, and the pretty fair woman Lady Margaret Penshore. The other woman is a Miss Thorpe-Hatton. Macheson probably knows more about them than I do!"

Macheson ignored the remark. He whispered something in his neighbour's ear, which made her laugh heartily. The temporary check to their merriment passed away. Macheson was soon laughing and talking as much as any of them.

"Supper," he declared, "would be the most delightful meal of the day in any other country except England. In a quarter of an hour the lights will be out."

"But it is barbarous," Mademoiselle Rosine declared. "Ah! Monsieur Macheson, you should come to Paris! There it is that one may enjoy oneself."

"I will come," Macheson answered, "whenever you will take me."

She clapped her hands.

"Agreed," she cried. "I have finished rehearsing. I have a week's 'vacance.' We will go to Paris to-morrow, all four of us!"

"I'm on," Davenant declared promptly. "I was going anyway in a week or two."

Mademoiselle Rosine clapped her hands again.

"Bravo!" she cried. "And you, Mademoiselle?"

The girl hesitated. She glanced at Macheson.

"We will both come," Macheson declared. "Miss Merriam will do me the honour to go as my guest."

"We'll stay at the Vivandiére," Davenant said. "I've a pal there who knows the ropes right up to date. What about the two-twenty to-morrow? We shall get there in time to change and have supper at Noyeau's."

"And afterwards — *au Rat Mort* ——" Mademoiselle Rosine cried. "We will drink a glass of champagne with *cher* Monsieur François."

Davenant raised his glass.

"One more toast, then, before the bally lights go out!" he exclaimed. "To Paris — and our trip!"

Some one touched Macheson on the arm. He turned sharply round. Deyes was standing there. Tall and immaculately attired, there was something a little ghostly in the pallor of his worn, beardless face, with its many wrinkles and tired eyes.

"Forgive me for interrupting you, my dear fellow," he said. "We are having our coffee outside, just on the left there. Miss Thorpe-Hatton wants you to stop for a moment on your way out."

Macheson hesitated perceptibly. A dull flush of colour stained his cheek, fading away almost immediately. He set his teeth hard.

"I shall be very happy," he said, "to stop for a second."

Deyes bowed and turned away. The room now was almost in darkness, and the people were streaming out into the foyer. Macheson paid the bill and followed in the wake of the others. Seeing

him approach alone, Wilhelmina welcomed him
with a smile, and drew her skirts on one side to
make room for him to sit down. He glanced doubtfully around. She raised her eyebrows.

"Your friends," she said, "are in no hurry. They
can spare you for a moment."

There was nothing in her tone to indicate any
surprise at finding him there, or in such company.
She made a few casual remarks in her somewhat
languid fashion, and recalled him to the recollection of Lady Peggy, who was to all appearance
flirting desperately with Lord Westerdean. Deyes
had strolled across to a neighbouring group, and
was talking to a well-known actor. Wilhelmina
leaned towards him.

"Has it ever occurred to you," she asked quietly,
"that you left me a little abruptly the other afternoon?"

His eyes blazed into hers. He found it hard to
emulate the quiet restraint of her tone and manner.
It was a trick which he had never cultivated, never
inherited, this playing with the passions in kid
gloves, this muzzling and harnessing of the emotions.

"You know why," he said.

She inclined her head ever so slightly to where
his late companions were seated.

"And this?" she asked. "Am I responsible for
this, too?"

He laughed shortly.

"It would never have occurred to me to suggest
such a thing," he declared. "I am amusing myself
a little. Why not?"

"Are you?" she asked calmly.

Her eyes drew his. He almost fancied that the quiver at the corners of her lips was of mirth.

"Somehow," she continued, "I am not sure of that. I watched you now and then in there. It seemed to me that you were playing a part — rather a ghastly part! There's nothing so wearisome, you know, as pretending to enjoy yourself."

"I had a headache to-night," he said, frowning.

She bent towards him.

"Is it better now?" she whispered, smiling.

He threw out his hands with a quick fierce gesture. It was well that the great room was wrapped in the mysterious obscurity of semi-darkness, and that every one was occupied with the business of farewells. He sprang to his feet.

"I am going," he said thickly. "My friends are expecting me."

She shook her head.

"Those are not your friends," she said. "You know very well that they never could be. You can go and wish them good night. You are going to see me home."

"No!" he declared.

"If you please," she begged softly.

He crossed the room unsteadily, and made his excuses with the best grace he could. Mademoiselle Rosine made a wry face. Miss Ella laid her fingers upon his arm and looked anxiously up at him.

"Say you won't disappoint us to-morrow," she said. "It's all fixed up about Paris, isn't it? Two-twenty from Charing Cross."

" Yes! " he answered. " I will let you know if anything turns up."

They all stood around him. Davenant laid his hand upon his shoulder.

" Look here, old chap," he said, "no backing out. We've promised the girls, and we mustn't disappoint them."

" Monsieur Macheson would not be so cruel," Mademoiselle Rosine pleaded. " He has promised, and Englishmen never break their work. Is it not so? A party of four, yes! that is very well. But alone with Herbert here I could not go. If you do not come, all is spoilt! Is it not so, my friends? "

" Rather! " Davenant declared.

The other girl's fingers tightened upon his arm.

" Don't go away now," she whispered. " Come round to my flat and we'll all talk it over. I will sing you my new song. I'm crazy about it."

Macheson detached himself as well as he could.

" I must leave you now," he declared. ' I can assure you that I mean to come to-morrow."

He hurried after Wilhelmina, who was saying good night to her friends. A few minutes later they were being whirled westwards in her brougham.

CHAPTER II

PLAYING WITH FIRE

"AND now," she said, throwing herself into an easy-chair and taking up a fan," "we can talk."

He refused the chair which she had motioned him to wheel up to the fire. He stood glowering down upon her, pale, stern, yet not wholly master of himself. Against the sombre black of her dress, her neck and bosom shone like alabaster. She played with her pearls, and looked up at him with that faint maddening curl of the lips which he so loved and so hated.

"So you won't sit down. I wonder why a man always feels that he can bully a woman so much better standing up."

"There is no question of bullying you," he answered shortly. "You are responsible for my coming here. What is it that you want with me?"

"Suppose," she murmured, looking up at him, "that I were to say — another kiss!"

"Suppose, on the other hand," he answered roughly, "you were to tell me the truth."

She sighed gently.

"You jump so rapidly at conclusions," she

"I WONDER WHY A MAN ALWAYS FEELS THAT HE CAN BULLY
A WOMAN SO MUCH BETTER STANDING UP." Page 180

declared. "Are you sure that it would not be the truth!"

"If it were," he began fiercely.

"If it were," she interrupted, "well?"

"I would rather kiss Mademoiselle Rosine or whatever her name is," he said. "I would sooner go out into the street and kiss the first woman I met."

She shook her head.

"What an impossible person you are!" she murmured. "Of course, I don't believe you."

He shrugged his shoulders, and glanced at the clock.

"Are you going to keep me here long?" he asked roughly. "I am going to Paris to-morrow, and I have to pack my clothes."

"To Paris? With Mademoiselle Rosine?"

"Yes!"

She laughed softly.

"Oh! I think not," she declared. "That sort of thing wouldn't amuse you a bit."

"We shall see!" he muttered.

"I am sure that you will not go," she repeated.

"Why not?" he demanded.

"Because — I beg you not to!"

"You!" he exclaimed. "You! Do you think that I am another of those creatures of straw and putty, to dance to your whims, to be whistled to your heel, to be fed with stray kisses, and an occasional kind word? I think not! If I am to go to the Devil, I will go my own way."

"You inconsistent creature!" she said. "Why not mine?"

"I'll take my soul with me, such as it is," he

answered. "I'll not make away with it while my feet are on the earth."

"Do you know that you are really a very extraordinary person?" she said.

"What I am you are responsible for," he answered. "I was all right when you first knew me. I may have been ignorant, perhaps, but at any rate I was sincere. I had a conscience and an ideal. Oh! I suppose you found me very amusing — a missioner who thought it worth while to give a part of his life to help his fellows climb a few steps higher up. What devil was it that sent you stealing down the lane that night from your house, I wonder?"

She nodded slowly.

"I'm sorry you can speak of it like that," she said. "To me it was the most delightful piece of sentiment! Almost like a poem!"

"A poem! It was the Devil's own poetry you breathed into me! What a poor mad fool I became! You saw how easily I gave my work up, how I sulked up to London, fighting with it all the time, with this madness — this ——"

"Dear me," she said, "what an Adam you are! My dear Victor, isn't it — you are very, very young. There is no need for you to manufacture a huge tragedy out of a woman's kiss."

"What else is it but a tragedy," he demanded, "the kiss that is a lie — or worse? You brought me here, you let me hold you in my arms, you filled my brain with mad thoughts, you drove everything good and worth having out of life, you filled it with what? Yourself! And then — you pat me on the cheek and tell me to come, and be kissed some other day, when you feel in the humour, a wet afternoon, perhaps, or when you are feeling bored, and want to hunt up a few new emotions! It may be the way with you and your kind. I call it hellish!"

"Well," she said, "tell me exactly what it is that you want?"

"To be laughed at — as you did before?" he answered fiercely. "Never mind. It was the truth. You have lain in my arms, you came willingly, your lips have been mine! You belong to me!"

"To be quite explicit," she murmured, "you think I ought to marry you."

"Yes!" he declared firmly. "A kiss is a promise! You seem to want to live as a 'poseuse,' to make playthings of your emotions and mine. I wanted to build up my life firmly, to make it a stable and a useful thing. You came and wrecked it, and you won't even help me to rebuild."

"Let us understand one another thoroughly," she said. "Your complaint is, then, that I will not marry you?"

The word, the surprising, amazing word, left her lips again so calmly that Macheson was staggered a little, confused by its marvellous significance. He was thrown off his balance, and she smiled as a wrestler who has tripped his adversary. Henceforth she expected to find him easier to deal with.

"You know — that it is not that — altogether," he faltered.

"What is it that you want then?" she asked calmly. "There are not many men in the world who have kissed — even my hand. There are fewer still — whom I have kissed. I thought that I had been rather kind to you."

"Kind!" he threw out his arms with a despairing gesture. "You call it kindness, the drop of magic you pour into a man's veins, the touch of your body, the breath of your lips vouchsafed for a second, the elixir of a new life. What is it to you? A caprice! A little dabbling in the emotions, a device to make a few minutes of the long days pass more smoothly. Perhaps it's the way in your world, this! You cheat yourself of a wholehearted happiness by making physiological experiments, frittering away the great chance out of sheer curiosity — or something worse. And we who don't understand the game — we are the victims!"

"Really," she said pleasantly, "you are very eloquent."

"And you," he said, "are ——"

Her hand flashed out almost to his lips, long shapely fingers, ablaze with the dull fire of emeralds.

"Stop," she commanded, "you are not quite yourself this evening. I am afraid that you will say something which you will regret. Now listen. You have made a most eloquent attack upon me, but you must admit that it is a perfect tangle of generalities. Won't you condescend to look me in the face, leave off vague complaints, and tell me precisely why you have placed me in the dock and yourself upon the bench? In plain words, mind. No evasions. I want the truth."

"You shall have it," he answered grimly. "Listen, then. I began at Thorpe. You were at

once rude and kind to me. I was a simple ass, of
course, and you were a mistress in all the arts which
go to a man's undoing. It wasn't an equal fight.
I struggled a little, but I thanked God that I had
an excuse to give up my work. I came to London,
but the poison was working. Every morning
before you were up, and every night after dark,
I walked round your square — and the days I saw
you were the days that counted."

"Dear me, how interesting!" she interrupted
softly. "And to think that I never knew!"

"I never meant you to know," he declared. "A
fool I was from the first, but never fool enough to
misunderstand. When I brought Letty Foulton to
you, I brought her against my will. It was for the
child's sake. And you were angry, and then I saw
you again — and you were kind!"

She smiled at him.

"I'm glad you admit that," she said gently. "I
thought that I was very kind indeed. And you
repaid me — how?"

"Kind!" he cried fiercely. "Yes! you were
kind! You were mine for the moment, you lay in
my arms, you gave me your lips! It was an impression! It amused you to see any human being so
much in earnest. Then the mood passed. Your
dole of charity had been given! I must sit apart and
you must smooth your hair. What did it all amount
to? An episode, a trifling debauch in sentiment —
and for me — God knows!"

"To return once more," she said patiently,
"to your complaint. Is it that I will not marry
you?"

"I did not ask that — at first," he answered. "It is a good deal, I know."

"Then do you want to come and kiss me every day?" she asked, "because I don't think that that would suit me either."

"I can believe it," he said.

"I am inclined to think," she said, "that you are a very grasping and unreasonable person. I have permitted you privileges which more men than my modesty permits me to tell you of have begged for in vain. You have accepted them — I promised nothing beyond, nor have you asked for it. Yet because I was obliged to talk reasonably to you, you flung yourself out of my house, and I am left to rescue you at the expense of my pride, perhaps also of my reputation, from associations which you ought to be ashamed of."

"To talk reasonably to me," he repeated slowly. "Do you remember what you said?"

She shrugged her shoulders.

"Naturally! And what I said was true enough."

"I was to be content with scraps. To go away and forget you, until chance or a whim of yours should bring us together again."

"Did you want so much more?" she asked, with a swift maddening glance at him.

He fell on his knees before her couch.

"Oh! I love you!" he said. "Forgive me if I am unreasonable or foolish. I can't help it. You came so unexpectedly, so wonderfully! And you see I lost my head as well as my heart. I have so little to offer you — and I want so much."

Her hands rested for a moment caressingly upon

his shoulders. A whole world of wonderful things was shining out of her eyes. It was only her lips that were cruel.

"My dear boy," she said, "you want what I may not give. I am very, very sorry. I think there must have been some sorcery in the air that night, the spell of the roses must have crept into my blood. I am sorry for what I did. I am very sorry that I did not leave you alone."

He rose heavily to his feet. His face was grey with suffering.

"I ought to have known," he said. "I think that I did know."

"All the same," she continued, laying her hand upon his arm, "I think that you are a rank extremist."

He shook his head.

"I don't understand," he said.

"Shall I teach you?" she whispered.

He flung her hand away.

"No!" he said savagely.

She sighed.

"I am afraid you had better go away," she said.

As he closed the door he fancied that he heard a sob. But it might have been only fancy.

CHAPTER III

MONSIEUR S'AMUSE

"TO-NIGHT," young Davenant declared, with something which was suspiciously like a yawn, "I really think that we must chuck it just a little earlier. Shall we say that we leave here at two, and get back to the hotel?"

Mademoiselle Rosine pouted, but said nothing. The young lady from America tried to take Macheson's hand.

"Yes!" she murmured. "Do let's! I'm dead tired."

She whispered something in Macheson's ear which he affected not to hear. He leaned back in his cushioned seat and laughed.

"What, go home without seeing François!" he exclaimed. "He's keeping the corner table for us, and we're all going to dance the Maxixe with the little Russian girl."

"We could telephone," Davenant suggested. "Do you know that we haven't been to bed before six one morning since we arrived in Paris?"

"Well, isn't that what we came for?" Macheson exclaimed. "We can go to bed at half-past twelve in London. Maître d'hôtel, the wine! My friends

are getting sleepy. What's become of the music?
Tell our friend there — ah! Monsieur Henri!"

He beckoned to the leader of the orchestra, who
came up bowing, with his violin under his arm.

"Monsieur Henri, my friends are '*triste*,'" he
explained. "They say there is no music here, no
life. They speak of going home to bed. Look at
mademoiselle here! She yawns! We did not come
to Paris to yawn. Something of the liveliest.
You understand? Perhaps mademoiselle there will
dance."

"Parfaitement, monsieur."

The man bowed himself away, with a twenty-
franc piece in the palm of his hand. The orchestra
began a gay two-step. Macheson, starting up,
passed his arm round the waist of a little fair-
haired Parisienne just arriving. She threw her gold
satchel on to a table, and they danced round the
room. Davenant watched them with unwilling
admiration.

"Well, Macheson's a fair knockout," he declared.
"I'm hanged if he can keep still for five minutes.
And when I knew him at Oxford, he was one of
the most studious chaps in the college. Gad! he's
dancing with another girl now — look, he's drinking
champagne out of her glass. Shouldn't stand it,
Ella."

Ella was watching him. Her eyes were very
bright, and there was more colour than usual in
her cheeks.

"It's nothing to me what Mr. Macheson does,"
she said, with a catch in her voice. "I don't
understand him a bit. I think he's mad."

Mademoiselle Rosine leaned across and whispered in her ear. Ella shook her head.

"You see — it is any girl with him," she said. "He dances with them, pays their bills — see, he pays for Annette there, and away he goes — laughing, You see it is so with them, too. He has finished with them now. He comes back to us. Guess I'm not sure I want him."

Nevertheless she moved her skirts and made room for him by her side. Macheson came up out of breath, and poured himself out a glass of wine.

"What a time they are serving supper!" he exclaimed.

Davenant groaned.

"My dear fellow," he exclaimed, "remember our dinner at Lesueur's. You can't be hungry!"

"But I am," Macheson declared. "What are we here for but to eat and drink and enjoy ourselves? Jove! this is good champagne! Mademoiselle Rosine!"

He raised his glass and bowed. Mademoiselle Rosine laughed at him out of her big black eyes. He was rather a fascinating figure, this tall, good-looking young Englishman, who spoke French so perfectly and danced so well.

"I would make you come and sit by me, Monsieur Macheson," she declared, "but Ella would be jealous."

"What about me?" Davenant exclaimed.

"Oh! là, là!" she answered, pinching his arm.

"I'm sure I don't mind," Ella declared. "I guess we're all free to talk to whom we please."

Macheson drew up a chair and sat opposite to them.

"I choose to look at you both," he said, banging the table with his knife. "Garçon, we did nct come here to eat your flowers or your immaculate table-cloth. We ordered supper half an hour ago. Good! It arrives."

No one but Macheson seemed to have much appetite. He ate and he drank, and he talked almost alone. He ordered another bottle of wine, and the tongues of the others became a little looser. The music was going now all the time, and many couples were dancing. The fair-haired girl, dancing with an older woman, touched him on the shoulder as she passed, and laughed into his face.

"There is no one," she murmured, "who dances like monsieur."

He sprang up from his seat and whirled her round the room. She leaned against his arm and whispered in his ear. Ella watched her with darkening face.

"It is little Flossie from the *Folies Marigny,*" Mademoiselle Rosine remarked. "You must have a care, Ella. She has followed Monsieur Macheson everywhere with her eyes."

He returned to his place and continued his supper.

"Hang it all, you people are dull to-night," he exclaimed. "Drink some more wine, Davenant, and look after mademoiselle. Miss Ella!"

He filled her glass and she leaned over the table.

"Every one else seems to make love to you," she whispered. "I guess I'll have to begin. If you call me Miss Ella again I shall box your ears."

"Ella then, what you will," he exclaimed. "Remember, all of you, that we are here to have a good time, not to mope. Davenant, if you don't sparkle up, I shall come and sit between the girls myself."

"Come along," they both cried. Mademoiselle Rosine held out her arms, but Macheson kept his seat.

"Let's go up to the *Rat Mort* if we're going," Ella exclaimed. "It's dull here, and I'm tired of seeing that yellow-headed girl make eyes at you."

Macheson laughed and drained his glass.

"*Au Rat Mort!*" he cried. "Good!"

They paid the bill and all trooped out. The fair-haired girl caught at Macheson's hand as he passed.

"*Au Rat Mort?*" she whispered.

She threw a meaning glance at Ella.

"Monsieur is well guarded," she said softly.

"Malheureusement!" he answered, smiling.

Davenant drew him on one side as the girls went for their cloaks.

"I say, old chap," he began, "aren't you trying Ella a bit high? She's not a bad-tempered girl, you know, but I'm afraid there'll be a row soon."

Macheson paused to light a cigarette.

"A row?" he answered. "I don't see why."

"You're a bit catholic in your attentions, you know," Davenant remarked.

"Why not?" Macheson answered. "Ella is nothing to me. No more are the rest of them. I amuse myself — that's all."

Davenant looked as he felt, puzzled.

"Well," he said. "I'm not sure that Ella sees it in that light."

"Why shouldn't she?" Macheson demanded.

"Well, hang it all, you brought her over, didn't you?" Davenant reminded him.

"She came over as my guest," Macheson answered. "That is to say, I pay for her whenever she chooses to come out with us, and I pay or shall pay her hotel bill. Beyond that, I imagine that we are both of us free to amuse ourselves as we please."

"I don't believe Ella looks at it in that light," Davenant said hesitatingly. "You mean to say that there is nothing — er ——"

"Of course not," Macheson interrupted.

"Hasn't she ——"

"Oh! shut up," Macheson exclaimed. "Here they come."

Ella passed her arm through his. Mademciselle Rosine had told her while she stood on tiptoe and dabbed at her cheeks with a powder-puff, that she was too cold. The Messieurs Anglais were often so difficult. They needed encouragement, so very much encouragement. Then there were more confidences, and Madame Rosine was very much astonished. What sort of a man was this Monsieur Macheson, yet so gallant, so gay! She promised herself that she would watch him.

"We will drive up together, you and I," Ella whispered in his ear, but Macheson only laughed.

"I've hired a motor car for the night," he said. "In you get! I'm going to sit in front with the chauffeur and sing."

"You will do nothing of the sort," Ella declared, almost sharply. "You will come inside with us."

"Anywhere, anyhow," he answered. "To the

little hell at the top of the hill, Jean, and drive fast," he directed. "Jove! it's two o'clock! Hurry up, Davenant. We shall have no time there at all."

There was barely room for four. Mademoiselle Rosine perched herself daintily on Davenant's knee. Ella tried to draw Macheson into her arms, but he sank on to the floor, and sat with his hands round his knees singing a French music-hall song of the moment. They shouted to him to leave off, but he only sang the louder. Then, in a block, he sprang from the car, seized the whole stock of a pavement flower-seller, and, paying her magnificently, emptied them through the window of the car into the girls' laps, and turning round as suddenly — disappeared.

"He's mad — quite mad," Ella declared, with a sigh. "I don't believe we shall see him again to-night."

Nevertheless, he was on the pavement outside the *Rat Mort* awaiting them, chaffing the commissionnaire. He threw open the door and welcomed them.

"They are turning people away here," he declared. "Heaps of fun going on! All the artistes from the Circus are here, and a party of Spaniards. François has kept our table. Come along."

Ella hung on to him as they climbed the narrow, shabby staircase.

"Say," she pleaded in his ear, "don't you want to be a little nicer to me to-night?"

"Command me," he answered. "I am in a most amenable temper."

"Sit with me instead of wandering round so.

You don't want to talk to every pretty girl, do
you?"

He laughed.

"Why not? Aren't we all on the same quest?
It is the 'camaraderie' of pleasure!"

They reached the bend of the stairs. From
above they could hear the music, the rattle of plates,
the hum of voices. She leaned towards him.

"Kiss me, please," she whispered.

He stooped down and raised her hand to his lips.
She drew it slowly away and looked at him curiously.

"Your lips are cold," she said.

He laughed.

"The night is young," he answered. "See, there
is François."

They passed on. Ella was a little more content.
It was the most promising thing he had said to her.

CHAPTER IV

AT THE " DEAD RAT "

MONSIEUR FRANÇOIS piloted the little party himself to the corner table which he had reserved for them. He had taken a fancy to this tall young Englishman, whose French, save for a trifle of accent, was as perfect as his own, who spent money with both hands, who was gay as the gayest, and yet who had the air of being little more than a looker-on at the merriment which he did so much to promote.

"We are full to-night, monsieur," he said. "There will be a great crowd. Yet you see your table waits. Mademoiselle Bolero herself begged for it, but I said always — 'No! no! no! It is for monsieur and his friends.'"

"You are a prince," Macheson exclaimed as they filed into their places. "To-night we are going to prove to ourselves that we are indeed in Paris! Sommelier, the same wine — in magnums to-night! My friend is sleepy. We must wake him up. Ah, mademoiselle!" he waved his hand to the little short-skirted danseuse. "You must take a glass of wine with us, and afterwards — the Maxixe! Waiter, a glass, a chair for mademoiselle!"

Mademoiselle came pirouetting up to them.   Monsieur was very kind. She would take a glass of champagne, and afterwards — yes! the Maxixe, if they desired it!

They sat with their backs to the wall, facing the little space along which the visitors to the café came and went, and where, under difficulties, one danced. The leader of the orchestra came bowing and smiling towards them, playing an American waltz, and Macheson, with a laugh, sprang up and guided mademoiselle through the throng of people and hurrying waiters.

"Monsieur comes often to Paris?" she asked, as they whirled around.

"For the first time in my life," Macheson answered. "We are here on a quest! We want to understand what pleasure means!"

Mademoiselle sighed ever so slightly under the powder with which her pretty face was disfigured.

"One is gay here always," she said somewhat doubtfully, "but it is the people who come seldom who enjoy themselves the most."

Macheson laughed as he led her back to their table.

"You are right," he declared. "Pleasure is a subtle thing.   It does not do to analyse."

Macheson filled her glass.

"Sit down," he said, "and tell us about the people. It is early yet, I suppose?"

She nodded.

"Yes," she answered. "There are many who come every night who have not yet arrived."

Ella leaned forward to ask a question, and mademoiselle nodded. Yes! that was Bolero at the small table opposite. She sat with three men, one of whom was busy sketching on the back of the menu card. Bolero, with her wonderful string of pearls, smileless, stolid, with the boredom in her face of the woman who sees no more worlds to conquer. Monsieur with the ruffled hair and black eyes? Yes! a Russian certainly. Mademoiselle, with a smile which belied her words, was not sure of his name, but François spoke always of His Highness! The gentleman with the smooth-shaven face, who read a newspaper and supped alone? Mademoiselle looked around. She hesitated. After all, monsieur and his friends were only casual visitors. It was not for them to repeat it, but the gentleman was a detective — one of the most famous. He had watched for some one for many nights. In the end it would happen. Ah! Some one was asking for a cake-walk? Mademoiselle finished her wine hastily and sprang up. She will return? But certainly, if monsieur pleases!

The band struck up something American. Mademoiselle danced up and down the little space between the tables. Ella laid her hand upon Macheson's shoulder.

" Why do you want to talk to every one? " she whispered. " I think you forget sometimes that you are not alone."

Macheson laughed impatiently.

" My dear young lady," he said, "you too forget that we are on a quest. We are here to understand what pleasure means — how to win it. We must talk to every one, do everything everybody else does. It's no good looking on all the time."

"But you never talk to me at all," she objected.
"Rubbish!" he answered lightly. "You don't listen. Come, I am getting hungry. Davenant, we must order supper."

Davenant, whose hair Mademoiselle Rosine had been ruffling, whose tie was no longer immaculate, and who was beginning to realize that he had drunk a good deal of wine, leaned forward and regarded Macheson with admiration.

"Old man," he declared, "you're great! Order what you like. We will eat it — somehow, won't we, Rosine?"

She laughed assent.

"For me," she begged, "some caviare, and afterwards an omelette."

"Consommé and dry biscuits — and some fruit!" Ella suggested.

Macheson gave the order and filled their glasses. It was half-past two, and people were beginning to stream in. Unattached ladies strolled down the room — looking for a friend — or to make one. Their more fortunate sisters of the "haute demi-monde" were beginning to arrive with their escorts, from the restaurants and cafés. Greetings were shouted up and down the room. Suddenly Ella's face clouded over again. It was the girl in blue, with whom Macheson had danced at Lesueur's, who had just entered with a party of friends, women in lace coats and wonderful opera cloaks, the men all silk-hatted — the shiniest silk hats in Europe — white gloves, supercilious and immaculate. A burst of applause greeted her, as, with her blue skirts daringly lifted, she danced down the room to the

table which was hastily being prepared for them.
Her piquant face was wreathed with smiles, she
shouted greetings everywhere, and when she saw
Macheson, she threw him kisses with both hands,
which he stood up and gallantly returned. She was
the centre of attraction until Mademoiselle Anna
from the Circus arrived, and to reach her place
leaped lightly over an intervening table, with a
wonderful display of red silk stocking and filmy
lingerie. The place became gayer and noisier every
moment. Greetings were shouted from table to
table. The spirit of Bohemianism seemed to flash
about the place like quicksilver. People who were
complete strangers drank one another's health across
the room. The hard-worked waiters were rushing
frantically about. The popping of corks was almost incessant, a blue haze of tobacco smoke hung
about the room. Macheson, leaning back in his
place, watched with eyes that missed little. He saw
the keen-faced little man whose identity mademoiselle had disclosed, calmly fold up his paper, light a
cigarette, and stroll across the room to a table nearly
opposite. A man was sitting there with a couple
of women — a big man with a flushed face and tumbled hair. The waiter was opening a magnum of
champagne — everything seemed to promise a cheerful time for the trio. Then a word was whispered
in his ear. The newcomer bowed apologetically to
the ladies and accepted a glass of wine. But a
moment later the two men left the place together —
and neither returned.

"What are you staring at?" Ella demanded
curiously.

Macheson looked away from the door and smiled quietly.

"I was wondering," he answered, "what it was like — outside?"

"Would you like to go?" she whispered eagerly in his ear. "I'm ready. The others could come on afterwards."

"What, without supper?" he exclaimed. "My dear girl, I'm starving. Besides — I didn't mean that altogether."

"It's rather hard to know what you do mean," she remarked with a sigh. "Say, I don't understand you a little bit!"

"How should you," he answered, "when I'm in the same fix myself?"

"I wish you were like other boys," she remarked. "You're so difficult!"

He looked at her — without the mask — for a moment, and she drew back, wondering. For his eyes were very weary, and they spoke to her of things which she did not understand.

"Don't try," he said. "It wouldn't be any good."

Mademoiselle sank into her chair opposite to them, breathless and hot. She accepted a glass of wine and begged for a cigarette. She whispered in Macheson's ear that the big man was a forger, an affair of the year before last. He was safe away from Paris, but the price of his liberty was more than he could pay. The man there to the left with the lady in pink, no! not the Vicomte, the one beyond, he was tried for murder a month ago. There was a witness missing — the case fell through, but — mademoiselle shook her shoulders significantly. The

lady with fair hair and dark eyes, Macheson asked,
was she English? But certainly, mademoiselle assured him. She was the divorced wife of an English nobleman. "To-night she is alone," mademoiselle added, "but it is not often! Ah, monsieur!"
Mademoiselle shook her finger across the table.
Macheson's too curious glance had provoked a smile
of invitation from the lady!

"I really think you might remember that I am
here," Ella remarked. "It is very interesting to
hear you talk French, but I get tired of it!"
Mademoiselle took the hint and flitted away.
Supper arrived and created a diversion. Nevertheless, Macheson alone of the little party seemed to have
absorbed successfully the spirit of the place. He
was almost recklessly gay. He drank toasts right
and left. He was the centre from which the hilarity
of the room seemed to radiate. Davenant was half
muddled with wine, and sleepy. He sat with his
arm about Rosine, who looked more often towards
Macheson. Ella, who had refused to eat anything,
was looking flushed and angry. She had tried to link
her arm in her companion's, but he had gently dis-
engaged it. She kept whispering in his ear, and sat
with her eyes glued upon Mademoiselle Flossie,
whose glances and smiles were all for Macheson.
And soon after the end came. The band began a
waltz — "L'Amoureuse" — it was apparently mademoiselle herself who had commanded it. With the
first bars, she sprang to her feet and came floating
down the room, her arms stretched out towards
Macheson. She leaned over the table, her body
swaying towards him, her gesture of invitation

HER ARMS STRETCHED OUT TOWARDS MACHESON. Page 202

piquant, bewitching. Macheson, springing at once
to his feet, rested his hand for a moment upon the
table which hemmed him in, and vaulted lightly into
the room. A chorus of laughter and bravoes greeted
his feat.

"But he is un homme galant, this Englishman,"
a Frenchwoman cried out, delighted. Every one
was watching the couple. But Ella rose to her feet
and called a waiter to move the table.

"I am going," she said angrily. "I have had
enough of this. You people can come when you
like."

They tried to stop her, but it was useless. She
swept down the room, taking not the slightest notice
of Macheson and his companion, a spot of angry
colour burning in her cheeks. Davenant and Mademoiselle Rosine stood up, preparing to follow her.
The former shouted to Macheson, who brought his
partner up to their table and poured her out a glass
of champagne.

"Ella's gone!" Davenant exclaimed. "You'll
catch it!"

Macheson smiled.

"I'm sorry," he said quietly. "Are you off too?"

"As soon as the Johnny brings the bill," Davenant answered.

"I'll settle up," Macheson declared. "Take the
automobile. I'll follow you in a few minutes."

Mademoiselle Flossie, called back to her own table,
hurried off with a parting squeeze of Macheson's
hand. He sat down alone for a moment. At the
other end of the room, a darkey with a doll's hat upon
his head was singing a coon song!

CHAPTER V

THE AWAKENING

ALONE for the first moment of the evening, it seemed to Macheson that a sudden wave of confounding thoughts surged into his brain, at war from the first with all that was sensuous and brilliant in this new and swiftly developed phase of his personality. He closed his eyes for a moment, and when again he opened them it seemed indeed as though a miracle had taken place. The whole atmosphere of the room was changed. He looked around, incredulous, amazed. The men especially were different. Such good fellows as they had seemed a few moments ago — from his altered point of view Macheson regarded them now in scornful curiosity. Their ties were awry, their hair was ruffled, their faces were paled or flushed. The laughter of women rang still through the place, but the music had gone from their mirth. It seemed to him that he saw suddenly through the smiles that wreathed their lips, saw underneath the barren mockery of it all. This hideous travesty of life in its gentler moods had but one end — the cold, relentless path to oblivion. Louder and louder the laughter rang, until Macheson felt that he must close his ears. The Devil was using his whip indeed.

Mademoiselle la Danseuse, seeing him alone, paused at his table on her way through the room.

"Monsieur is *triste*," she remarked, "because his friends have departed."

Macheson shook his head.

"I am off, too, in a few minutes," he answered.

A waiter with immovable face slipped a note into his hand, under cover of presenting the bill. Macheson read it and glanced across the room. Mademoiselle Flossie was watching him with uplifted eyebrows and expectant smile. Macheson shook his head, slightly but unmistakably. The young lady in blue shrugged her shoulders and pouted.

Mademoiselle la Danseuse was watching him curiously.

"I wonder," she said softly, "why monsieur comes here."

"In search of pleasure," Macheson answered grimly.

She looked at him fixedly, and Macheson, momentarily interested, returned her gaze. Then he saw that underneath the false smile, for a moment laid aside, there was something human in her face.

"Monsieur makes a brave show, but he does not succeed," she remarked.

"And you?" he asked. "Why do you come here?"

"It pays — very well," she answered quietly, and left him.

Macheson settled his bill and called for the vestiaire. In the further corner of the room two women were quarrelling. The languid senses of those who still lingered in the place were stirred.

The place was electrified instantly with a new excitement. A fight, perhaps — every one crowded around. Unnoticed, Macheson walked out.

Down the narrow stairs he groped his way, with the music of the orchestra, the fierce hysterical cries of the women, the mock cheering of those who crowded round, in his ears. He passed out into the blue-grey dawn. The stars were faint in the sky, and away eastwards little fleecy red clouds were strewn over the house-tops. He stood on the pavement and drew in a long breath. The morning breeze was like a draught of cold water; it was as though he had come back to life again after an interlude spent in some other world. Overhead he could still hear the music of the "Valse Amoureuse," the swell of voices. He shivered, with the cold perhaps — or the memory of the nightmare!

The commissionnaire, hat in hand, summoned a coupé, and Macheson took his place in the small open carriage. Down the cobbled street they went, the crazy vehicle swaying upon its worn rubber tyres, past other night resorts with their blaze of lights and string of waiting cabs; past women in light boots, in strange costumes, artificial in colour and shape, painted, bold-eyed, uncanny pilgrims in the City of Pleasure; past the great churches, silent and stern in the cold morning light; past weary-eyed scavengers into the heart of the city, where a thin stream of early morning toilers went on their relentless way. Once more he entered the obscurity of his dimly lit hotel, where sleepy-eyed servants were sweeping, and retired to his room, into which he let himself at last with a sigh

HE WAITED UNTIL HE HEARD THE QUIET, RELUCTANT FOOTSTEPS
PASS AWAY DOWN THE CORRIDOR. Page 207

of relief. He threw up the blinds and opened the windows. To be alone within those four walls was a blessed thing.

He threw off his coat and glanced at his watch. It was half-past five. His eyes were hot, but he had no desire for sleep. He walked restlessly up and down for a few minutes, and then threw himself into an easy-chair. Suddenly he looked up.

Some one was knocking softly at his door. He walked slowly towards it and paused. All his senses were still pulsating with a curious sense of excitement; when he stood still he could almost hear his heart beat. From outside came the soft rustling of a woman's gown — he knew very well who it was that waited there. He stood still and waited. Again there came the knocking, to him almost like a symbolical thing in its stealthy, muffled insistence. He felt himself battling with a sudden wave of emotions, struggling with a passionate, unexpected desire to answer the summons. He took a quick step forwards. Then sanity came, and the moment seemed far away — a part of the nightmare left behind. He waited until he heard the quiet, reluctant footsteps pass away down the corridor. Then he muttered something to himself, which sounded like a prayer. He sank into a chair and passed his hand across his forehead. The recollection of that moment was horrible to him. He stared at the door with fascinated eyes. What if he had opened it!

He still had no desire for sleep, but he began slowly to undress. His clothes, his tie, everything he had been wearing, seemed to him to reek of ac-

cumulated perfumes of the night, and he flung them
from him with feverish disgust. There was a small
bath-room opening from his sleeping chamber, and
with a desire for complete cleanliness which was not
wholly physical, he filled the bath and plunged in.
The touch of the cold water was inspiring and he
stepped out again into a new world. Much of the
horror of so short a time ago had gone, but with his
new self had come an ever-increasing distaste for
any resumption, in any shape or form, of his associations of the last few days. He must get away.
He rummaged through his things and found a time-
table. In less than an hour he was dressed, his
clothes were packed, and the bill was paid. He
wrote a short note to Davenant and a shorter one
to Ella. Ignoring the events of the last night, he
spoke of a summons home. He enclosed the re-
ceipted hotel bill, and something with which he
begged her to purchase a souvenir of her visit.
Then he drank some coffee, and with a somewhat
stealthy air made his way to the lift, and thence
to the courtyard of the hotel. Already a small
victoria was laden with his luggage; the concierge,
the baggage-master, the porters, were all tipped
with a prodigality almost reckless. Shaven, and
with a sting of the cold water still upon his skin, in
homely flannel shirt and grey tweed travelling
clothes, he felt like a man restored to sanity and
health as his cab lumbered over the long cobbled
street, on its way to the Gare du Nord. It was only
a matter of a few hours, and yet how sweet and fresh
the streets seemed in the early morning sunshine.
The shops were all open, and the busy housewives

were hard at work with their bargaining, the toilers
of the city thronged the pavements, everywhere there
was evidence of a real and rational life. The city
of those few hours ago was surely a city of night-
mares.   The impassable river flowed between.
Macheson leaned back in his carriage and his eyes
were fixed upon the blue sunlit sky.   His lips moved;
a song of gratitude was in his heart.   He felt like
the prisoner before whom the iron gates have been
rolled back, disclosing the smiling world!

CHAPTER VI

THE ECHO OF A CRIME

"MACHESON, by Jove! Where on earth have you sprung from?"

Holderness threw down his pen and held out both his hands. Macheson drew a long sigh of relief.

"From the pigsties, Dick. Whew! It's good to see you again — to be here!"

Holderness surveyed his friend critically.

"What have you been up to?" he asked. "Look washed out, as though you'd had a fever or something. I've been expecting to see you every day."

"I've been on a pleasure trip to Paris," Macheson answered. "Don't talk about it, for God's sake."

Holderness roared with laughter.

"You poor idiot!" he exclaimed. "Been on the razzle-dazzle, I believe. I wish I'd known. I'd have come."

"It's all very well to laugh," Macheson answered. "I feel like a man who's been living in a sewer."

"Are you cured?" Holderness asked abruptly.

Macheson hesitated. As yet he had not dared to ask himself that question. Holderness watched the struggle in his face.

"I'm sorry I asked you that," he said quietly. "Look here! I know what you've come to me for, and I can give it you. You can start at once if you like."

"Work?" Macheson asked eagerly. "You mean that?"

"Of course! Tons of it! Henwood's at his wits' end in Stepney. He's started lecturing, and the thing's taken on, but he can't go on night after night. We don't want anything second-rate either. Then I want help with the paper."

"I'll help you with the paper as soon as you like," Macheson declared. "I'd like to go to Stepney, too, but could we hit it, Henwood and I?"

"Of course," Holderness answered. "What are you thinking of, man? You haven't become a straw-splitter, have you?"

"Not I," Macheson answered "but you have crystallized your ideas into a cult, haven't you? I might find myself on the other side of the traces."

"Rot!" Holderness answered vigorously. "Look here! This is what we call ugliness and dirt. We say that these things make for misery. We say that it is every man's duty, and every woman's, too, to keep themselves clean and clean-living, for the sake of the community. We take the Christian code. It is the most complete, the most philosophic, the most beautiful. We preach it not from the Christian standpoint, but from the point of view of the man of common sense. Doctrinal religions are all very well in their way, but the great bald fact remains that the truth has not been vouchsafed to us through any of them. Therefore we say live the life and wait.

From a scientific point of view we believe, of course, in a future state. It may be that the truth awaits us there. You can work to that, can't you?"

"Of course," Macheson answered, "but don't you rather overlook the support which doctrine gives to the weak and superstitious?"

"Bah! There are the strong to be considered," Holderness declared. "Think how many men of average intelligence chuck the whole thing because they can't stomach doctrine. Besides, these people all think, if you want to confirm 'em or baptize 'em or anything of that sort, that you've your own axe to grind. Jolly suspicious lot the East-Enders, I can tell you."

"I'll go and see Henwood," Macheson declared.

Holderness glanced at his watch.

"We'll have something to eat and go together," he declared. "Look here, I'm really pushed or I wouldn't bother you. Can you do me a country walk in November for the paper? I have two a month. You can take the last number and see the sort of thing."

"I'll try," Macheson promised. "You can give me a couple of days, I suppose?"

"A week — only I want it off my mind. You can get out somewhere and rub up your impressions. We'll dine for half a crown in Soho, and you shall tell me about Paris."

Macheson groaned.

"Shut up about Paris," he begged. "The thought of it's like a nightmare to me — a nightmare full of puppet gnomes, with human masks and the faces of devils underneath."

"The masks came off?" Holderness asked.

Macheson shivered.

"They did," he answered.

"Do you good," Holderness declared coolly, locking his desk. "I've been through it. So long as the masks came off it's all right. What was it sent you there, Victor?"

"A piece of madness," Macheson answered in a low tone, "supreme, utter madness."

"Cured?"

"Oh! I hope so," Macheson answered. "If not — well, I can fight."

Holderness stood still for a moment. There was a queer look in his eyes.

"There was a woman once, Victor," he said, "who nearly made mincemeat of my life. She could have done it if she liked — and she wasn't the sort who spares. She died — thank God! You see I know something about it."

They walked out arm in arm, and not a word passed between them till they reached the street. Then Holderness called a hansom.

"I feel like steak," he declared. "Entre-côte with potatoes, maître d'hôtel. Somehow I feel particularly like steak. We will chuck Soho and dine at the Café Royal."

They talked mostly of Henwood and his work. Holderness spoke of it as successful, but the man himself was weakly. The strain of holding his difficult audience night after night had begun to tell on him. Macheson's help would be invaluable. There was a complete school of night classes running in connexion with the work, and also a library.

"You can guess where the money came from for those," he added, smiling. "On the women's side there was only the cookery, and the care of the children. All very imperfect, but with the making of great things about it."

They went into the Café proper for their coffee, sitting at a marble-topped table, and Holderness called for dominoes. But they had scarcely begun their game before Macheson started from his seat, and without a word of explanation strode towards the door. He was just in time to stop the egress of the man whom he had seen slip from his seat and try to leave the place.

"Look here," he said, touching him on the shoulder. "I want to talk to you."

The man made no further attempt at escape. He was very shabby and thin, but Macheson had recognized him at once. It was the man who had come stealing down the lane from Thorpe on that memorable night— the man for whose escape from justice he was responsible.

"My friend won't interfere with us," Macheson said, leading him back to their seats. "Sit down here."

The man sat down quietly. Holderness took up a paper.

"Go ahead," he said. "I shan't listen."

"If I am to talk," the man said, "I must have some absinthe. My throat is dry. I have things to say to you, too."

Macheson called a waiter and ordered it.

"Look here," the man said, "I know all that you want to say to me. I can save you time. It was I

who called upon old Mr. Hurd. It was out of
kindness that I went. He has a daughter whom I
cannot find. She is in danger, and I went to warn
him. He struck me first. He lost his temper.
He would not tell me where to find her, he would
not give me even the money I had spent on my
journey. I, too, lost my temper. I returned the
blow. He fell down — and I was frightened. So
I ran away."

Macheson nodded.

"Well," he said, "you seem to have struck an
old man because he would not let you blackmail
him, and I, like a fool, helped you to escape."

"Blackmail!" The man looked around him as
though afraid of the word. His cheeks were
sunken, but his brown eyes were still bright. "It
wasn't that," he said. "I brought information
that was really valuable. There is a young lady
somewhere who is in danger of her life. I came to
warn him; I believed what I had always been told,
that she was his daughter. I found out that it was
a lie. It was a conspiracy against me. He never
had a daughter. But I am going to find out who
she is!"

"What if I give you up to the police?" Macheson
asked.

"For the sake of the woman whom the old man
Hurd was shielding you had better not. You had
very much better not," was the hoarse reply. "If
you do, it may cost a woman her life."

"Why are you staying on in England?" Macheson
asked.

"To find that woman, and I will find her," he

added, with glittering eyes. "Listen! I have seen her riding in a carriage, beautifully dressed, with coachman and footman upon the box, an aristocrat. I always said that she was that. It was a plot against us — to call her that old man's daughter."

"All this has nothing to do with me," Macheson said quietly. "The only thing I have to consider is whether I ought or ought not to hand you over to the police."

The man eyed him craftily. He had little fear.

"If you did, sir," he said, "it would be an injustice. I only touched the old man in self-defence."

Macheson looked at him gravely.

"I hope that that is the truth," he said. "You can go."

The man stood up. He did not immediately depart.

"What is it?" Macheson asked.

"I was wondering, sir," he said, in a confidential whisper, "whether you could not give me an idea as to who the lady was who called herself Stephen Hurd's daughter in Paris six years ago."

Macheson shook his head.

"I have no idea," he answered curtly.

The man shuffled away. Macheson lit a cigarette and watched him for a moment steadfastly through the large gilt-framed mirror.

"Queer sort of Johnny, your friend," Holderness remarked.

"He's a bad lot, I'm afraid," Macheson answered. "Somehow or other I can't help wishing that I hadn't seen him."

Holderness laughed.

"Man alive," he said, "it's a good thing you've come back to me, or you'd be a bundle of nerves in no time. We'll get along now, if you're ready. You might find something to say to 'em to-night. I know Henwood's pretty well pumped dry."

They left the place, and took an omnibus city-wards.

CHAPTER VII

A COUNTRY WALK

IT was exactly such a day as he would have chosen
for his purpose when Macheson stepped out of
the train at the wayside station and set his face towards Thorpe. A strong blustering wind, blowing
down from the hills, had dried the road of all save a
slight coating of mud, a wind fresh from the forest, so
fresh and strong that he walked with his cap in his
hand and his head thrown back, glad to breathe it
in his lungs and feel the sting of it on his cheeks.
It seemed to him that he had been away for months,
as he climbed the long hill towards the village. The
fields now were brown instead of green, a pungent
smell of freshly turned earth and burning wood was
in his nostrils. The hedges and trees were bare; he
caught a glimpse of the great house itself from an
unexpected point. Everywhere he was receiving
familiar impressions. He came to the avenue up
which he had passed on his first visit to the house,
continually he met carts bearing her name, and
villagers, most of whom he noticed with some surprise, looked at him doubtfully. Presently he arrived at the village itself, and stopped before the
long, low, white house where Stephen Hurd lived.

He paused for a moment, hesitating whether to fulfil this part of his mission now, or to wait until later in the day Eventually, with the idea of getting the thing over, he opened the gate and rang the front-door bell.

He was shown into the study, and in a few minutes Stephen Hurd came in, smoking a pipe, his hands in his pockets. When he saw who his visitor was he stopped short. He did not offer his hand or ask Macheson to sit down. He looked at him with a heavy frown upon his face.

"You wished to see me?" he said.

"I did," Macheson answered. "Perhaps my call is inopportune. I have come from London practically for no other reason than to ask you a single question."

Hurd laughed shortly.

"You had better ask it then," he said. "I thought that you might have other business in the neighbourhood. Preaching off, eh?"

"My question is simply this," Macheson said calmly. "Have you, or had you, ever a sister?"

A dull red flush streamed into the young man's face. He removed his pipe from his mouth and stared at Macheson. His silence for several moments seemed to arise from the fact that surprise had robbed him of the powers of speech.

"Who put you up to asking that?" he demanded sharply.

Macheson raised his eyebrows slightly.

"My question is a simple one," he said. "If you do not choose to answer it, it is easy for me to procure the information from elsewhere. The first villager I met would tell me. I preferred to come to you."

"I have no sister," Hurd said slowly. "I never had. Now you must tell me why you have come here to ask me this."

"I am told," Macheson said, "that years ago a girl in Paris represented herself as being your father's daughter. She is being inquired for in a somewhat mysterious way."

"And what business is it of yours?" Hurd demanded curtly.

"None — apparently," Macheson answered. "I am obliged to you for your information. I will not detain you any longer."

But Stephen Hurd barred the way. Looking into his face, Macheson saw alreacy the signs of a change there. His eyes were a little wild, and though it was early in the morning he smelt of spirits.

"No! you don't," he declared truculently. "You're not going till you tell me what you mean by that question."

"I am afraid," Macheson answered, "that I have nothing more to tell you."

"You will tell me who this mysterious person is," Hurd declared.

Macheson shook his head.

"No!" he said. "I think that you had better let me pass."

"Not yet," Hurd answered. "Look here! You've been in communication with the man who came here and murdered my father. You know where he is."

"Scarcely that, was it?" Macheson answered.

"There was a struggle, but your father's death was partly owing to other causes. However, I did not come here to discuss that with you. I came to ask you a question, which you have answered. If you will permit me to pass I shall be obliged."

Hurd hesitated for a moment.

"Look here," he said, with an assumption of good nature, "there's no reason why you and I should quarrel. I want to know who put you up to asking me that question. It isn't that I want to do him any harm. I'll guarantee his safety, if you like, so far as I am concerned. Only I'm anxious to meet him."

Macheson shook his head.

"I do not know where he is myself," he answered. "In any case, I could not give you any information."

Stephen Hurd stood squarely in front of the door.

"You'll have to," he said doggedly. "That's all there is about it."

Macheson took a step forward.

"Look here," he said, "I shouldn't try that on if I were you. I am stronger than you are, and I have studied boxing. I don't care about fighting, but I am going to leave this room — at once."

"The devil you are," Hurd cried, striking at him. "Take that, you canting hypocrite."

Macheson evaded the blow with ease. Exactly how it happened he never knew, but Hurd found himself a few seconds later on his back — and alone in the room. He sprang up and rushed after Macheson, who was already in the front garden. His attack was so violent that Macheson had no alternative. He knocked him into the middle of his rose bushes, and opened the gate, to find himself face to face with the last person in the world whom he expected to see in Thorpe. It was Wilhelmina herself who was a spectator of the scene!

"Mr. Macheson," she said gravely, "what is the meaning of this?"

Macheson was taken too completely by surprise to frame an immediate answer. Stephen Hurd rose slowly to his feet, dabbing his mouth with his handkerchief.

"A little disagreement between us," he said, with an evil attempt at a smile. "We will settle it another time."

"You will settle it now," the lady of the Manor said, with authority in her tone. "Shake hands, if you please. At once! I cannot have this sort of thing going on in the village."

Macheson held out his hand without hesitation.

"The quarrel was not of my seeking," he said. "I bear you no ill-will, Hurd. Will you shake hands?"

"No!" Stephen Hurd answered fiercely.

Macheson's hand fell to his side.

"I am sorry," he said.

"You will reconsider that, Mr. Hurd," Wilhelmina said quietly.

"No!" he answered. "I am sorry, Miss Thorpe-Hatton, to seem ungracious, but there are reasons why I cannot accept his hand. He knows them well enough. We cannot possibly be friends. Don't let us be hypocrites."

Wilhelmina turned away coldly.

"Very well," she said. "Mr. Macheson, will you

walk with me a little way? I have something to
say to you."

"With pleasure," he answered. "I'm sorry,
Hurd," he added, turning round.

There was no answer. Together they walked
up the village street. Already the shock of seeing
her had passed away, and he was fighting hard
against the gladness which possessed him. He had
paid dearly enough already for his folly. He was
determined that there should be no return of it.

"Which way were you going?" she asked.

"To the hills," he answered. "I can leave you
at the church entrance. But before you go ——"

"I am not going," she answered. "I should
love a walk. I will come with you to the hills."

He looked at her doubtfully. She appeared to him
so different a person in her country clothes — a dark
brown tailor-made suit, with short skirt, a brown
tam-o'-shanter and veil. She was not much more
than a child after all. Her mouth was a little sad,
and she was very pale and seemed tired.

"If you care to walk so far," he said gravely —
"and with me!"

"What am I expected to say to that?" she asked
demurely.

"I think that you know what I mean," he answered, avoiding her eyes. "Your villagers will
certainly think it strange to see their mistress
walking with the poor missioner who wasn't allowed
to hold his services."

"I am afraid," she answered, "that my people
have learnt to expect the unexpected from me.
Now tell me," she continued, "what has brought

you back to the scene of your persecutions? I am hoping you are going to tell me that it is to apologize for the shockingly rude way you left me last time we met."

" I did not know that you were here," he answered. " I came for two reasons — first, to collect materials for a short article in a friend's magazine, and secondly, to ask a question of Stephen Hurd."

" Apparently," she remarked, " your question annoyed him."

" He seemed annoyed before I asked it," Macheson remarked; " I seem to have offended him somehow or other."

" I should imagine," she said drily, " that that is not altogether incomprehensible to you."

So she knew or guessed who it was that had been Letty Foulton's companion in London. Macheson was silent. They walked on for some distance, climbing all the time, till Wilhelmina paused, breathless, and leaned against a gate.

" I hope," said she, " that you are collecting your impressions. If so, I am sure they must be in the air, for you have not looked to the right or to the left."

He smiled and stood by her side, looking downwards. The village lay almost at their feet, and away beyond spread the mist-wreathed country, still and silent in the November afternoon. The wind had fallen, the birds were songless, nothing remained of the busy chorus of summer sounds. They stood on the edge of a plantation — the peculiar fragrance of freshly turned earth from the ploughed fields opposite, and of the carpet of wet leaves be-

neath their feet, had taken the place of all those
sweeter perfumes which a short while ago had seemed
to belong naturally to the place.

"To tell you the truth," he said, "I have been
thinking more about something which I have to say
to you."

"Is it something serious?" she asked.

"Rather," he admitted.

Her eyebrows were faintly contracted. She
looked up at him pathetically.

"It will keep for a little time," she said. "Let
us finish our walk first. I am down here alone, and
have been dull. This exercise is what I wanted.
It is doing me good. I will not have my afternoon
spoilt. See, I have the key of the gate here, we will
go through the plantation and up to the back of
the beacon."

She led the way, giving him no time to protest,
and he followed her, vaguely uneasy. Through the
plantation their feet fell noiselessly upon a carpet of
wet leaves; outside on the springy turf the rabbits
scampered away in hundreds to their holes. Then
they began to climb. Beneath them the country
expanded and rolled away like a piece of patchwork,
dimly seen through a veil of mist. Wilhelmina
turned towards him with a laugh. There was more
colour now in her cheeks. She was breathless before
they reached the summit and laid her hand upon
his arm for support.

"Confess," she said, "you like me better here than
in London, don't you?"

"You are more natural," he answered. "You are
more like what I would have you be."

She sat down on a piece of grey rock. They were at the summit now. Below was the great house with its magnificent avenues and park, the tiny village, and the quaint church. Beyond, a spreading landscape of undulating meadows and well-tilled land. The same thought came to both of them.

"Behold," she murmured, "my possessions."

He nodded.

"You should be very proud of your home," he said quietly. "It is very beautiful."

She turned towards him. Her face was as cold and destitute of emotion as the stone on which she sat.

"Do you wonder," she asked, "why I have never married?"

He shrugged his shoulders.

"A matter of temperament, perhaps," he said. "You are inclined to be independent, aren't you?"

"There have been things in my life — a very secret chamber," she said slowly. "I think that some day I shall tell you about it, for I may need help."

"I shall be glad," he said simply. "You know that!"

She rose and shook out her skirts.

"Come," she said, "it is too cold to sit down. I am going to take you to Onetree Farm. Mrs. Foulton must give us some tea. I have a reason, too," she added more slowly, "for taking you there."

CHAPTER VIII

THE MISSING LETTY

MACHESON knew directly they entered the farm that Wilhelmina had brought him here for some purpose. For Mrs. Foulton straightened herself at the sight of him, and forgot even her usual respectful courtesy to the lady of the Manor.

"I have brought Mr. Macheson to see you, Mrs. Foulton," Wilhelmina said. "We want you to give us some tea — and there is a question which I think you ought to ask him."

The woman was trembling. She seemed for the moment to have no words.

"If you like," Wilhelmina continued calmly, "I will ask it for you. Did you know, Mr. Macheson, that Letty Foulton has left home and has gone away without a word to her mother?"

"I did not know it," Macheson answered gravely. "I am very sorry."

"You — didn't know it? You don't know where she is?" the woman demanded fiercely.

"Certainly not," Macheson answered. "How should I?"

The woman looked bewildered. She turned towards Wilhelmina as though for an explanation.

"Mr. Macheson has himself to blame," Wilhelmina said, "if his action in bringing your daughter to me that night has been misunderstood. At any rate, he cannot refuse to tell you now what he refused to tell me. You understand, Mr. Macheson," she added, turning towards him, "Mrs. Foulton insists upon knowing with whom you found her daughter having supper that night in London."

Macheson hesitated only for a moment.

"Your daughter was with Mr. Stephen Hurd, Mrs. Foulton," he said.

The woman threw her apron over her head and hastened away. They heard her sobbing in the kitchen. Wilhelmina shrugged her shoulders.

"What a bore!" she remarked. "We shan't get any tea. People of this sort have no self-control."

Macheson looked at her sternly.

"Have the people here," he asked, "been connecting me with this child's disappearance? "

"I suppose so," she answered carelessly. "Rather a new line for you, isn't it — the gay Lothario! It's your own fault. You shouldn't be so mysterious."

"You didn't believe it?" he said shortly.

"Why not? You've been — seeing life lately, haven't you?"

"You didn't believe it?" he repeated, keeping his eyes fixed upon her.

She came over to him and laid her hands upon his shoulders. Her pale face was upturned to his. It seemed open to him to transform her attitude into a caress.

"Of course not, dear," she answered. "If — any one else did, they will soon know the truth."

"All the same," he muttered, "it's horrible. We must do something!"

She moved away from him wearily. His thoughts were full of the tragedy of Letty Foulton's disappearance. He seemed scarcely to know that she had been almost in his arms. He turned to her suddenly.

"I shall go back," he said, "to speak once more with Stephen Hurd."

She looked into his face and saw things there which terrified her. He had moved already towards the door, but she stood in his way.

"No!" she cried. "It is not your affair. Let me deal with him!"

He shook his head.

"It is no matter," he said, "for a woman to interfere in."

"He will not listen to you," she continued eagerly. "He will tell you that it is not your concern."

"It is the concern of every honest man," he interrupted. "You must please let me go!"

She was holding his arm, and she refused to withdraw her fingers. Then Mrs. Foulton intervened.

She had smoothed her hair and was carrying a tea-tray. They both looked at her as though fascinated.

"I hope I have not kept you waiting, madam," she said quietly. "I had to send Ruth up for the cream. The boy's at Loughborough market, and I'm a bit shorthanded."

"I — oh! I'm sorry you bothered about the tea, Mrs. Foulton," Wilhelmina said, with an effort. "But how good it looks! Come, Mr. Macheson! I don't know whether you've had any lunch, but I haven't. I'm perfectly ravenous."

"I've some sandwiches in my pocket," Macheson answered, moving slowly to the table, "but to tell you the truth, I'd forgotten them."

She drew off her gloves and seated herself before the teapot. All the time her eyes were fixed upon Macheson. She was feverishly anxious to have him also seat himself, and he could scarcely look away from the woman who, with a face like a mask, was calmly arranging the things from the tray upon the table. When she left the room he drew a little breath.

"Do they feel — really, these people," he asked, "or are they Stoics?"

"We feel through our nerves," she answered, "and they haven't many. Is that too much cream? — and pass the strawberry jam, please."

He ate and drank mechanically. The charm of this simple meal alone with her was gone — it seemed to him that there was tragedy in the arrangement of the table. She talked to him lightly, and he answered — what he scarcely knew. Suddenly he interposed a question.

"When did this girl Letty leave home?" he asked.

"I am not sure," she answered. "We will ask Mrs. Foulton."

Mrs. Foulton came silently in.

"We want to know, Mrs. Foulton, when Letty went away," Wilhelmina asked.

"A week ago to-morrow, madam," Mrs. Foulton answered. "Is there anything else you will be wanting?"

"Nothing, thank you," Wilhelmina answered, and then, seeing that the woman lingered, she continued:

"Are you wanting to get rid of us?"

The woman hesitated.

"It isn't that, madam," she said, "but I'm wanting to step out as soon as possible."

The same idea occurred at once to both Wilhelmina and Macheson.

"You are going down to the village, Mrs. Foulton?" Wilhelmina asked gravely.

"I'm going down to have a bit of talk with Mr. Stephen Hurd, madam," she answered grimly. "I'd be glad to clear away as soon as convenient."

Wilhelmina turned round in her chair, and laid her hand upon the woman's arm.

"Mrs. Foulton," she said, "Mr. Macheson and I are going to see him at once. Leave it to us, please."

Mrs. Foulton shook her head doubtfully.

"Letty's my daughter, madam, thank you kindly," she said. "I must go myself."

Wilhelmina shook her head.

"No!" she said firmly. "You can go and see him afterwards, if you like. Mr. Macheson and I are going to see what we can do first. Believe me, Mrs. Foulton, it will be better for Letty."

The woman was shaken and Wilhelmina pushed home her advantage.

"We are going straight to the village now, Mrs. Foulton," she said. "You will only have to be patient for a very short time. Come, Mr. Macheson. If you are ready we will start."

They walked briskly along the country lane, through the early twilight. They said little to one another.

Macheson was profoundly moved by the tragedy of Letty's disappearance. With his marvellous gift of sympathy, he had understood very well the suffering of the woman whom they had just left. He shivered when he thought of the child. With every step they took, his face resolved itself into grimmer lines. Wilhelmina was forced at last to protest.

"After all," she said, touching his arm, "this young man will scarcely run away. Please remember that I am not an athletic person — and I have not much breath left."

He slackened his pace at once.

"I am sorry," he said. "I was forgetting."

"Yes," she answered simply, "you were forgetting. I — noticed it!"

To Macheson, her irritation seemed childish — unworthy. He knew so little of women — or their moods.

"What are you going to say to Stephen Hurd?" he asked abruptly.

"I shall make him marry Letty Foulton," she answered.

"Can you do it?" he demanded.

"He must marry her or go," she declared. "I will make that quite clear."

Macheson drew a little breath. He suddenly realized that for all his impetuosity, the woman who walked so calmly by his side held the cards. He slackened his pace. The lane had narrowed now,

and on either side of them was a tall holly hedge.
Her hand stole through his arm.

"Well," she said softly, "you have not told
me yet whether your pilgrimage to Paris was a
success."

He turned upon her almost fiercely.

"Yes!" he answered. "It was! A complete
success! I haven't an atom of sentiment left!
Thank goodness!"

She laughed softly.

"I don't believe it," she whispered in his ear.
"You went abroad to be cured of an incurable
disease. Do you imagine that the Mademoiselle
Rosines of the world count for anything? You
foolish, foolish person. Do you imagine that if I
had not known you — I should have let you go?"

"I am not one of your tenants," he answered
grimly.

"You might be," she laughed.

"You are very kind," he declared. "But I
need not tell you that nothing in this world would
induce me to become one."

She walked on, humming to herself. He was hard
to tame, she told herself, but the end was so sure.
Yet all her experience of his sex had shown her
nothing like this. It was the first time she had
played such a part. Was it only the novelty which
she found attractive? She stole an upward glance
at him through the twilight. Taller and more
powerful than ever he seemed in the gathering
darkness — so far as looks were concerned he was
certainly desirable enough. And yet the world
— her world, was full of handsome men. It must

be something else which he possessed, some other less obvious gift, perhaps that flavour of puritanism about his speech and deportment, of which she was always conscious. He resisted where other men not only succumbed but rushed to meet their fate. It must be that, or ——

She herself became suddenly serious. She looked straight ahead down the darkening lane. Fate could surely not play her a trick so scurvy as this. It could not be that she cared. Her hands were suddenly clenched; a little cry broke from her lips. Her heart was beating like a girl's; the delicious thrill of youth seemed to be thawing her long frozen blood. Not again! she prayed, not again! It was a catastrophe this; grotesque, impossible! She thrust out her hands, as though to guard herself from some impending danger. Macheson turned to look at her in surprise, and her eyes were glowing like stars.

"Is anything the matter?" he asked.

She laughed unnaturally.

"A memory," she answered, "a superstition if you like. Some one was walking over the grave of my forgotten days."

She pointed to the front of the low white house, now only a few yards away. A dogcart stood there waiting, with some luggage at the back. Stephen Hurd himself, dressed for travelling, was standing in the doorway.

CHAPTER IX

FOILED

"WE seem to be just in time, Mr. Hurd," Wilhelmina said. "Do you mind coming back for a moment into your study? Mr. Macheson and I have something to say to you."

He glanced at his watch. He was wholly unable to conceal his annoyance at their appearance.

"I am afraid," he said, with strained civility, "that I can only spare a couple of minutes."

"You are going to town?" she asked, as he reluctantly followed her.

"Yes!" he answered. "Mr. White wished to see me early to-morrow morning about the new leases, and I have to go before the committee about this Loughborough water scheme."

"These are my affairs," she said, "so if you should miss your train, the responsibility will be mine."

"I can spare five minutes," he answered, "but I cannot miss that train. I have some private engagements. And, madam," he continued, struggling with his anger, "I beg that you will not forget that even if I am in your employ, this is my house, and I will not have that man in it!"

He pointed to Macheson, who was standing upon the threshold. Wilhelmina stood between the two. "Mr. Hurd," she said, "please control yourself. There is no reason why we should any of us quarrel. Mr. Macheson and I are here to speak to you of a matter in which he has become concerned. I asked him to come here with me. We have come to see you about Letty!"

"What about her?" he demanded, with some attempt at bravado.

"We find that there is an impression in the village that Mr. Macheson is responsible for her disappearance."

Hurd seized his opportunity without a second's hesitation.

"How do you know that it isn't the truth?" he demanded. "He wouldn't be the first of these psalm-singing missioners who have turned out to be hypocrites!"

Macheson never flinched. Wilhelmina only shrugged her shoulders.

"Mr. Hurd," she said, "we will not waste time. Mr. Macheson and I are both perfectly aware that you are responsible for Letty's disappearance."

"It's — it's false!" he declared, swallowing with an effort a more obnoxious word. "Why, I haven't left the village since the day she went away."

"But you are going — to-night," Wilhelmina remarked.

He flushed.

"I'm going away on business," he answered. "I don't see why it should be taken for granted that I'm going to see her."

"Nevertheless," Wilhelmina said quietly, "between us three there isn't the slightest doubt about it. I tell you frankly that the details of your private life in an ordinary way do not interest me in the least. But, on the other hand, I will not have you playing the Don Juan amongst the daughters of my tenants. You have been very foolish and you will have to pay for it. I do not wish to make you lose your train to-night, but you must understand that if you ever return to Thorpe, you must bring back Letty Foulton as your wife."

He stared at her incredulously.

"As my — wife!" he exclaimed.

"Precisely," Wilhelmina answered. "I will give her a wedding present of a thousand pounds, and I will see that your own position here is made a permanent one."

He had the appearance of a man beside himself with anger. Was this to be the end of his schemes and hopes! He, to marry the pretty uneducated daughter of a working farmer — a girl, too, who was his already for the asking. He struggled with a torrent of ugly words.

"I — I must refuse!" he said, denying himself more vigorous terms with an effort.

She looked at him steadily.

"Better think it over, Mr. Hurd," she said. "I am in earnest."

He hesitated for a moment, and then, with a glance at the clock, moved towards the door.

"Very well," he said, "I will think it over. I will let you know immediately I return from London."

She shook her head.

"You can take as long as you like to reflect," she answered, "but it must be here in this room. Mr. Macheson and I will wait."

He turned towards her.

"Miss Thorpe-Hatton," he said, "will you allow me to speak to you alone for two minutes?"

She shook her head.

"It is not necessary," she answered. "Mr. Macheson does not count. You can say whatever you will before him."

A smile that was half a sneer curved his lips. He was like a rat in a corner, and he knew that he must fight. He must use the weapon which he had feared with a coward's fear.

"The matter on which I wish to speak to you," he said, looking straight at her, "is not directly connected with the affair which we have been discussing. If you will give me two minutes, I think I can make you understand."

She met his challenge without flinching. She was a shade paler, perhaps; the little glow which the walk through the enchanted twilight had brought into her cheeks had faded away. But her gaze was as cool and contemptuous as before. She showed no sign of any fear — of any desire to conciliate.

"I think," she said, "that I can understand without. You can consider that we are alone. Whatever you may have to say to me, I should prefer that Mr. Macheson also heard."

Macheson looked from one to the other uneasily.

"Shall I wait in the passage?" he asked. "I should be within call."

"Certainly not," she answered. "This person,"

she continued, indicating Stephen with a scornful gesture, "is, I believe, about to make a bungling attempt to blackmail me! I should much prefer that you were present."

Stephen Hurd drew a sharp breath. Her words stung like whips.

"I don't know — about blackmail," he said, still holding himself in. "I want nothing from you. I only ask to be left alone. Stop this nonsense about Letty Foulton and let me catch my train. That's all I want."

Wilhelmina shrugged her shoulders.

"You are a very wearisome person," she declared. " Did you ever know me to change my mind? Every word I have said to you I absolutely mean. No more, no less! "

One of the veins at his temple was protruding. He was passionately angry.

"You think it wise," he cried threateningly, "to make an enemy of me!"

She laughed derisively, a laugh as soft as velvet, but to him maddening.

"My dear young man," she said carelessly, "I think I should prefer you in that capacity. I should probably see less of you."

He took a quick stride forward. He thrust his face almost into hers. She drew back with a gesture of disgust.

"You," he cried, striking the table with his clenched fist, "to pretend to care what becomes of any fool of a girl who chooses to take a lover! Is it because you're in love with this would-be saint here?"

He struck the table again. He was absolutely beside himself with rage. He seemed even to find a physical difficulty in speech. Wilhelmina raised her eyebrows.

"Go on," she said coolly. "I am curious to hear the rest."

Macheson suddenly intervened. He stepped between the two.

"This has gone far enough," he said sternly. "Hurd, you are losing your head. You are saying things you will be sorry for afterwards. And I cannot allow you to speak like this to a woman — in my presence!"

"Let him go on," Wilhelmina said calmly. "I am beginning to find him interesting."

Hurd laughed fiercely.

"What!" he cried. "You want to hear of your 'Apache' lover, the man you took from the gutters of Paris into ——"

Macheson struck him full across the mouth, but Wilhelmina caught at his arm. She had overestimated her courage or her strength — he was only just in time to save her from falling.

"Brute!" she muttered, and the colour fled from her cheeks like breath from a looking-glass.

Macheson laid her on the couch and rang the bell. Suddenly he realized that they were alone. From outside came the sound of wheels. He sprang up listening. Wilhelmina, too, opened her eyes. She waved him away feebly. He smiled back his comprehension.

"The servants are coming," he said. "I can hear them. I promise you that if he catches the train, I will!"

"Go on," she said coolly, "I am curious to hear the rest." Page 240

He vaulted through the window which he had already opened. The sound of wheels had died away, but he set his face at once towards the station, running with long easy strides, and gradually increasing his pace. Stephen Hurd, with his handkerchief to his mouth, and with all his nerves tingling with a sense of fierce excitement, looked behind him continually, but saw nothing. Long before he reached the station he had abandoned all fear of pursuit. Yet during the last half-mile Macheson was never more than a few yards from him, and on St. Pancras platform he was almost the first person he encountered.

"Macheson! By God!"

He almost dropped the coat he was carrying. He looked at Macheson as one might look at a visitor from Mars. It was not possible that this could be the man from whom he had fled. Macheson smiled at him grimly.

"How did — how did you get here?" the young man faltered.

"By the same train as you," Macheson answered. "How else? Where are you going to meet Letty?"

Hurd answered with a curse.

"Why the devil can't you mind your own business?" he demanded.

"This is my business," Macheson answered.

Then he turned abruptly round towards the hesitating figure of the girl who had suddenly paused in her swift approach.

"It is my business to take you home, Letty," he said. "I have come to fetch you!"

Letty looked appealingly towards Stephen Hurd.

What she saw in his face, however, only terrified her.

"Look here," he said thickly, "I've had almost enough of this. You can go to the devil — you and Miss Thorpe-Hatton, too! I won't allow any one to meddle in my private concerns. Come along, Letty."

He would have led her away, but Macheson was not to be shaken off. He kept his place by the girl's side.

"Letty," he said, "are you married to him?"

"Not yet," she answered hesitatingly. "But we are going to be."

"Where are you going to now?"

She glanced towards Stephen.

"I am going to take her away with me," he declared sullenly, "as soon as I can get my luggage on this cab."

"Letty," Macheson said, "a few hours ago Miss Thorpe-Hatton offered Stephen Hurd a dowry for you of a thousand pounds, if he would promise to bring you back as his wife. He refused. He has not the slightest intention of making you his wife. I am sorry to have to speak so plainly, but you see we haven't much time for beating about the bush, have we? I want you to come with me to Berkeley Square. Mrs. Brown will look after you."

She turned towards the young man piteously.

"Stephen," she said, "tell Mr. Macheson that he is mistaken. We are going to be married, aren't we?"

"Yes," he answered. "At least I always meant to marry you. What I shall do if every one starts bullying me I'm sure I don't know. Out the whole lot of you, I think, and be off to the Colonies."

"You don't mean that, Stephen," she begged.

He pointed to the cab laden now with his luggage.

"Will you get in or won't you, Letty?" he asked.

She shrank back.

"Stephen," she said, "I thought that you were going to bring mother up with you."

He laughed hardly.

"Your mother wasn't ready," he said. "We can send for her later."

"Don't you think, Stephen," she pleaded, "that it would be nice for me to stay with Mrs. Brown until — until we are married?"

"If you go to Mrs. Brown," he said gruffly, "you can stay with her. That's all! I won't be fooled about any longer. Once and for all, are you coming?"

She took a hesitating step forward, but Macheson led her firmly towards another hansom.

"No!" he answered, "she is not. You know where she will be when you have the marriage license."

Stephen sprang into his cab with an oath. Even then Letty would have followed him, but Macheson held her arm.

"You stay here, Letty," he said firmly.

She covered her face with her hands, but she obeyed.

CHAPTER X

THAT night, and for many nights afterwards, Macheson devoted himself to his work in the East End. The fascination of the thing grew upon him; he threw himself into his task with an energy which carried him often out of his own life and made forgetfulness an easy task. Night after night they came, these tired, white-faced women, with a sprinkling of sullen, dejected-looking men; night after night he pleaded and reasoned with them, striving with almost passionate earnestness to show them how to make the best of the poor thing they called life. Gradually his efforts began to tell upon himself. He grew thinner, there were shadows under his eyes, a curious intangible depression seemed to settle upon him. Holderness one night sought him out and insisted upon dinner together.

"Look here, Victor," he said, "I have a bone to pick with you. You'd better listen! Don't sit there staring round the place as though you saw ghosts everywhere."

Macheson smiled mirthlessly.

"But that is just what I do see," he answered. "The conscience of every man who knows must be

haunted with them! The ghosts of starving men
and unsexed women! What keeps their hands from
our throats, Dick?''

"Common sense, you idiot," Holderness answered
cheerfully. "There's a refuse heap for every one of
nature's functions. You may try to rake it out and
cleanse it, but there isn't much to be done. Hang
that mission work, Victor! It's broken more hearts
than anything else on earth! A man can but do
what he may."

"The refuse heap is man's work!" Macheson
muttered.

"But not wholly his responsibility," Holderness
declared. "We're part of the machine, but remember the wheels are driven by fate, or God, or whatever the hidden motive force of the universe may
be. Don't lose yourself, Macheson! Sentiment's
a good thing under control. It's a sickly master."

"You call it sentiment, if one feels the horror of
this garbage heap! Come to-night and look into
their faces."

"I've done it," Holderness declared. "I've been
through it all. Hang it all, do you forget that I'm
the editor of a Socialist magazine? No! feel it
you must, but don't let it upset your mental balance.
Don't lose your values!"

Macheson left his friend in a saner frame of mind.
His words came back to him that night as he watched
the little stream of people file out from the bare
white-washed building, with its rows of cheap cane
chairs. It was so true! To give way to despair
was simply to indulge in a sentimental debauch.
Yet in a sense he had never felt so completely the

pitiful ineffectiveness of his task. How could he preach the Christian morality, expound the Christian doctrines, to a people whose very sufferings, whose constant agony, was a hideous and glaring proof that by the greater part of the world those doctrines were ignored!

A man was shown into his room afterwards, as he was putting on his overcoat. Almost with relief Macheson saw that he at least had no pitiful tale to tell. He was a small dapper man, well dressed, and spoke with a slight American accent.

"Mr. Macheson," he said, "I'm taking the liberty of introducing myself. Peter Drayton my name is, never mind my profession. It wouldn't interest you."

Macheson nodded.

"What can I do for you?" he asked, with some curiosity.

"Say, I've been very much interested in these talks of yours to the people," Mr. Drayton remarked. "But it's occurred to me that you're on the wrong end of the stick. That's why I'm here. You're saying the right things, and you've got the knack of saying them so that people have just got to listen, but you're saying them to the wrong crowd."

"I don't understand," Macheson was forced to confess.

"Well, I reckon it's simple enough," Drayton answered. "These people here don't need to have their own misery thrust down their throats, even while you're trying to show them how to bear it. It's the parties who are responsible for it all that you want to go for. See what I mean?"

"I think so," Macheson admitted, "bu⸗ ——"

"Look here," Drayton interrupted, "you're a man of common sense, and you know that life's more or less a stand-up fight. Those that are licked live here in Whitechapel — if you can call it living — and those who win get to Belgravia! It's a pitiless sort of affair this fight, but there it is. Now which of the two do you think need preaching to, these people, or the people who are responsible for them? You've started a mission in White-chapel — it would have been more logical, if there's a word of truth in your religion, to have started it in Mayfair."

Macheson laughed.

"They wouldn't listen to me," he declared.

"I'd see to that," Drayton answered quickly. "It's my business.   I want you to give a course of — well, we'd call them lectures, in the West End. You can say what you like. You can pitch into 'em as hot as Hell! I'll guarantee you a crowded audience every time."

"I have no interest in those people," Macheson said. "Why should I go and lecture to them? My sympathies are all down here."

"Exactly," Drayton answered. "I want you to stir up the people who can really help, people who can give millions, pull down these miles of fever-tainted rat holes, endow farms here and abroad. Lash them till their conscience squeaks! See? What's the good of preaching to these people? That won't do any good! You want to preach to the really ignorant, the really depraved, the West-Enders!"

"Do I understand," Macheson asked, "that you have a definite scheme in which you are inviting me to take part?"

Drayton lit a cigarette and led the way out.

"Look here," he said, "I'll walk with you as far as you're going, and tell you all about it." . . .

It was a sort of pilgrimage which Macheson undertook during these restless nights, a walk seemingly purposeless, the sole luxury which he permitted himself. Always about the same hour he found himself on the garden side of Berkeley Square, always he stood and looked, for a period of time of which he took no count, at the tall, dimly lit house, across whose portals he had once passed into fairyland. Then came a night when everything was changed. Lights flashed from the windows, freshly painted window-boxes had been filled with flowers, scarce enough now; everything seemed to denote a sudden spirit of activity. Macheson stood and watched with a curious sense of excitement stirring in his blood. He knew very well what was happening. She was coming, perhaps had already arrived in town. He realized as he stood there, a silent motionless figure, how far gone in his folly he really was, how closely woven were the bonds that held him. For time seemed to him of no account beside the chance of seeing her, if only for a moment, as she passed in or out. He never knew how long he waited there — it was long enough, however, for his patience to be rewarded. Smoothly, with flashing lights, a little electric brougham turned into the Square and pulled up immediately opposite to him. The tall footman sprang to the ground, the door flew open, he saw a slim, familiar figure, veiled and dressed in a dark travelling costume, pass leisurely up the steps and into the arc of light which streamed through the open door. The brougham glided away, the door was closed, she was gone. Still Macheson leaned forward, watching the spot where she had been, his heart thumping against his sices, his senses thrilled with the excitement of her coming. Suddenly his attention was diverted in a curious manner. He became conscious that he was not the only watcher under the chestnut trees. A man had stolen out from amongst the deeper shadows close up to the railings, and was standing by his side. Macheson recognized him with a start.

"What are you doing here?" he asked abruptly.

His fellow-watcher, too, showed signs of excitement. His cheeks were flushed. He pointed across the road with shaking finger, and looked up into Macheson's face with a triumphant chuckle.

"Run to earth at last!" he exclaimed. "You saw her! You saw her, too!"

"I saw a lady enter that house," Macheson answered. "What of it?"

The man whom he had once befriended drew a breath between his clenched teeth.

"There she goes!" he muttered. "The woman who dared to call herself the daughter of a poor land agent! The woman who is deceiving her world to day as she deceived us—once! Bah! It is finished!"

He started to cross the road. Macheson kept by his side.

"Where are you off to?" he asked.

The man pointed to the brilliantly lit house.

"There!" he answered fiercely. "I am going to see her. To-night! At once! She shall not escape me this time!"

"What do you want with her?" Macheson asked.

"Money — or exposure, such an exposure," the man answered. "But she will pay. She owes a good deal; but she will pay."

"And supposing," Macheson said, "that I were to tell you that this lady is a friend of mine, and that I will not have you intrude upon her — what then?"

Something venomous gleamed in the man's eyes. A short unpleasant laugh escaped him.

"Not all the devils in hell," he declared, "would keep me from going to her. For five years she's fooled us! Not a day longer, not an hour!"

Macheson's hand rested lightly upon the man's shoulder.

"Can you reach her from prison?" he asked calmly.

The man turned and snarled at him. He knew well enough that escape or resistance alike was hopeless. He was like a pigmy in the hands of the man who held him.

"This isn't your affair," he pleaded earnestly. "Let me go, or I shall do you a mischief some day. Remember it was you who helped me to escape. You can't give me away now."

"I helped you to escape," Macheson said, "but I did not know what you had done. There is another matter. You have to go away from here quietly and swear never to molest ——"

The man ducked with a sudden backward movement, and tried to escape, but Macheson was on his guard.

"It is the man who visited your father on the night of his death." Page 251

"You are a fool," the man hissed out, his small bead-like eyes glittering as though touched with fire, his thick red lips parted, showing his ugly teeth. "It is money alone I want from her. I have but to breathe her name and this address in a certain quarter of Paris, and there are others who would take her life. Let me go!"

Then Macheson was conscious of a familiar figure crossing the street in their direction. He had seen him come furtively out of the house they had been watching, and had recognized him at once. It was Stephen Hurd. Keeping his grasp upon his captive's shoulder, Macheson intercepted him.

"Hurd," he said, "I want to speak to you."

Hurd started, and his face darkened with anger when he saw who it was that had accosted him. Macheson continued hurriedly.

"Look here," he said. "I owe you this at any rate. I have just caught our friend here watching this house. Have you ever seen him before?"

Hurd looked down into the face of the man who, with an evil shrug of the shoulders, had resigned himself — for the present — to the inevitable.

"Never," he answered. "Can't say I'm particularly anxious to see him again. Convert of yours?" he asked, with a sneer.

"He is the man who visited your father on the night of his death," Macheson said.

Stephen Hurd was like a man electrified. He seized hold of the other's arm in excitement.

"Is this true?" he demanded.

The man blinked his eyes.

"You have to prove it," he said. "I admit nothing."

"You can leave him to me," Stephen Hurd said, turning to Macheson.

Macheson nodded and prepared to walk on.

"There is a police-station behind to the left," he remarked.

Hurd took no notice. He had thrust his arm tightly through the other man's.

"I have been looking for you," he said eagerly. "We must have a talk together. We will take this hansom," he added, hailing one.

The man drew back.

"Are you going to take me to the police-station?" he demanded.

"Police-station, no!" Hurd answered roughly. "What good would that do me? Get in! Café Monico!"

CHAPTER XI

THE WAY OF SALVATION

HOLDERNESS leaned back in his worn leather chair and shouted with laughter. He treated with absolute indifference the white anger in Macheson's face.

"Victor," he cried, "don't look at me as though you wanted to punch my head. Down on your knees, man, and pray for a sense of humour. It's the very salt of life."

"That's all very well," Macheson answered, "but I can't exactly see ——"

"That's because you're deficient," Holderness shouted, wiping the tears from his eyes. "I haven't laughed so much for ages. Here you come from the East to the West, with all the world's tragedy tearing at your heart, flowing from your lips, a flagellator, a hater of the people to whom you speak, seeking only to strike and to wound, and they accept you as a new sensation! They bare their back to your whip! They have made you the fashion! Oh! this funny, funny world of ours!"

Macheson smiled grimly.

"I'll grant you the elements of humour in the situation," he said, "but you can scarcely expect me to appreciate it, can you? I never came here to play the mountebank, to provide a new sensation for these tired dolls of Society. Dick, do you think St. Paul could have opened their eyes?"

Holderness shook his head.

"I don't know," he declared. "They're a difficult class — you see, they have pluck, and a sort of fantastic philosophy which goes with breeding. They're not easily scared."

Macheson thought of his friend's words later in the afternoon, when he stood on the slightly raised platform of the fashionable room where his lectures were given. Not a chair was empty. Macheson, as he entered, gazed long and steadily into those rows of tired, distinguished-looking faces, and felt in the atmosphere the delicate wave of perfume shaken from their clothes — the indescribable effect of femininity. There were men there, too, mostly as escorts, correctly dressed, bored, vacuous, from intent rather than lack of intelligence. Macheson himself, carelessly dressed from design, his fine figure ill-clad, with untidy boots and shock hair, felt his anger slowly rising as he marked the stir which his coming had caused. He to be the showman of such a crowd! It was maddening! That day he spoke to them without even the ghost of a smile parting his lips. He sought to create no sympathy. He cracked his whip with the cool deliberation of a Russian executioner.

. . . . "I was asked the other day," he remarked, "by an enterprising journalist, what made me decide to come here and deliver these lectures to you. I did not tell him. It is because I wanted to speak to the most ignorant class in Christendom. You are that class. If you have intelligence, you make it the servant of your whims. If you have imagination, you use it to enlarge the sphere of your vices. You are worse than the ostrich who buries his head in the sand — you prefer to go underground altogether. . . .

"As you sit here — with every tick of your jewelled watches, out in the world of which in your sublime selfishness you know nothing, a child dies, a woman is given to sin, a man's heart is broken. What do you care? What do you know of that infernal, that everlasting tragedy of sin and suffering that seethes around you? Why should you care? Your life is attuned to the most pagan philosophy which all the ages of sin have evolved. You have sunk so low that you are content to sit and listen to the story of your ignominy. . . ."

What fascination was it that kept them in their places? Holderness, who was sitting in the last row, fully expected to see them leave their seats and stream out; Macheson himself would not have been surprised. His voice had no particular charm, his words were simple words of abuse, he attempted no rhetorical flourishes, nor any of the tricks of oratory. He stood there like a disgusted schoolmaster lecturing a rebellious and backward school. Holderness, when he saw that no one left, chuckled to himself. Macheson, aware that his powers of invective were spent, suddenly changed his tone.

Consciously or unconsciously, he told them, every one was seeking to fashion his life according to some hidden philosophy, some unrealized ideal.

With religion, as it was commonly understood, he had, in that place at any rate, nothing to do. Even the selfish drifting down the stream of idle pleasures, which constituted life for most of them, was the passive acceptance in their consciousness of the old "fainéant" philosophy of "laissez faire." Had they any idea of the magnificent stimulus which work could give to the emptiest life! For health's sake alone, they were willing sometimes to step out of the rut of their easy-going existence, to discipline their bodies at foreign watering-places, to take up courses of physical exercises, as prescribed by the fashionable crank of the moment. What they would do for their bodies, why should they not try for their souls! The one was surely as near decay as the other — the care of it, if only they would realize it, was ten thousand times more important! He had called them, perhaps, many hard names. There was one he could not call them. He could not call them cowards. On the contrary, he thought them the bravest people he had ever known, to live the lives they did, and await the end with the equanimity they showed. The equivalent of Hell, whatever it might be, had evidently no terrors for them. . . .

He concluded his address abruptly, as his custom was, a few minutes later, and turned at once to leave the platform. But this afternoon an unexpected incident occurred. A man from the middle of the audience rose up and called to him by name.

Macheson, surprised, paused and turned round. It was Deyes who stood there, immaculately dressed in morning clothes, his long face pale as ever, his manner absolutely and entirely composed. He was swinging his eyeglass by its narrow black ribbon, and leaning a little forward.

"Sir," he said, once more addressing Macheson, "as one of the audience whose shortcomings have so — er — profoundly impressed you, may I take the liberty of asking you a question? I ask it of you publicly because I imagine that there are many others here besides myself to whom your answer may prove interesting."

Macheson came slowly to the front of the platform.

"Ask your question, sir, by all means," he said.

Deyes bowed.

"You remind me, if I may be permitted to say so," he continued, "of the prophet who went about with sackcloth and ashes on his head, crying 'Woe! woe! woe!' but who was either unable or unwilling to suggest any means by which that doleful cry might be replaced by one of more cheerful import. In plain words, sir, according to your lights — what must we do to be saved?"

There was a murmur of interest amongst the audience. There were many upon whom Macheson's stinging words and direct denunciation had left their mark. They sat up eagerly and waited for his answer. He came to the edge of the platform and looked thoughtfully into their faces.

"In this city," he said, "it should not be necessary for any one to ask that question. My answer may seem trite and hackneyed. Yet if you will accept it, you may come to the truth. Take a hansom cab, and drive as far, say, as Whitechapel. Walk — in any direction — for half a mile. Look into the faces of the men, the women and the children.

Then go home and think. You will say at first
nothing can be done for these people. They have
dropped down too low, they have lost their humanity, they only justify the natural law of the survival
of the fittest. Think again! A hemisphere may
divide the East and the West of this great city;
but these are human beings as you are a human
being, they are your brothers and your sisters. Consider for a moment this natural law of yours. It is
based upon the principle of the see-saw. Those
who are down, are down because the others are up.
Those men are beasts, those women are unsexed,
those children are growing up with dirt upon their
bodies and sin in their hearts, because you others
are what you are. Because! Consider that. Consider it well, and take up your responsibility. They
die that you may flourish! Do you think that the
sea-saw will be always one way? A revolution in
this world, or justice in the next! Which would you
rather face?"

Deyes bowed slightly.

"You have given me an answer, sir, for which I
thank you," he answered. "But you must allow me
to remind you of the great stream of gold which
flows all the while from the West to the East. Hos-
pitals, mission houses, orphanages, colonial farms —
are we to have no credit for these?"

"Very little," Macheson answered, "for you give
of your superfluity. Charity has little to do with
the cheque-book. Besides, you must remember
this. I am not here to-day to plead the cause of
the East. I am here to talk to you of your own
lives. I represent, if you are pleased to have it

so, the Sandow of your spiritual body. I ask you to submit your souls to my treatment, as the professor of physical culture would ask for your bodies. This is not a matter of religion at all. It is a matter, if you choose to call it so, of philosophy. Your souls need exercise. You need a course of thinking and working for the good of some one else — not for your own benefit. Give up one sin in your life, and replace it with a whole-hearted effort to rescue one unfortunate person from sin and despair, and you will gain what I understand to be the desire of all of you — a new pleasure. Briefly, for your own sakes, from your own point of view, it is a personal charity which I am advocating, as distinguished from the charity of the cheque-book."

"One more question, Mr. Macheson," Deyes continued quietly. "Where do we find the lost souls — I mean upon what principle of selection do we work?"

"There are many excellent institutions through which you can come into touch with them," Macheson answered. "You can hear of these through the clergyman of your own parish, or the Bishop of London."

Deyes thanked him and sat down. The lecture was over, and the people slowly dispersed. Macheson passed into the room at the back of the platform. Drayton, who was waiting for him there, pushed over a box of cigarettes. He knew that Macheson loved to smoke directly he had finished talking.

"Macheson," he said solemnly, "you're a marvel. Why, in my country, I guess they'd come and scratch your eyes out before they'd stand plain speaking like that."

Macheson was looking away into vacancy.

"I wonder," he said softly, "if it does any good — any real good?"

Drayton, who was looking through a cash-book with gleaming eyes, opened his lips to speak, but thought better of it. He pointed instead towards the table.

The usual pile of notes was there — all the latest novelties in fancy stationery were represented there, crested, coroneted, scented. Macheson began to tear them open and as rapidly destroy them with a little gesture of disgust. They were mostly of the same type. The girls were all so anxious to do a little good, so tired of the wearisome round of Society, wouldn't Mr. Macheson be very kind and give them some personal advice? Couldn't he meet them somewhere, or might they come and see him? They did hope that he wouldn't think them bold! It would be such a help to talk to him. The married ladies were bolder still. They felt the same craving for advice, but their proposals were more definite. Mr. Macheson must come and see them! They would be quite alone (underlined), there should be no one else there to worry him. Then followed times and addresses. One lady, whose coronet and motto were familiar to him, would take no denial. He was to come that afternoon. Her carriage was waiting at the side door and would bring him directly to her. Macheson looked up quickly. Through the window he could see a small brougham, with cockaded footman and coachman, waiting outside. He swept all the notes into the flames.

"For Heaven's sake, go and send that carriage away, Drayton," he begged.

Drayton laughed and disappeared. On the table there remained one more note — a square envelope, less conspicuous perhaps than the others, but more distinguished-looking. Macheson broke the seal. On half a sheet of paper were scrawled these few lines only.

"For Heaven's sake, come to me at once. — Wilhelmina."

He started and caught up his hat. In a few minutes he was on his way to Berkeley Square.

CHAPTER XII

OVER a marble-topped table in a retired corner of the café Stephen Hurd listened to the story of the man whom Macheson had delivered over to him, and the longer he listened the more interesting he found it. When at last all was told, the table itself was strewn with cigarette stumps, and their glasses had three times been replenished. The faces of both men were flushed.

"You see," the little man said, glancing for a moment at his yellow-stained fingers, and then beginning to puff furiously at a fresh cigarette, "the time is of the shortest. Jean le Roi — well, his time is up! He may be here to-morrow, the next day, who can tell? And when he comes he will kill her! That is certain!"

Hurd shuddered and drank some of his whisky.

"Look here," he said, "we mustn't have that. Revenge, of course, he will want — but there are other ways."

The little man blinked his eyes.

"You do not know Jean le Roi," he said. "To him it is a pastime to kill! For myself I do not know the passions as he would know them. Where

there was money I would not kill.   It would be as
you have said — there are other ways.   But Jean le
Roi is different."

"Jean le Roi, as you call him, must be tamed,
then," Hurd said.   "You speak of money.   I have
been her agent, so I can tell you.   What do you
think might be the income of this lady?"

Johnson was deeply interested.   He leaned across
the table.   His little black eyes were alight with
cupidity.

"Who can tell?" he murmured.   "It might be
two, perhaps three, four thousand English pounds
a year.   Eh?"

Stephen Hurd laughed scornfully.

"Four thousand a year!" he repeated.   "Bah!
She fooled you all to some purpose!   Her income is
— listen — is forty thousand pounds a year!   You
hear that, my friend?   Forty thousand pounds a
year!"

The little man's face was a study in varying ex-
pressions.   He leaned back in his chair, and then
crouched forward over the table.   His beady eyes
were almost protruding, a spot of deeper colour, an
ugly purple patch, burned upon his cheeks.   The
words seemed frozen upon his lips.   Twice he opened
his mouth to speak and said nothing.

Stephen Hurd took off his hat and placed it upon
the table before him.   His listener's emotion was
catching.

"Forty thousand pounds," he said softly, "livres
you call it!   It is a great fortune.   She has deceived you, too!   You must make her pay for it."

Johnson was recovering himself slowly.   His

voice when he spoke shook, but it was with the dawn of a vicious anger!

"Yes!" he muttered, speaking as though to himself, "she has deceived us! She must pay! God, how she must pay!"

His fingers twitched upon the table. He was blinking rapidly.

"There is the money," he said softly, "and there is Jean le Roi!"

It was a night of shocks for him. Again his eyes were dilated. He shrank back in his chair and clutched at Hurd's sleeve.

"It is himself!" he whispered hoarsely. "It is Jean le Roi! God in Heaven, he will kill us!"

Johnson collapsed for a moment. In his face were all the evidences of an abject fear, and Stephen Hurd was in very nearly as evil a plight. The man who was threading his way through the tables towards them was alarming enough in his appearance and expression to have cowed braver men.

"Jean le Roi — he fears nothing — he cares for nothing, not even for me, his father," Johnson muttered with chattering teeth. "If he feels like it he will kill us as we sit here."

Hurd, who was facing the man, watched him with fascinated eyes. He was over six feet high, and magnificently formed. Notwithstanding his ready made clothes, fresh from a French tailor, his brown hat ludicrously too small and the blue stubble of a recently cropped beard, he was almost as impressively handsome as he was repulsive to look at. He walked with the grace of a savage animal in his native woods; there was something indeed not alto-

gether human in the gleam of his white teeth and
stealthy, faultless movements. He came straight
to where they sat, and his hand fell like a vice upon
the shoulder of the shrinking elder man. It was
further characteristic of this strange being that
when he spoke there was no anger in his tone. His
voice indeed was scarcely raised above a whisper.

"What are you doing here, old man?" he asked.
"Why did you not meet me? Eh?"

"I will tell you, tell you everything, Jean," Johnson answered. "Sit down here and drink with us.
Everything shall be made quite clear to you. I
came for your sake — to get money, Jean. Sit down,
my boy."

Jean le Roi sat down.

"I sit with you," he said, "and I will drink with
you, because I have no money to pay for myself. But we are not friends yet, old man! I
will hear first what you have done. And who is
this?"

His eyes flashed as he looked upon Hurd. Johnson interposed quickly.

"A friend, a good friend," he exclaimed. "He
will be of service to us, great service. Only a few
minutes ago he told me something astounding,
something for you also to hear, dear Jean. It is
wonderful news."

Jean le Roi interrupted.

"What I want to hear from you," he said, in a
soft, vicious whisper, "is why, when they let me out
of that cursed place, you were not there with money
and clothes for me, as I ordered. But for the poor
faithful Annette, whom I did not desire to see, I

might have starved on the day of my release.
Stop! ——" he held up his hand as Johnson was on
the point of pouring out a copious explanation,
"order me brandy first. Tell them to bring me the
bottle. Do not speak till I have drunk."

They called a waiter and gave the order. They
waited in an uneasy silence until it arrived. Jean
le Roi drank at first sparingly, but his eyes rested
lovingly upon the bottle.

"Now speak," he commanded.

Johnson told his story with appropriate gestures.

"After it was all over," he began rapidly, "and
one saw that a rescue was impossible, I followed
madame! It was a moment of fury, I thought.
She will repent, she will pay for lawyers for his
defence. So I hung about her hotel, only to find
that she had left, stolen away. As you know, she
did not appear at the trial! It was a bargain with
the police that they should not call her if she betrayed you! She escaped me, Jean, and as you
know, I had no money. All, every penny had been
spent on your clothes and your horse and carriage,
to make you a gentleman."

Jean le Roi extended his hands. "Money well
spent indeed! Let the old man continue!"

"She escaped me, Jean, and it was many months
before I found a clue on an old label — just the words
'Thorpe, England.' So I wrote there, and the letter
did not come back as the others. I waited a little
time and I wrote again, this time to receive an
answer! It was a stern, angry letter from a man
who called himself her father, and signed himself
Stephen Hurd. He was what is called here an

estate agent, and he had not very much money. He would not send one pound. He said that the marriage was illegal, and if one came to England he threatened the law! I wrote again — humbly, piteously. I spoke of your hardships. I told how all the time you raved of your dear wife, how you repented your madness — how it was for love of her only that you had committed such a crime! There came no answer. I forwarded the letters which you had written to her — I begged, oh! how I begged for just a little money for the small luxuries, the good wine, the tobacco, the newspapers. They sent nothing!"

Jean le Roi drew in his breath with a gasp.

"Oh!" he muttered. "So they sent nothing!"

"Not one sou, Jean — not one sou! And all the while the time of your release was drawing near. What could I do! Well, I raised the money. How I will not tell you, my boy, but I went on a fruit boat from Havre to Southampton, and from there down to Thorpe. I saw the old man Stephen Hurd. It was on a Sunday night that I arrived, and I found him alone. He was as hard, Jean, as his letters. When I pressed him he ordered me out of the house. I would not go. I said that I would see my daughter-in-law. I would remain until I saw her, I said, even if I slept under a hedge. Again he ordered me out of the house. I was firm; I refused. Then he struck me, there was a quarrel, and he fell. I thought at first that he was unconscious, but when I examined him — he was dead."

Johnson finished his speech in a stealthy whisper,

leaning half way across the table. Jean le Roi poured himself out more brandy, but he was unmoved.

"The old trick, I suppose," he remarked carelessly, making a swift movement with his hand.

"No! no!" Johnson declared earnestly. "I used no weapon! It was an accident, a pure accident. Remember that this is his son. He would not be here if it was not quite certain that it was accident — and accident alone."

Jean le Roi lifted his head and gazed curiously at Stephen Hurd.

"So you," he murmured, "are my brother-in-law?"

Johnson leaned once more across the table.

"It is where you, where we all have been deceived," he said impressively. "Listen. She was never the daughter of Stephen Hurd at all. It was a schoolgirl's freak to take that name, when she was eluding her chaperon and amusing herself in Paris. Stephen Hurd was her servant."

"And she?" Jean le Roi asked softly.

Johnson spread out his yellow-stained fingers. His voice trembled, his eyes shone. It was like speaking of something holy.

"She is a great lady," he said. "She goes to Court, she has houses, and horses and carriages, troops of servants, a yacht, motor-cars. She is rich — fabulously rich, Jean. She has — listen — forty thousand pounds, livres mind, a year."

"More than that," Hurd muttered.

"More than that," Johnson repeated.

Jean le Roi was no longer unmoved. He drew a

long breath and his teeth seemed to come together
with a click.

"There is no mistake?" he asked softly. "An
income of forty thousand pounds?"

"There is no mistake," Stephen Hurd assured
him. "I will answer for that."

Jean le Roi's face was white and vicious. Yet
for a time he said nothing and his two companions
watched him anxiously. There was something
uncanny about his silence.

"It is a great deal of money," he said at last.
"Often in prison I was hungry, I had no cigarettes.
I was forced to drink water. A great deal of money!
And she is my wife! Half of what she has belongs
to me! That is the law, eh?"

"I don't know about that," Stephen Hurd said,
"but she has certainly treated you very badly."

Jean le Roi struck the table with his fist not
violently, and yet somehow with a force which made
itself felt.

"It is over — that!" he said. "I am a man who
knows when he has been ill-treated; who knows,
too, what it is that a wife owes to her husband.
Tell me where it is that she lives, old man. Write
it down."

Johnson drew from his pocket a stump of pencil
and the back of an envelope. He wrote slowly and
with care. Jean le Roi extended the palm of his
hand to Stephen Hurd.

"He will warn madame, perhaps," he suggested.
"Why does he sit here with us, this young man? Is
it that he, too, wants money?"

"No! no! my son," Johnson intervened hastily.

"Madame treated him badly. He would not be sorry to see her humiliated."

Jean le Roi smiled.

"It shall be done," he promised. "But from one of you I must have money. I cannot present myself before my wife so altered. No one would believe my story."

"How much do you want?" Hurd asked uneasily.

"Twenty pounds English," Jean le Roi answered. "I cannot resume my appearance as a gentleman on less."

Hurd took out some notes.

"I will lend you that," he said slowly.

Jean le Roi's long fingers took firm hold of the notes. He buttoned them up in his pocket, slapped the place where they were, and poured out more brandy.

"Now," he said, "I am prepared. Madame shall discover what it means to deceive her fond husband!"

Hurd moved in his seat uneasily. There was something ominous in the villainous curve of the man's lips — in the utter absence of any direct threats. What was it that was passing in his mind?

"You are not thinking of any violence?" he asked. "Remember she is a proud woman, and you cannot punish her more than by simply appearing and declaring yourself."

Jean le Roi smiled.

"We shall see," he declared.

CHAPTER XIII

THE KING OF THE APACHES

WILHELMINA was resting — and looked in need of it. All the delicate colours and fluttering ribbons of her Doucet dressing-jacket could not hide the pallor of her cheeks, or the hollows under her eyes. Macheson, who came in sternly enough, felt himself moved to a troublous pity. Nothing seemed left of the great lady — or the "poseuse"!

"You are kind," she murmured, "to come so soon. Sit down, please!"

"Is there any trouble?" he asked. "You look worried."

She laughed unnaturally.

"No wonder," she answered. "For five years I have been living more or less on the brink of a volcano. From what I have heard, I fancy that an eruption is about due."

"Tell me about it," he asked.

She passed him a telegram. It was from Paris, and it was signed Gilbert Deyes.

"Jean le Roi was free yesterday. Left immediately for England."

Macheson looked up. He did not understand.

"And who," he asked, "is Jean le Roi?"

She looked him in the eyes.

"My husband," she told him quietly. "At least that is what I suppose the law would say that he was."

Macheson had been prepared for something surprising, but not for this. He looked at her incredulously. He found himself aimlessly repeating her words.

"Your husband?"

"I was married five years ago in Paris," she said in a dull, emotionless tone. "No one over here knows about it, or has seen him, because he has been in prison all the time. It was I who sent him there."

"I can't believe this," he said, in a low tone. "It is too amazing."

Then a light broke in upon him and he began to understand.

"He is in England now," she said, "and I am afraid."

"Jean le Roi?" he muttered.

"King of the Apaches," she answered bitterly. " 'The greatest rogue in Paris,' they said, when they sentenced him."

"Sentenced him!" he repeated, bewildered.

"He has been in prison since the day we were married," she continued. "It was I who sent him there."

He bowed his head. He felt that it was not right to look at her. An infinite wave of tenderness swept through his whole being. He was ashamed of his past thoughts of her, of his hasty

judgments. All the time she had been carrying
this in her bosom. Her very pride seemed to him
now magnificent. He felt suddenly like a querulous
child.

"What can I do to help you?" he asked softly.

She came a little nearer to him.

"I am afraid," she said, dropping her voice
almost to a whisper. "Ever since I heard the story
of his life, as it was told in court, I have been afraid.
When he was taken, he swore to be revenged. For
the last twenty-four hours I have felt somehow that
he was near! Read this!"

She passed him a letter. The notepaper was
thick and expensive, and headed by a small coronet.

"My dearest wife," it began. "At last this
miserable separation comes to an end! I am here
in London, on my way to you! Prepare to throw
yourself into my arms. How much too long has
our happiness been deferred!

"I should have been with you before, dear
Wilhelmina, but for more sordid considerations. I
need money. I need money very badly. Send me,
please, a thousand pounds to-morrow between
three and four — or shall I come and fetch it, and
you?

"As you will.

"Your devoted husband,

"Jean."

He gave her back the letter gravely.

"What was your answer?" he asked.

"I sent nothing," she declared. "I did not reply. But I am afraid — horribly afraid! He is a terrible man. If we were alone, he would kill me as you or I would a fly. If only they could have proved the things at the trial which were known to be true, he would never have seen the daylight again. But even the witnesses were terrified. They dared not give evidence against him."

"Will you tell me," Macheson asked, "how it all came about? Not unless you like," he added, after a moment's hesitation. "Not if it is painful to you."

She sat down upon the couch, curling herself up at the further end of it, and building up the pillows at the further end to support her head. Against the soft green silk, her face was like the face of a tired child. Something seemed to have gone out of her. She was no longer playing a part — not even to him — not even to herself. There was nothing left of the woman of the world. It was the child who told him her story.

"You must listen," she said, "and you may laugh at me if you like, but you must not be angry. My story is the story of a fool! Sit down, please — at the end of the couch if you don't mind! I like to have you between me and the door."

He obeyed her in silence, and she continued. She spoke like a child repeating her lesson. She held a crumpled-up lace handkerchief in her hand, and her eyes, large and intent, never left his.

"This is the story of a girl," she said, "an orphan

who went abroad with a chaperon to travel in
Europe and perfect her French. In Paris the
chaperon fell ill, the girl hired a guide recommended
by the hotel, to show her the sights.

"They saw all that the tourist sees, and the
chaperon was still ill. The girl thought that she
would like to see something of the Parisians themselves; she was tired of Cook's English people and
Americans. So she gave the guide money to buy
himself clothes, and bade him take her to the
restaurants and places where the world of Paris
assembled. It was known at the hotel, perhaps
through the servants, that the girl was rich. The
guide heard it and told some one else. Between
them they concocted a plot. The girl was to be
the victim. She was only eighteen.

"One day they were lunching at the Café de
Paris — the guide and the girl — when a young man
entered. He was exceedingly handsome, and very
wonderfully turned out after the fashion of the
French dandy. The guide, as the young man
passed, rose up and bowed respectfully. The young
man nodded carelessly. Then he saw the girl, and
he looked at her as no man had ever looked before.
And the girl ought to have been angry, but wasn't.

"She asked the guide who the young man was.
He told her that it was the Duke of Languerois, head
of one of the oldest families in France. His father
and grandfather, and for a time he himself, had been
in their service! The girl looked across at the young
man with interest, and the young man returned her
gaze. That was what he was there for.

"As they left the restaurant her guide fell behind

for a moment, and when she looked round she saw him talking to the young man. Of course she wanted to know what they had been saying, and with much apparent reluctance the guide told her. The young man had been inquiring about mademoiselle, where they spent their time, how he could meet them. Of course he had told nothing. But the young man was very persistent and very much in earnest! She encouraged the guide to talk about him, and she believed what she was told. He was rich, noble, adored in French society, and he was in love with mademoiselle. She was very soon given to understand this.

"For several days the young man was always in evidence. He was perfectly respectful, he never attempted to address her. It was all most cunningly planned. Then one evening, when she was driving with her guide through a narrow street, a man sprang suddenly upon the step of her carriage and snatched at her jewels. Another on the other side had passed his arm round the guide's neck and almost throttled him, and a third was struggling with the coachman. It was one of those lightning-like attacks by Apaches, which were common enough then — at least it seemed like one. The girl screamed, and, of course, the young man, who had been following in another voiture, appeared. One of the thieves he threw on to the pavement, the others fled. And the young man was a hero! It was well arranged!"

Her voice broke for a moment, and Macheson moved uneasily upon the sofa. If he could he would have stopped her. He could guess as much of the

"And the young man was a hero! It was well arranged." Page 276

miserable story as it was necessary for him to know!
But she ignored his threatened interruption. She
was determined, having kept her secret for so long,
that he should know now the whole truth.

"After that, things moved rapidly. The girl was
as near her own mistress as a child of her age could
be. She was lonely and the young man proved a
delightful companion. He had many attractive
gifts, and he knew how to make use of them. All
the time he made love to her. For a time she
resisted, but she had very little chance. She was
just at the age when all girls are more or less fools.
In the end she consented to a secret marriage.
Afterwards he was to take her to his family. But
that time never came.

"They were married at eleven o'clock one morning, and went afterwards to a café for déjeûner.
The young man that day was ill at ease and nervous.
He kept looking about him as though he was afraid
of being followed. He spoke vaguely of danger
from the anger of his noble relations. They were
scarcely seated at luncheon before a man came
quietly into the place and whispered a few words
in his ear. Whatever those few words were, the
young man went suddenly pale and called for his
hat and stick. He wrote an address on a piece of
paper and gave it to the girl. He begged her to
follow him in an hour — he would introduce her then
to his friends. And he left her alone. The girl
was troubled and uneasy. He had gone off without
even paying for the luncheon. He had the air of a
desperate man. She began to realize what she
had done.

" She was preparing to depart when an Englishman, who had been lunching at the other end of
the room, came over, and, with a word of apology,
sat down by her side. He saw that she was young,
and a fellow-countryman, and he told her very
gravely that he was sure she could not be aware of
the character of the man with whom she had been
lunching. Her eyes grew wide open with horror.
The man, he said, was the illegitimate son of a
French nobleman, and his mother had been married
to a guide — her guide! He had perhaps the worst
character of any man in Paris. He had been tried
for murder, imprisoned for forgery, and he was
now suspected of being the leader of a band of
desperate criminals who were dreaded all over
Paris. This and other things he told her of the
man whom she had just married. The girl listened
as though turned to stone, with the piece of paper
which he had given her crumpled up in her hands.
Then the police came. They asked her questions.
She pretended at first to know nothing. At last
she addressed the commissionary. If she gave him
the address where this young man could be found,
he and all his friends, might she depart without
mention being made of her, or her name appearing
in any way? The commissionary agreed, and she
gave him the piece of paper. The Englishman —
it was Gilbert Deyes — took her back to her hotel,
and the police captured Jean le Roi and the whole
band of his associates. The girl returned to England
that night. Jean le Roi was sentenced to six years'
penal servitude. His time was up last week."

"What a diabolical plot!" Macheson exclaimed.

"But the marriage! It could have been annulled, surely?"

"Perhaps," she answered, "but I did not dare to face the publicity. I felt that I should never be able to look any one in the face again. I had given my name to the guide Johnson as Clara Hurd. I hoped that they might never find me."

"They cannot do you any harm," Macheson declared. "Let me go with you to the lawyers. They will see that you are not molested."

She shook her head.

"It is not so easy," she said. "The marriage was quite legal. To have it annulled I should have to enter a suit. The whole story would come out. I could never live in England afterwards."

"But you don't mean," he protested, "to remain bound to this blackguard all your life!"

"How can I free myself," she asked, "except by making myself the laughing-stock of the country?"

"Why did you send for me?" he asked bluntly.

"To ask for your advice — and to protect me," she added, with a shiver. "It is not only money that Jean le Roi wants! It is vengeance because I betrayed him."

"As for that, I won't leave you except when you send me away," he declared. "And my advice! If you want that, the right thing to me seems simple enough. Go at once to your lawyers. They will tell you the proper course. At the worst, the man could be bought off for the present."

She raised her head.

"I will not give him one penny," she declared. "I have always sworn that."

"But I'm afraid if you won't try to divorce him that he can claim some," Macheson said.

"Then he must come and take it by force," she declared.

There was silence between them. Then she rose to her feet and came and stood before him.

"I ought to have told you all this long ago," she said simply. "To-day I felt that I must tell you without another hour's delay. Now that you know, I am not so terrified. But you must promise to come and see me every day while that brute remains in London."

"Yes! I promise that," he answered, also rising to his feet.

They heard her maid moving about in the bed-room.

"Hortense is reminding me that I must dress for dinner," she remarked with a faint smile. "One must dine, you know, even in the midst of tragedies."

Macheson prepared to take his departure.

"I shall come to-morrow," he said, "if you do not send for me before."

CHAPTER XIV

LADY PEGGY was fussing round the drawing-room, talking to all her guests at once.

"I haven't the least idea who takes anybody in," she declared. "James said he'd see to that, so you might just as well put your hand in a lucky-bag. And I'm not at all sure that you'll get any dinner. I've got a new *chef* — drives up in a high dog-cart with such a sweet little groom. He may be all right. Jules, the maître d'hôtel at Claridge's, got him for me, and, Wilhelmina, sooner than come out like a ghost, I'd really take lessons in the use of the rouge-pot. My new maid's a perfect treasure at it. No one can ever tell whether my colour's natural or not. I don't mind telling you people it generally isn't. But anyhow, it isn't daubed on like Lady Sydney's — makes her look for all the world like one of 'ces dames,' doesn't it? I'm sure I'd be afraid to be seen speaking to her if I were a man. Gilbert," she broke off, addressing Deyes, who was just being ushered in, "how dare you come to dinner without being asked? I'm sure I have not asked you. Don't say I did, now. You refused me eight times running, and I crossed you off my list."

Deyes held out a card as he bowed over his hostess's fingers.

"My dear lady," he said, "here is the proof that I am not an intruder. I am down to take in our hostess of Thorpe!"

"You have bribed James," she declared. "I hope it cost you a great deal of money. I will not believe that I asked you. However, since you are here, go and tell Wilhelmina some of your stories. I hate pale cheeks, and Wilhelmina blushes easily. No use looking at the clock, Duke. Dinner will be at least half an hour late, I'm sure. These foreign *chefs* have no idea of punctuality. What's that? Dinner served! Two minutes before time. Well, we're all here, aren't we? I knew it would be either too early or too late. Duke, you will have to take me in. By the time we get there the soup will probably be cold. You'd better pray that we're starting with caviare and oysters! Such a slow crowd, aren't they — and such chatterboxes! I wish they'd move on a little faster and talk a little less. No! Only thirty. Nice sociable number, I call it, for a round table. I asked Victor Macheson, the man who's so rude to us all every Thursday afternoon for a guinea a time — I don't know why we pay it to be abused, — but he wouldn't come. I met him before he developed, and I don't think he liked me."

"You got my telegram?" Deyes asked, as he unfolded his napkin.

Wilhelmina nodded.

"Yes!" she answered. "It was very good of you to warn me. I have had — a letter already. The campaign has begun."

Deyes nodded.

"Chosen your weapons yet?" he asked.

"I haven't much choice, have I?" she answered, a little bitterly. "I fight, of course."

Deyes was carefully scanning the menu through his horn-rimmed eyeglass.

"Becassine à la Broche," he murmured. "I must remember that."

Then he turned in his chair and looked at Wilhelmina.

"You are worrying," he declared abruptly.

She shrugged her shoulders, alabaster white, rising from the unrelieved black of her velvet gown.

"My maid's fault," she added. "I ought to have worn white. Of course I'm worrying. I don't care about carrying the signs of it about with me though. I think I shall have to adopt Peggy's advice, and go to the rouge-pot."

"Perhaps," he said deliberately, "it will not be necessary."

She looked up at him quickly. His words sounded encouraging.

"What do you mean?"

"I mean that a way may be found to induce a certain gentleman to return to his native country and stay there," Deyes said smoothly. "After dinner we are going to have some talk. Please oblige me now by abandoning the discussion and eating something. Ah! that champagne will do you good."

Her neighbour on the other side addressed her, and Wilhelmina was conscious of a sudden lighten-

ing of the load upon her heart. Like every one
else, she had confidence in this tall, self-contained
man whose life was somewhat of a mystery even to
his friends, and who had about him that suggestion
of power which reticence nearly always brings. He
was going to help her. She pushed all those miserable thoughts away from her. She became herself
again.

"Let no one imagine," Lady Peggy said, carefully knocking the end of a cigarette upon the table,
"that I am going to try to catch the eyes of all you
women, and go sailing away with my nose in the
air to look at engravings in the drawing-room. You
can just get up and go when you like, any or all of
you. There are bridge tables laid out for you in
the library, music and a hopping girl — I don't call
it dancing — in the drawing-room, a pool in the
billiard-room, or flirtation in the winter-garden.
Coffee and liqueurs will follow you wherever you go.
Take your choice, good people. For myself, the
Duke is telling me stories of Cairo. J'y suis, j'y reste.
I'm only thankful no one else can hear them!"

The party at the great round table dispersed
slowly by two and threes. Wilhelmina and Deyes
strolled into the winter-garden. Deyes lit a cigarette
and stood with his hands behind him. Wilhelmina
was leaning against the back of a chair. She was
too excited to sit down.

"Please!" she begged.

Deyes threw his cigarette away. His face seemed
to harden and soften at the same time. His mouth
was suddenly firm, but his eyes glowed. All the boredom was gone from his manner and expression.

"Wilhelmina," he said, "I have wanted to marry you ever since I saw you in the Café de Paris with that atrocious blackguard who has caused you so much suffering. You may remember that I have hinted as much to you before!"

She was startled — visibly disturbed.

"You know very well," she said, "that you are speaking of impossible things!"

"Things that were impossible, Wilhelmina," he said. "Suppose I take Jean le Roi off your hands? Suppose I promise to send him back to his own country like a rat to his hole? Suppose I promise that your marriage shall be annulled without a line in the newspapers, without a single vestige of publicity?"

"You cannot do it," she murmured eagerly.

"You want your freedom, then?" he asked.

"Yes! I want my freedom," she answered. "I have a right to it, haven't I?"

"And I," he said slowly, "want you!"

There was a short pause. Through the palms came the faint wailing of a violin, the crash of pianoforte chords, the clear soft notes of a singer. Wilhelmina felt her eyes fill with tears. She was overwrought, and there were new things, things that were strange to her, in the worn, lined face of the man who was bending towards her.

"Wilhelmina," he said softly, "life, our life, does its best to strangle the emotions. One feels that one does best with a pulse which has forgotten how to quicken, and a heart which beats to the will of its owner. But the most hardened of us come to grief sometimes. I am afraid that I have come — very much to grief!"

"I am sorry," she said quietly.

He drew away and his face became like marble.

"You mean — that it isn't any use?" he asked hoarsely.

She looked at him, and he did not press for words.

"Is it — the missioner?" he asked.

Her head sank a little lower, but still she did not answer. Gilbert Deyes drew himself upright. He remembered the cigarette which had burnt itself out between his fingers, and he carefully relit it.

"I am now," he said, blowing a cloud of blue smoke into the heart of a yellow rose, "confronted by a somewhat hackneyed, but always interesting problem. Do I care for you enough — or too little— or too much — to continue your friend, when my aid will probably ensure the loss of you for ever! It is not a problem to be hurried over, this!"

"There is no need for haste," she answered. "I know you, Gilbert, better than you know yourself. I am very sure that you will help me — if you can."

He laughed bitterly.

"You are a good deal surer of me than I am of myself," he answered. "Why should I give you up to a boy who hasn't learnt yet the first lesson of life?"

"What is it?" she asked. "I am not clear that I have graduated."

"You can see it blazoned over the portals as you pass through the gates," he answered, " 'Abandon all enthusiasm, ye who enter here.' The pathways of life are heaped with the corpses of those who will

" Is it—the Missioner ? " he asked.   Page 286

not understand. Do you think that this boy will
fare better than the rest, with his preaching and
lectures and East End work? It's sheer impertinence! Man, the individual, is only a pawn in the
game of life. Why should he imagine that he can
alter the things that are?"

"Even the striving to alter them," she said, "may
tend towards betterment."

"A platitude," he declared — "and hopeless!"

She raised her eyes to his.

"Anyhow," she said softly, "I care for him."

He bowed low.

"Incomprehensible," he murmured. "Take your
freedom and marry this young man if you must.
But I warn you that you will be miserable. Apples
and green figs don't grow on the same tree."

He drew an envelope from his pocket and handed
it to her.

"Jean le Roi," he said, "was married to Annette
Hurier, in the town of Châlons, two years before he
posed before you as the Duke of Languerois. You
will find Annette's address in there. It took me a
year to trace this out — a wasted year! Bah! you
women are all disappointments. We will go and
play bridge."

Lady Peggy stared at Wilhelmina when they
entered the library a few minutes later.

"What on earth have you been doing to her,
Gilbert?" she demanded. "She's a changed woman!"

"Making love to her!" Deyes answered.

Lady Peggy laughed.

"If I believed you," she declared, "I'd give up
this rubber and go and lose myself amongst the

palms with you. Come and cut in — you too, Wilhelmina."

But Wilhelmina excused herself. She drove homewards with a soft smile upon her lips, and the dead weight lifted from her heart.

CHAPTER XV

IT was a round table, too, at which Macheson dined that night, but with a different company. For they were all men who sat there, men with earnest faces and thoughtful eyes. The graces of evening dress and society talk they knew nothing of. They were the friends of Macheson's college days, the men who had sworn amongst themselves that, however they might live, they would devote the greater part of their life to their fellow-creatures.

They were smoking pipes, and a great bowl of tobacco was on the table. Few of them took wine, but Macheson and Holderness were drinking whisky. Holderness, their senior, was usually the one who started their informal talk.

"My work's been easy enough all the time," he remarked, leaning forward. "There were no end of labour-papers, but all being run either for the trades' unions, or some special industrial branch. I started a labour magazine — Macheson found the money, of course — and I'm paying my way now. I don't know whether the thing does any good. At any rate it's an effort! I've been hearing about your colony, Franklin. I shall want an article on it presently."

A tall, thin young man removed his pipe from his mouth.

"You shall have it as soon as I can find time," he answered. "We're going strong, but really there's very little credit due to me. It was Macheson's money and Macheson's idea. We've got an entire village now near Llandirog, and the whole population come from the prisons. Macheson and I used to attend the police-courts ourselves, hear all the cases, and form our own conclusions as to the prisoners. If we thought there was any hope for them, we made a note, met them when they came out, and offered them a job, on probation — in our village. We have to leave it to the chaplains now — I can't spare time to be always in London. We've two woollen mills, a saw-mill, and a bakery, besides all the shops, and nearly a thousand acres of well-farmed land. At first the people round were terribly shy of us, but that's all over now. Why, we have less trouble with the police in our village than any for miles around. We're paying our way, too."

"You've done thundering well, Franklin," Macheson declared. "I remember what a rough time you had at first. Uphill work, wasn't it?"

"That's what makes it such a relief to have pulled through," Franklin declared, re-lighting his pipe. "I shouldn't like to say how much I had to draw from Macheson before we turned the corner. Glad to say we've paid a bit back now, though. Tell us about your idea, Holroyd. They tell me it's working well in some of the large cities."

"It's simple enough," Holroyd answered, smiling. "It was just the application of common sense to the laws of charity. Nearly every one's charitable by instinct — only sometimes it's so difficult for a busy man to know exactly when and how to give. I started in one of the big cities, looking up prosperous middle-class families. I'd try to induce them, instead of just writing cheques for institutions and making things for bazaars, to take a personal interest in a family of about the same size as their own who were in a bad way. When they promised, all I had to do was to find the poor family and bring them together, and it was astonishing how much the one could do for the other without undue effort. There were the clothes, of course, and old housekeeping things, odd bits of furniture, food from the kitchen, a job for one of the boys in the garden, a day's work for one of the girls in the house. I tell you I have lists of hundreds of poor families, who feel now that they have some one to fall back upon, and the richer half of the combination take a tremendous interest in their foster-family, as some of them call it. Sometimes there is trouble, but the world is governed by majorities, and in the majority of cases the thing has turned out excellently."

"There's the essence of charity in the idea — the personal note," Macheson remarked. "How's the Canadian farm going, Finlayson?"

"We're paying our way," Finlayson answered, "and you should see our boys. They come out thin and white — all skin and bones. You wouldn't recognize one of them in six months! They're good workers, too. We've nine hundred altogether in the

North-West, and we want more. I'm hoping to take a hundred back with me."

"It's a grand country," Macheson said. "I'm glad it's part of the Empire, Finlayson, or I should grudge you those boys. We can't spare too many. Hinton, your work speaks for itself."

Hinton, the only one in clerical dress, smiled a little wearily.

"Sometimes," he said, "I wish it would speak a little louder. East End work is all the same. One feels ashamed of preaching religion to a starving people."

Macheson nodded his sympathy.

"I know what you mean," he said. "It drove me from the East to the West. We should preach at the one and feed the other! . . . Of course, I personally have always been handicapped. I haven't been able to subscribe to any of the established churches. But I do believe in the laws of retribution, whether you call them human or Divine. One's moral delinquencies pay one out just as bodily excesses do. Always one's debts are to be paid, and it's a terrible burden the drones must carry. After all, I've come to the conclusion that there's heaps of sound moral teaching to be drummed into our fellow-creatures without the necessity of being orthodox!"

"You speak lightly of your own work, Macheson," Franklin said, "but there is one thing we must none of us forget. Our schools, our farms, our colonies, all our attempts, indeed, owe their very being to your open purse ——"

Macheson held out his hand.

" Franklin," he said, " I want to tell you something which I think none of you know. I want
to tell you where most of my money came from,
and you'll understand then why I've been so anxious
to get rid of it — or a part of it — in this way. Did
you ever hear of Ferguson Davis, the money-lender?
Yes, I can see by your faces you did. Well, he
was my mother's brother, and he died without a
will when I was a child, and the whole lot came
to me! "

" A million and a quarter," some one murmured.

" More," Macheson answered. " I was at Oxford
when I understood exactly the whole business, and
it seemed like nothing but a curse to me. Then
I talked to the dear old professor, and he showed
me the way. I can honestly say that not one
penny of that money has ever been spent, directly
or indirectly, upon myself. I believe that if the
old man could come to life and read my bank-book
he'd have a worse fit than the one which carried
him off. I appointed myself the trustee of his
fortune, and it's spread pretty well all over the
world. I've never refused to stand at the back
of any reasonable scheme for the betterment of
our fellow-creatures. There have been a few failures
perhaps, but many successes. The Davis buildings
are mine — in trust, of course. They've done
well. I've a larger scheme on hand now on the
same lines. And in spite of it all the money grows!
I can't get rid of it. The old man chose his investments well, and many of our purely philanthropic
schemes are beginning to pay their way. It isn't
that I care a fig about the money, but you must

try to make these things self-supporting, or you injure the character of those who benefit by them. Now I've told you all the truth, but don't let it go out of this room. You can consider yourselves fellow-trustees with me, if you like. Show me an honest way to use money for the real benefit of the world's unfortunates, and it's yours as much as mine."

"It's magnificent," Franklin murmured.

"It's justice," Macheson answered. "The money was wrung from the poor, and it goes back to them. Perhaps it's a saner distribution, for it's the improvident and shiftless of the world who go to the money-lender."

There was a knock at the door. The hall-porter of the club in which they were holding their informal meeting entered and addressed Macheson.

"I beg your parden, sir," he said, "but there is a young man here who wants to see you at once. He would not give his name, but he says that his business is urgent."

"Where is he?" Macheson asked.

"In the smaller strangers' room, sir."

Macheson excused himself, and, crossing the hall, entered the barely furnished apartment, on the left of the entrance. A young man was walking up and down with fierce, restless movements. He was pale, untidily dressed, and in his eyes there was a curious look of terror, as though all the time he saw beyond the walls of the room things which kept him breathless with fear. Macheson, pausing for a moment on the threshold, failed on the instant to recognize him. Then he closed the door and advanced into the room.

"Hurd!" he exclaimed. "What do you want? What is the matter?"

"Matter enough," Hurd declared wildly. "I have been a fool and a blackguard. Those two got round me — the old man and his cursed step-son! I must have been mad!"

"What have you done?" Macheson asked sharply.

"She treated me badly," Hurd continued, "made a fool of me before you, and turned me away from Thorpe. I wanted to cry quits with her, and those two got hold of me. Jean le Roi is her husband. She refused to see him — to hear from him. Letty Foulton is there, and I have been allowed to visit her. I knew the back way in, and I took Jean le Roi there — an hour ago — and he is waiting in her room until she comes home!"

"Good God!" Macheson murmured. "You unspeakable blackguard!"

He glanced at the clock. It was past midnight.

"What time was she expected home?" he demanded.

"Soon after eleven! She was only dining out. He — he swore that he only wanted to talk to her, to threaten her with exposure. She deserved that! But he is a madman. When I left him I was afraid. He carries a knife always, and he kept on saying that she was his wife. I left him there waiting — and when I wanted him to promise that there should be no violence, he laughed at me. He is hidden in her room. I thought that it was only money he wanted — but — but ——"

Macheson flung him on one side. He caught up his hat and rushed out of the club.

CHAPTER XVI

MAN TO MAN

HORTENSE smiled softly to herself as she laid down the ivory-backed brushes. What did it mean, she wondered, when her mistress went out with tired eyes and pallid cheeks, and came home with the colour of a rose and eyes like stars, humming an old French love-song, and her feet moving all the time to some unheard music? It was years since she had seen her like this! Hortense knew the signs and was well pleased. At last, then, the household was to be properly established. A woman as beautiful as her mistress without a lover was to Hortense an incomprehensible thing.

"You can go now, Hortense," her mistress ordered. "I will have my coffee half an hour earlier to-morrow morning."

"Very good, madame," the girl answered. "There is nothing else to-night, then?"

"Nothing, thank you," Wilhelmina answered. "You had better go to bed now. I have been keeping you up rather late the last few evenings. We must both turn over a new leaf."

Hortense departed, smiling to herself. It was always like this — when it came. One thought of others and one wanted to be alone. She, too, hummed a few bars of that love-song as she climbed the stairs to her room.

Wilhelmina rose from her chair and stood for a moment looking at herself in the long, oval looking-glass. Hortense had chosen for her a French dressing-jacket, with the palest of light blue ribbons drawn through the lace. Wilhelmina looked at herself and smiled. Was it the light, the colouring, or was she really still so good to look at? Her hair, falling over her shoulders, was long and silky, the lines seemed to have been smoothed out of her face — she was like herself when she had been a girl! She followed the slender lines of her figure, down past the lace of her petticoat to her feet, still encased in her evening slippers with diamond buckles, and she laughed softly to herself. What was she yet but a girl? Fate had cheated her of some of the years, but she was barely twenty-five. How wonderful to be young still and feel one's blood flow to music like this! Her thoughts ran riot. Her mouth trembled and a deeper colour stained her cheeks. Then she heard a voice behind her, a living voice in her room. And as swiftly as those other mysterious thoughts had stolen into her heart, came the chill of a deadly, indescribable fear.

"Charming! Ravishing! It is almost worth the six years of waiting, dear wife!"

She began to tremble. She could not have called out or framed any intelligible sentence to save her life. It was like a nightmare. The horror was there, without the power of movement or speech.

He moved his position and came within the range

of her terrified vision. Hurd's twenty pounds and a little more added to it had done wonders. He wore correct evening clothes, correctly worn. Except for his good looks — the good looks of a devil — he would have attracted notice nowhere. He leaned against the couch, and though his lips curled into a sneer, there was a flame in his eyes, a horrible admiration.

She tried to pray.

"You are overcome," he murmured softly. "Ah! Why not? Six years since our happiness was snatched from us, chérie! Ah! but it was cruel! You have thought of me, I trust! You have pitied me! Ah! how often I have lain awake at night in my cell, fondly imagining some such reunion — as this."

She forced herself to speak through lips suddenly pale. What strange words they sounded, frozen things, scarcely audible! Yet the effort hurt her.

"I will give you — the money," she said. "More, if you will!"

"Ah!" he said reflectively, "the money! I had forgotten that. It was not kind of you to run away and hide, little woman! It was not kind of you to send me nothing when I was in prison! Oh! I suffered, I can tell you! There is a good deal to be made up for! Pet, if you had not reminded me, just now these things seem so little. Dear little wife, you are enchanting. Almost you turn my head."

He came slowly towards her. She threw up her hands.

"Wait!" she begged, "oh, wait! Listen! I am in your power. I admit it. I will make terms. I will sign anything. What is it that you want?

You shall be rich, but you must go away. You must
leave me now!"

He looked at her steadily and it seemed to her
that his eyes were on fire with evil things.

"Little wife," he said, with a shade of mockery
in his lowered tone. "I cannot do that. Consider
how you were snatched from my arms! Consider
the cruelty of it. As for the money — bah! I have
come to claim my own. Don't you understand,
you bewitching little fool? It is you I want! The
money can wait! I cannot!"

He came nearer still and she shrank, like a terrified
dumb thing, against her magnificent dressing-table,
with its load of priceless trinkets. She tried to call
out, but her voice seemed gone, and he only laughed
as he laid his hand over her mouth and drew her
gently towards him. With a sudden unnatural
strength she wrested herself from his arms.

"Oh! listen to me, listen to me for one moment
first," she begged frantically. "It's true that I
married you, but it was all a plot — and I was a
child! You shall have your share of my money!
Leave me alone and I swear it! You shall be rich!
You can go back to Paris and be an adventurer
no longer. You shall spend your own money. You
can live your own life!"

Even then her brain moved quickly. She dared
not speak of Annette, for fear of making him desperate. It was his cupidity to which she appealed.

"I am no wife of yours," she moaned. "You
shall have more money than you ever had before in
your life. But don't make me kill myself! For I
shall, if you touch me!"

He was so close to her now that his hot breath scorched her cheek.

"Is it that another has taken my place?" he asked.

"Yes! — no! that is, there is some one whom I love," she cried. "Listen! You know what you can do with money in Paris. Anything! Everything!"

He was so close to her now that the words died away upon her lips.

"Little wife," he whispered, "don't you understand — that I am a man, and that it is you I want?"

Again she tried to scream, but his hand covered her mouth. His arm was suddenly around her. Then he started back with an oath and looked towards the door of her bedroom.

"Who is in that room?" he asked quickly.

"My maid," she lied.

He took a quick step across the room. The door was flung open and Macheson entered. Wilhelmina fainted, but forced herself back into consciousness with a sheer effort of will. Sobbing and laughing at the same time, she tried to drag herself towards the bell, but Jean le Roi stood in the way. Jean le Roi was calm but wicked.

"What are you doing in my wife's bedroom?" he asked.

"I am here to see you out of the house," Macheson answered, with one breathless glance around the room. "Will you come quietly?"

"Out of my own house?" Jean le Roi said softly. "Out of my wife's room? Who are you?"

"Never mind," Macheson answered. "Her friend!

THE BONE SNAPPED, AND THE KNIFE FELL FROM THE NERVELESS
FINGERS. Page 301

Let that be enough. And let me tell you this. If I had come too late I would have wrung your neck."

Jean le Roi sprang at him like a cat, his legs off the ground, one arm around the other's neck, and something gleaming in his right hand. Nothing but Macheson's superb strength saved him. He risked being throttled, and caught Jean le Roi's right arm in such a grip that he swung him half round the room. The bone snapped, and the knife fell from the nerveless fingers. But Macheson let go a second too soon. Jean le Roi had all the courage and the insensibility to pain of a brute animal. He stretched out his foot, and with a trick of his old days, tripped Macheson so that he fell heavily. Jean le Roi bent over him on his knees, breathing heavily, and with murder in his eyes. Macheson scarcely breathed! He lay perfectly still. Jean le Roi staggered to his feet and turned towards Wilhelmina.

"You see, madame," he said, seizing her by the wrist, "how I shall deal with your lovers if there are any more of them. No use tugging at that bell. I saw to that before you came! I'm used to fighting for what I want, and I think I've won you!"

He caught her into his arms, but suddenly released her with a low animal cry. He knew that this was the end, for he was pinioned from behind, a child in the mighty grip which held him powerless. "You are a little too hasty, my friend," Macheson remarked. "I was afraid I might not be so quick as you on my feet, so I rested for a moment. But no man has ever escaped from this grip till I chose to let him go. Now," he added, turning to Wilhelmina,

" the way is clear. Will you go outside and rouse the servants? Don't come back."

" You are — quite safe? " she faltered.

" Absolutely," he answered. " I could hold him with one hand."

Jean le Roi lifted his head. His brain was working swiftly.

" Listen! " he exclaimed. " It is finished! I am beaten! I, Jean le Roi, admit defeat. Why call in servants? The affair is better finished between ourselves."

Wilhelmina paused. In that first great rush of relief, she had not stopped to think that with Jean le Roi a prisoner, and herself as prosecutrix, the whole miserable story must be published. He continued.

" Give me money," he said, " only a half of what you offered me just now, and you shall have your freedom."

Wilhelmina smiled. Something of the joy of a few hours ago came faintly back to her.

" I have already that," she answered. " I learnt the truth to-night."

Jean le Roi shrugged his shoulders. The game was up then! What an evening of disasters!

" Let me go," he said. " I ask no more."

Wilhelmina and Macheson exchanged glances. She vanished into her room for a moment, and reappeared in a long wrapper.

" Come with me softly," she said, " and I will let you out."

So they three went on tiptoe down the broad stairs. Macheson and Wilhelmina exchanged no words. Yet they both felt that the future was different for them.

"You can give Mr. Macheson your address," Wilhelmina said, as they stood at the front door. "I will send you something to help you make a fresh start."

But Jean le Roi laughed.

"I play only for the great stakes," he murmured, with a swagger, "and when I lose — I lose."

So he vanished into the darkness, and Macheson and Wilhelmina remained with clasped hands.

"To-morrow," he whispered, stooping and kissing her fingers.

"To-morrow," she repeated. "Thank God you came to-night!"

She was too weary, too happy to ask for explanations, and he offered none. All the time, as he crossed the Square and turned towards his house, those words rang in his ears — To-morrow!

CHAPTER XVII

LORD AND LADY BOUNTIFUL

D EYES caught a vision of blue in the window, and crossed the lawn. Lady Peggy leaned over the low sill. Between them was only a fragrant border of hyacinths.

"You know that our host and hostess have deserted us?" she asked.

He nodded.

"They have gone over to this wonderful Convalescent Home that Macheson is building in the hills," he remarked. "I am not sure that I consider it good manners to leave us to entertain one another."

"I am not sure," she said, "that it is proper. Wilhelmina should have considered that we are her only guests."

She sat down in the window-sill and leaned back against the corner. She had slept well, and she was not afraid of the sunshine—blue, too, was her most becoming colour. He looked at her admiringly.

"You are really looking very well this morning," he said.

"Thank you," she answered. "I was expecting that."

"I wonder," he said, "how you others discover the secret of eternal youth. You and Macheson and Wilhelmina all look younger than you did last year. I seem to be getting older all by myself."

She looked at him critically. There were certainly more lines about his face and the suspicion of crow's-feet about his tired eyes.

"Age," she said, "is simply a matter of volition. You wear yourself out fretting for the impossible!"

"One has one's desires," he murmured.

"But you should learn," she said, "to let your desires be governed by your reason. It is a foolish thing to want what you may not have."

"You think that it is like that with me?" he asked.

"All the world knows," she answered, "that you are in love with Wilhelmina!"

"One must be in love with someone," he remarked.

"Naturally! But why choose a woman who is head and ears in love with some one else?"

"It cannot last," he answered, "she has married him."

Lady Peggy reached out for a cushion and placed it behind her head.

"That certainly would seem hopeful in the case of an ordinary woman— myself, for instance," she said. "But Wilhelmina is not an ordinary woman. She always would do things differently from other people. I don't want to make you more unhappy than you are, but I honestly believe that Wilhelmina is going to set a new fashion. She is going to try and re-establish the life domestic amongst the upper classes."

"She always was such a reformer," he sighed.

Lady Peggy nodded sympathetically.

"Of course, one can't tell how it may turn out," she continued, "but at present they seem to have turned life into a sort of Garden of Eden, and do you know I can't help fancying that there isn't the slightest chance for the serpent. Wilhelmina is so fearfully obstinate."

"The thing will cloy!" he declared.

"I fancy not," she answered. "You see, they don't live on sugar-plums. Victor Macheson is by way of being a masterful person, and Wilhelmina is only just beginning to realize the fascination of being ruled. Frankly, Gilbert, I don't think there's the slightest chance for you!"

He sighed.

"I am afraid you are right," he said regretfully. "I began to realize it last night, when we went into the library unexpectedly, and Wilhelmina blushed. No self-respecting woman ought to blush when she is discovered being kissed by her own husband."

"Wilhelmina," Lady Peggy said, stretching out her hand for one of Deyes' cigarettes, "may live to astonish us yet, but of one thing I am convinced. She will never even realize the other sex except through her own husband. I am afraid she will grow narrow — I should hate to write as her epitaph that she was an affectionate wife and devoted mother — but I am perfectly certain that that is what it will come to."

"In that case," Deyes remarked gloomily, "I may as well go away."

"No! I shouldn't do that," Lady Peggy said.
" I should try to alter my point of view."

"Direct me, please," be begged.

"I should try," she continued, "to put a bridle
upon my desires and take up the reins.   You could
lead them in a more suitable direction."

"For instance?"

"There is myself," she declared.

He laughed quietly.

"You!" he repeated.   "Why, you are the most
incorrigible flirt in Christendom.   You would no
more tie yourself up with one man than enter a
nunnery."

She sighed.

"I have always been misunderstood," she declared, looking at him pathetically out of her
delightful eyes.   "What you call my flirtations
have been simply my attempts, more or less clumsy,
to gain a husband.   I have been most unlucky.   No
one ever proposes to me!"

He laughed derisively.

"Your victims have been too loquacious," he
replied.   "How about Gayton, who went to Africa
because you offered to be his friend, and Horris —
he came to my rooms to tell me all about it the day
you refused him, and Sammy Palliser — you treated
him shockingly!"

"I had forgotten them," she admitted.   "They
were nice men, too, all of them, but they all made
the same mistake.   I remember now they did pro-
pose to me.   That, of course, was fatal."

"I scarcely see ——" he began.

She patted him gently on the arm.

"My dear Gilbert," she said, "haven't I always said that I never intend to marry any one who proposes to me? When I have quite made up my mind, I am going to do the proposing myself!"

"Whether it is Leap Year or not?" he asked.

"Decidedly!" she answered. "Men can always shuffle out of a Leap Year declaration. My man won't be able to escape. I can promise you that."

"Does he — exist then?" Deyes asked.

She laughed softly.

"He's existed for a good many years more than I have," she answered. "I wasn't thinking of marrying a baby."

"Ah! Does he know?"

"Well, I'm not sure," she said thoughtfully. "He ought to, but he's such a stupid person."

It was then that Gilbert Deyes received the shock of his life. He discovered quite suddenly that her eyes were full of tears. For the first time for many years he nearly lost his head.

"Perhaps," he suggested, dropping his voice and astonished to find that it was not quite so steady as usual, "he has been waiting!"

"I am afraid not," she answered, looking down for a moment at the buckle in her waistband.

He looked round.

"If only he were here now," he said. "Could one conceive a more favourable opportunity? An April morning, sunshine, flowers, everything in the air to make him forget that he is an old fogey and doesn't deserve ——"

She lifted her eyes to his, now deliciously wet. Her brows were delicately uplifted.

"I couldn't do it," she murmured, "unless he were in the same room."

Deyes stepped over the hyacinths and vaulted through the window.

Wilhelmina selected a freshly cut tree-stump, carefully brushed away the sawdust, and sat down. Macheson chose another and lighted a cigarette. Eventually they decided that they were too far away, and selected a tree-trunk where there was room for both. Wilhelmina unrolled a plan, and glancing now and then at the forest of scaffold poles to their left, proceeded to try to realize the incomplete building. Macheson watched her with a smile.

"Victor," she exclaimed, "you are not to laugh at me! Remember this is my first attempt at doing anything — worth doing, and, of course, I'm keen about it. Are you sure we shall have enough bedrooms?"

"Enough for a start, at any rate," he answered. "We can always add to it."

She looked once more at that forest of poles, at the slowly rising walls, through whose empty windows one could see pictures of the valley below.

"One can build ——" she murmured, "one can build always. But think, Victor, what a lot of time I wasted before I knew you. I might have done so much."

He smiled reassuringly.

"There is plenty of time," he declared. "Better to start late and build on a sure foundation, you know. A good many of my houses had to come down as fast as they went up. Do you remember, for instance, how I wanted to convert all your villagers by storm?"

She smiled.

"Still — I'm glad you came to try," she said softly. "That horrid foreman is watching us, Victor. I am going to look the other way."

"He has gone now," Macheson said, slipping his arm around her waist. "Dear, do you know I don't think that one person can build very well alone. It's a cold sort of building when it's finished — the life built by a lonely man. I like the look of our palace better, Wilhelmina."

"I should like to know where my part comes in?" she asked.

"Every room," he answered, "will need adorning, and the lamps — one person alone can never keep them alight, and we don't want them to go out, Wilhelmina. Do you remember the old German, who said that beautiful thoughts were the finest pictures to hang upon your walls? Think of next spring, when we shall hear the children from that miserable town running about in the woods, picking primroses — do you see how yellow they are against the green moss?"

Wilhelmina rose.

"I must really go and pick some," she said. "What about your pheasants, Victor?"

He laughed.

"I'll find plenty of sport, never fear," he answered, "without keeping the kiddies shut out. Why, the country belongs to them! It's their birthright, not ours."

They walked through the plantation side by side.
The ground was still soft with the winter's rains, but
everywhere the sunlight came sweeping in, up the
glade and across the many stretching arms of tender
blossoming green. The ground was starred with
primroses, and in every sheltered nook were violets.
A soft west wind blew in their faces as they emerged
into the country lane. Below them was the valley,
hung with a faint blue mist; all around them the
song of birds, the growing sounds of the stirring
season. Stephen Hurd came cantering by, and
stopped for a moment to speak about some matter
connected with the estates.

"My love to Letty," Wilhelmina said graciously,
as he rode off. Then she turned to Macheson.

"Stephen Hurd is a little corner in your house,"
she remarked.

"In our house," he protested. "I should never
have considered him if he had not worked out his
own salvation. If he had reached me ten minutes
later —— "

She gripped his arm.

"Don't," she begged.

He laughed.

"Don't ever brood over grisly impossibilities," he
said. "The man never breathed who could have
kept you from me. Across the hills home, or are
your shoes too thin?"

He swung open the gate, and they passed through,
only to descend the other side, along the broad
green walk strewn with grey rocks and bordered
with gorse bushes, aglow with yellow blossom.
They skirted the fir plantation, received the respect-

ful greetings of Mrs. Green at the gamekeeper's cottage, and, crossing the lower range of hills, approached the house by the back avenue. And Wilhelmina laughed softly as they passed along the green lane, for her thoughts travelled back to one wild night when, with upraised skirts and flying, trembling footsteps, she had sped along into a new world. She clung to her husband's arm.

"I came this way, dear, when I set out that night — to kiss you."

He stooped down and kissed her full on the lips.

"A nice state you flung me into," he remarked.

"It was rather an exciting evening," she said demurely.

They walked straight into the morning-room, which was indiscreet, and Wilhelmina screamed.

"Peggy," she cried, "Peggy, you bad girl!"

The two women went off together, of course, to talk about it, and Deyes and Macheson, like Englishmen all the world over, muttered something barely comprehensible, and then looked at one another awkwardly.

"Care for a game of billiards?" Macheson suggested.

"Right oh!" Deyes answered, in immense relief.

THE END